FLINT KILL CREEK

FLINT KILL CREEK

CREEK

Stories of Mystery and Suspense

JOYCE CAROL OATES

THE MYSTERIOUS PRESS
NEW YORK

FLINT KILL CREEK

Mysterious Press
An Imprint of Penzler Publishers
58 Warren Street
New York, N.Y. 10007

First Mysterious Press edition

Interior design by Maria Fernandez

Library of Congress Control Number: 2024911693

ISBN: 978-1-61316-557-7
eBook ISBN: 978-1-61316-564-5

10 9 8 7 6 5 4 3 2 1

Printed in the United States of America
Distributed by W. W. Norton & Company

for Richard D. Smith
in whom high lonesome & eldritch conjoin

CONTENTS

FLINT KILL CREEK

1.

Flint Kill Creek originated in the Adirondack mountains and emptied into Lake Ontario forty miles to the west, one of numerous small tributaries emptying into the great lava-colored lake which in turn emptied into the turbulent Niagara River and that river into the vast St. Lawrence to empty finally into the Atlantic Ocean hundreds of miles to the east. *And so her body was carried that distance, lost in the Atlantic Ocean.*

Inga, her name had been. He remembered now.

2.

He knew little of creeks, rivers. He knew that there were freshwater streams and there were salt-saturated bodies of water but he had no clear idea of their origins or why they differed. He did know that "Flint Kill Creek" had been originally just "Flint Kill"—for "kill" was a Dutch term that meant creek. Dutch settlers had been the first Europeans to live and farm in this region of upstate New York, in the early 1600s.

He knew simple facts—water runs inexorably downhill, land slopes downhill to water, a powerful gravity draws us down, downward, like time; and it is not reversible. He knew that small tributaries yearn to be swallowed up in larger streams, borne away and identities obliterated in very vastness, a wide rushing river, a great wind-tortured lake.

Flint Kill Creek was relatively shallow for much of its hundred-mile length, rock strewn, spilling over its banks only during the spring thaw and after heavy rainfalls. When snow melted in the mountains and foothills in early April the creek became a cascade of lush clear water that seemed to render the very air above it scintillant, dazzling; very different from the gushing mud-colored water after a storm, a sickly hue, smelling of rot, excrement.

The creek ran along the eastern edge of the state university campus at Oriskany, New York, that sprawled over five thousand acres. He'd discovered it a few weeks after he'd arrived from the small city of Sparta. He'd been just slightly older than other first-year students—twenty. He'd lived off campus, he'd had few friends. He'd been fired with idealism: here was the beginning of his life, his *actual* life and not the accident of his birth.

How long ago that seemed now. Another lifetime for which he felt contempt as for a younger, naive, and ignorant self outgrown.

And how long had he lived in Oriskany, in all—six, or seven years—difficult to calculate time once you've detached yourself from the grid of a four-year college program or have been expelled from it, a door shut behind you, slammed, locked.

He'd seen the creek in all weathers, for it was *his* creek, he felt a kinship with it, that could not have been explained.

So many times in a trance of oblivion hiking the trail following Flint Kill Creek north of the campus to the old iron-girder bridge at the Rapids, and across that bridge, returning to the campus on the other side of the creek, a hike of about six miles. So many times a solitary hiker, desperate to get away from the neighborhood bordering the university, repelled by a sudden loathing for his own kind—*midtwenties, dog off leash, prowling hungry eyed.*

3.

First time she'd come with him on the Flint Kill trail. Impulsively he'd invited her.

Hey. Stay with me a while, okay?

It was the morning after their first night together. Things had happened swiftly, haphazardly. He'd been drinking. He hadn't been thinking clearly. Realizing. It had been a drought season, into early October. No rainfall for months, the creek had become shrunken, shallow.

It pained him, seeing the creek so diminished. A slow-sluggish current wheedling between ungainly bleached white like exposed bone. A smell wafted to their nostrils—brackish, rancid. He was feeling a sharp disappointment, Flint Kill Creek had betrayed him.

So easily smote down, his spirit. Sometimes, he had a vision of his mother slapping him on the head and shoulders with a broom, sobbing and cursing. *Bad bad bad! Why are you born.*

Frothy skeins of something like detergent were visible in the creek bed, clotted against boulders and underbrush. Broken bits of plastic, rabid-white Styrofoam. Hoped to Christ they wouldn't see torn condoms amid the debris. But in shallow water at shore he saw what appeared to be filth bobbing, he urged Inga along so that she wouldn't see.

Fury coursed through his veins. He'd wanted Flint Kill Creek to be beautiful to the girl, he'd wanted to impress her.

It was no secret that most of the streams in the region were polluted. Even in the Adirondacks, hundreds of miles from industrial sites. Acid rain fell in the mountains amid tall stands of fir trees and birches looking from a distance as if their beauty could endure forever.

Parts of Lake Ontario and Lake Erie had been designated "dead zones"—"hypoxic zones"—oxygen in the water so depleted that myriad organisms had died. More durable organisms had migrated elsewhere radically altering the lake ecosystem. Species of fish long native to the lakes were endangered, invasive species were moving in—sea lampreys, Russian carp, spiny water fleas. It was strongly advised that fish caught in Flint Kill Creek should not be consumed by human beings.

But Inga marveled at the creek, as a child might. As if she'd never seen a creek before.

It amused him, unless it annoyed him, that Inga exaggerated so much. Her moods, her exhilaration, her giddy high spirits.

Or was it that Inga was *in love*. This behavior, the way of a girl *in love*.

Before he could stop her Inga stepped into the creek, in water that barely came to her ankles. She was wearing open-toed sandals, her feet and legs were bare, white. In her playful mood she seemed oblivious of the befouled water, or indifferent to it; dark-feathered birds lifted from the creek bed emitting sharp angry cries, what were they?—some kind of blackbird?

Red-winged blackbirds, he told her.

Red-winged? She objected, their wings were black.

He wasn't going to argue. He was only just becoming acquainted with Inga—taken by surprise, and not altogether a pleasurable surprise.

She was an only child, he'd gathered from remarks she made. Born to older, doting parents. Accustomed to ignoring warnings. Knowing that, however childishly she behaved, she would be cherished, adored.

She was so *slight*. He might have picked her up in one muscled arm, marveling at her lithe squirming weight, birdlike, with a bird's hollow bones.

She could not go outdoors without wearing dark-tinted glasses, her eyes were hypersensitive to light. On her head, a cloth hat with a wide rim slanted across her forehead to shield her face, for her pale thin skin burnt easily.

Her mouth she'd made bloodred with a shiny lipstick, an exotic bloom out of the waxy pallor of her face. Her eyebrows were so pale, she seemed to have none. Behind the dark-tinted lenses, barely visible ghost eyes that appeared to be lashless.

It was a bright autumn day, the sky was a hard cobalt-blue. A sky promising no rain. A sky of merciless candor. They were new to each other, edgy. He was not even certain of her last name. He liked not knowing her last name so that, if things failed to work out between them, he might say negligently to anyone who inquired—*I never caught her last name.*

He had told her just his first name: Romulus. Which wasn't in fact his name but an artful variant of his (unartful) (ordinary) birth name.

Already a kind of sexual rivalry had begun between them—which of them would have dominion over the other. Which would emerge the stronger.

He wasn't going to scold her, if that was what she wanted. He was determined to keep his voice light: "The rocks might be sharp, Inga. You might cut your feet . . ."

Her name was startling in his mouth—*Inga*. He marveled that he spoke it so easily, so intimately, when he scarcely knew her, the name was exotic to him.

Inga seemed not to hear him. Her manner was childlike, willful. She splashed about in the water until he lost patience, seeing a thick scum of what looked like human excrement bobbing in the water amid clots of algae, and smelling a sharp stench.

It was possible, sewage drained into Flint Kill Creek somewhere upstream. There were old settlements north of Oriskany, in the foothills of the Adirondacks, with primitive methods for disposing of human waste.

"Inga, Christ! Come on."

He wasn't going to get his running shoes wet, he stood on a flat rock to reach for her, seizing her wrist. It was a surprise to them both, how his fingers closed about her thin wrist, tugging at her.

"Hey! What're you doing!"—Inga pulled away, aroused in opposition.

Shaking her arm to loosen his grip on her wrist but he only tightened his grip, and tugged at her, forcibly now, yanking her off-balance so that she nearly fell into the water. With his superior strength he hauled her back onto shore. She could not have weighed much more than one hundred pounds, he weighed at least one hundred sixty. Both were breathing hard. For a moment they were actually—almost—struggling, hot-faced and indignant; then, Inga decided to give in, with a sharp little laugh like ice being broken.

A short distance away two hikers were observing them. Waiting to see whether Inga would run from the aggressive young man who towered over her by six or more inches, or signal to them for help, to be protected from him; but Inga coolly ignored them.

It was a way of hers, ignoring the stares of others. Or perhaps with her weak eyes she was totally oblivious of others.

He'd first noticed Inga in a large lecture hall at the university, sitting in the first row of seats, virtually beneath the lectern on a raised platform; these were seats often taken by students with special needs, disabled in some way. In her dark glasses she might have been mistaken for a blind person, though she was taking notes by hand, leaning over a spiral notebook, her strikingly pale, ash-blond hair obscuring her face.

She looked unusually young, even among undergraduates. She seemed to be dressed to attract attention—shorts that exposed her thin, waxy-pale thighs and legs, bare feet in sandals, with red-polished toenails; a sleeveless, tight-fitting T-shirt, that exposed the thin pale arms of a ten-year-old. Her oversized dark glasses had white plastic frames. Her mouth was bloodred. Her hair fell straight past her shoulders, lacking luster, synthetic-looking as the hair on a doll.

He was sitting at the rear of the steeply banked lecture hall, in one of the unassigned seats. Not enrolled in the course but not an (official) auditor, either. A nomad, of a kind. No one would notice an interloper, no one would much care.

The girl he'd later know as Inga, fascinating to observe. She was very striking while not beautiful or conventionally attractive. There was something amiss in her, he thought. Something askew.

Was it—*albinoism*? Skin and hair lacking pigmentation. He felt a twinge of slightly repelled sympathy.

The impaired, the disabled, drew his rapt attention. You expected to see meekness in them, humility, even apology, but this girl did not exude such an air, rather one of self-confidence.

No. I don't see you. But I can feel you seeing me.

Inga was rubbing wryly at her wrist. Her pale eyes lifted to his, just visible inside the dark-tinted glasses, with a look he couldn't decipher: accusation? hurt? admiration?

He hadn't meant to hurt her—*of course*. She'd provoked him, and she knew it.

He asked her if she'd like to turn back and she shook her head curtly *No*.

They walked on. He'd been setting a brisk pace, now he would walk more slowly, for Inga's sake. By the time they reached the Rapids her wrist had begun to bruise: the imprint of his fingers was distinct.

He saw, and was astonished. He lifted her wrist to kiss it.

Turning the slender wrist, to kiss the faint blue arteries beneath the pale skin.

Not like him—"Romulus"—to behave so emotionally. His skin flushed with confused delight.

With a naive sort of boastfulness Inga explained to him that she'd been born with a certain *condition*. Her skin wasn't like others' skin, he'd probably noticed—it lacked pigmentation. She was highly susceptible to sunburn, skin cancer. Bright sunshine made her nearly blind. Yet, in darkened places, she could sometimes see better than persons with normal vision.

Normal. He had to smile, the way Inga uttered the word. As if it were synonymous with *ordinary, banal.*

Not once in the brief time he would know her did Inga utter the word *albinoism*. Nor did he. He understood that this term would

8

be offensive to her for it was clinical, impersonal. Inga's vanity was such, she had to believe that her *condition* was unique to her alone.

4.

Clutching hands. Her small daring hand, clutching *his*.

In a public place, taking his hand as if making a claim. Walking on Union Street. In the Chinese restaurant. In the Fourth Street diner. On the Flint Kill trail. He wasn't sure if he liked this—a girl taking *his* hand.

Neediness was repulsive to him, in others as in himself. Abruptly he ceased seeing girls who (unwisely) revealed to him how emotionally needy they were. And once he'd detached himself from them, they were likely to redouble their efforts to keep him—to keep him in some sort of emotional confinement, as in a strangling embrace—willing to humble themselves, pleading, bargaining.

But—I think I love you . . .

To such a claim, what reply? He felt his face heat with indignation, distaste. The mere utterance of the word *love* seemed to him shameless, repugnant; a declaration of weakness that never failed to convey an air of reproach.

But Inga didn't strike him as *needy*. Rather, her impetuous behavior was a repudiation of *needy*.

That she was near-blind in bright sunshine, even wearing dark glasses. That her delicate skin was so susceptible to sunshine, she had to wear a hat with a wide brim. That she bruised so easily . . . He felt half-faint, recalling.

In his arms, in his bed she was passive, yielding. Yet there was a kind of willfulness even in her passivity, an elusiveness that frustrated him.

And her eyes!—without the dark glasses her eyes were startlingly naked, raw, with lashes so pale as to seem invisible. The irises were so faint a blue they appeared transparent, with an interior glisten of the hue of faded blood.

Looking into these eyes he felt a touch of vertigo as if he were peering into the brain of another, too intimately.

When he was alone with her he soon began to feel uneasy, restless; what a relief to be free of her!

But when he was away from her he found himself thinking obsessively of her. This, he resented!

Initially he'd kept a distance from Inga. She was too young for him, and too-young girls could become very needy. And boring.

He'd been content to observe her in the lecture class and to follow her, for short interludes, after the class; he'd been curious about her as one might be curious about an exotic species of bird. (Indeed there was something birdlike about Inga: the ashy-pale hair falling straight past her slender shoulders like an exotic plumage.)

It happened then, seemingly by chance, that he was noticing her frequently—on campus, in the university library, on Union Street. In the secondhand bookstore in which he worked part-time.

They began to recognize each other. That is: Inga began to recognize him, and he nodded in response.

His greetings were courteous, reserved. It was to be Inga who smiled first at *him*.

In the university library he slipped into a seat at a table near her, behind her; if she glanced around, he would give no sign of noticing her, intent upon whatever he was reading, annotating. In the bookstore he observed her examining a display of books but did not approach her. In Starbucks he saw her seated in a booth with persons he knew, and allowed himself to be waved over, to slide into the booth beside her.

Inga, have you met Rom? Rom, this is Inga.

He did not correct the general misconception that he was a graduate student in an obscure subject—philosophy of language? Semantics, linguistics? It was known that he wrote poetry, prose poetry, he kept a black hardcover journal filled with such poetry and lines from classic literature—Lucretius's *On the Nature of Things*, Milton's *Paradise Lost*, Pound's *Cantos*.

It was boasted of him, by admirers, that he'd published prose poems in national publications—*Threepenny Review, American Poetry Review*.

Inga was impressed. Very likely she'd never heard of these publications but Inga was impressed and asked immediately if she could read the poems?—he had no choice but to say *yes of course*.

Of course: he was flattered.

(Not that Inga would understand the poems. He had no expectation that anyone he knew could appreciate his employment of language as an aesthetic dimension in itself, divorced from the literalness of meaning.)

Soon, they were meeting in Starbucks, in the Union Diner. They began to share meals together in the Chinese restaurant. They arranged to meet in the university library, he walked her to her residence hall at eleven P.M.

He was impressed, that Inga seemed to expect nothing of him. Other girls were too eager, too needy. Especially those nearer to his age.

Would've liked to establish with Inga a firmer relationship so that he knew exactly what she was doing at any hour of the day yet—of course—he couldn't bring himself to make such a request out of a fear of presenting a question to another person to which a possible answer was a coolly devastating *No thank you.*

Clutching hands. Her small daring hand, clutching his.

Late October. Their second hike on the Flint Kill trail.

To his relief the creek was higher now. In autumn sun its current was swift and glittering and there was a smell of sunshine on soft-rotted leaves.

It was still startling to him, the girl taking his hand as she did. For they did not really know each other so well, yet. Was the gesture possessive, or was it (merely) playful? Flirtatious?—as a naive young girl might be flirtatious, with no clear idea of what such an invitation might involve.

Inga was not a very sexual person, so far as he could judge; like other girls he'd known since coming to Oriskany she seemed to be inhabiting her body, self-conscious, vain, yet insecure. As a blind person might mimic the responses of a sighted person, in earnest pretense that she was *feeling* as intensely as another did.

In his relations with young women, *he* was the aggressor, if and when he cared to be. This, he'd taken for granted.

"'Bad dreams come to those who sleep unwisely.'"

Inga was quoting from a novel she'd been reading. He hadn't been listening closely and wasn't sure of the nature of the conversation.

"'Sleep unwisely'—what does that mean?"

"I think—not alone and protected. In some way unprotected."

Unprotected. Did she expect him to *protect* her? Or—was it another sort of protection, self-protection, she meant?

The first time he'd brought Inga back with him to his room to make love with her. The first time he'd brought anyone to that particular room on the second floor of the weathered brick house on East Union.

Hadn't expected that Inga would really come with him, or that he'd suggest that she come yet he seemed to have prepared for the possibility by tidying the room beforehand. He'd even made the bed, changed bedsheets, pulled the (slightly broken, begrimed) venetian blind down to the windowsill so no one could see inside. (It would be dark when they entered the room, he'd have to switch on a light.)

The room was oddly long, narrow, with a single tall window. In one corner a table he used for a desk piled high with books, papers. His clunky Dell computer, of another era.

"So *cozy*."

She'd laughed, out of nervousness perhaps. Now that they were alone together. Her playfulness, the girlish insouciant manner that shielded her so well in public, drawing eyes to her, waned abruptly; in the most elemental sense, here was a small-boned, young person at the mercy of another who was larger, stronger.

Her hands were cold. Her skin felt cold. Even her face, her mouth—that looked so avid in its redness, in a public place.

He wondered if he would regret bringing Inga to his room. He worried that she was too young—inexperienced. She'd claimed to be twenty years old but he doubted this was so. He was sure, though she tried to behave boldly with him, that she'd had very little sexual experience.

Her skin was so unnaturally white, astonishingly soft. Her small soft breasts, a young girl's breasts, he didn't want to bruise.

The first time he removed Inga's clothing she'd gripped his wrists as if to prevent him but she had not prevented him, she'd only just gripped his wrists. Staring up at him with the pale ghost eyes into which he did not wish to peer too intently.

In public places she was likely to chatter, brightly. But now in his room she was very quiet.

In such close quarters with her—as with anyone—he was likely to feel anxious. Since childhood he wasn't accustomed to emotions of a visceral kind—immediate and palpable as a beating heart.

Wading out, out of the shallows, into the deeper region of the stream where the current would move swiftly, knocking him off-balance. In love, undertow. He would be *swept off his feet.*

Nothing more ignominious, demeaning—*Swept off his feet.*

He'd felt anxiety that Inga would want to stay with him through the night, for she'd become so quiet. The wild thought came to him—*What if she never leaves?*

She'd been telling him how, when she was a little girl, her grandmother had read children's books to her, at bedtime. In so wistful a way, he had the idea Inga hoped he might read to her.

Ridiculous! Though he might—(he could imagine)—read his own work to her, drafts of his prose poetry, if things worked out between them . . .

He'd been worried that Inga wouldn't leave his room yet, when she insisted upon leaving promptly at eleven P.M., he felt a sharp surprise, disappointment.

Following this, he avoided Inga for several days. Slipped into the rear of the lecture hall for the psychology lecture, sitting where she couldn't easily see him, slipping away just as the lecture ended.

Not the first time he'd behaved this way, with a girl. There was a kind of ease to it, a zestfulness, a reverse sort of hunting.

Yet, by chance finding Inga in Starbucks with another friend he'd approached the girls with a confident smile, asking if he could join them?

Inga's veiled expression. Liquidy bloodred mouth. He'd seen some softness there, a mild frisson of relief at the sight of him.

Hi there!

Hel-lo. . . .

Unmistakable, an attraction between them. He would have sworn that it had grown in the interregnum of several days when he'd avoided her but had not avoided thinking of her.

"Come walk with me. Are you free?"

"By the creek?"—she was hesitating, for Flint Kill Creek trail was not close by.

"Yes. By the creek."

Gratifying to him, that she gave in. As he'd known she would.

Hiking along the trail, no one else in sight. They had left the university behind. They had left other hikers behind. In the creek flashed reflections of red-burnished leaves, a sky mottled like buttermilk.

Inga nudged her head against his shoulder.

"D'you think that, when we die, it's just—nothing?"

In his bed, in his arms, sometimes Inga spoke in this way, a hushed girl's voice, asking a question whose answer she dreaded.

He laughed and shrugged, *who knows.*

"It's hard to believe, so much fuss in our lives, so much religion, and people yammering at you how to live, then just— nothing . . ."

Inga was sounding so wistful, he squeezed her hand.

"That's why there is fuss and religion. To forestall the acknowl-edgment that there is nothing."

"Then—why are we here?"

He was becoming impatient with her, her naivete. Asking precisely those questions he'd asked himself, years before.

"'Here' is pretty damned good. Where's better?"

15

Flint Kill Creek, warm autumn sunshine, swift-moving water gliding and glistening over outcroppings of granite like enormous stepping stones.

Such beauty!—even when ordinary, it had the power to pierce his heart.

But Inga persisted: "You know what I mean. I mean—it won't last."

Pale eyes lifting to his in appeal, behind the dark lenses.

"—a beautiful day like today, and us together. And I am so happy. But—you know—it won't *last*."

He knew exactly what Inga meant. So he must deny it, laughing. "Well. Nothing does. Nothing lasts. At least we're *here*."

It was an awkward moment. He liked Inga much better when she was being playful, insincere. *Sincere* exuded no sexual attraction for him.

Yet Inga was so wistful, so childlike. So touching.

Halfway he wondered, was he falling in love? He did not want to *fall in love*, he did not want to *fall* in any way. Ridiculous!

Not love, but maybe—protection. He could *protect her*.

It was the instinct of the male, to protect the female. The instinct of the strong, to protect the weak. But instinct was a trap, to be resisted.

They were crossing the iron-girder bridge at the Rapids. The bridge had been constructed in 1939 and looked as if it had not been repaired in recent decades. The girders were streaked with rust, bird droppings. The bridge swayed as a pickup truck passed over.

The day seemed to have shifted, there was a faint sepia cast to the air. Below the bridge the creek's current was swift, urgent. Spilling noisily over rock. White-water froth, coursing like blood through an artery.

The Rapids had once been a Dutch settlement, centuries ago. A farming community, long fallen into desuetude. In the countryside were old, weatherworn stone houses still (evidently) inhabited, wood-frame farmhouses with collapsing outbuildings, more recently built "ranch houses," small mobile homes resting on concrete blocks in fields. What had been a country village had lately become a low-income suburb of Oriskany with a single Sunoco station, 7-Eleven store, housefront beauty salon. A wood-frame Methodist church built close to the road, an unkempt cemetery behind. The area remained primarily rural, there were no sidewalks and the roads were poorly maintained two-lane blacktop.

Beside the steep twin ramps to the ancient iron-girder bridge were concrete walls at about waist-height, badly crumbling. On the farther side of the bridge Inga boldly climbed up on one of these walls, as a child might do, not reckless so much as capricious, making her way in mincing steps, arms extended for balance. Ten feet below, the white-water rapids frothed and fumed.

He didn't like Inga taking risks like this. He had to wonder if, in her imagination, she was the female lead of a romantic film, invulnerable because the female lead in a romantic film. Though probably, there was little likelihood that she would slip and fall; and if she did, the rushing water below was no more than eighteen inches deep.

She *could* injure herself on the rocks, he supposed. But damned if he was going to chide her.

He should have been flattered, Inga was obviously performing for him. Often, she seemed to be performing for him. In the coffee shop, in the Chinese restaurant. Walking on campus. Calling attention to herself, as a way of displaying herself. To him.

Rightly she understood that an attractive girl, publicly attached to a man, was a kind of light playing upon him, enhancing him. And so, clearly she was behaving like this for *him*.

Another companion would have climbed up onto the wall with Inga, falling in with her caprice. But that didn't attract him. He didn't follow others in circumstances like these. Also, he wasn't as physically coordinated as other guys. High school athletics had made that clear. He'd been tall, lean, quick, intelligent and yet in the excitement and confusion of the moment—on the basketball court, on the soccer field—he'd fumbled the ball, stumbled too often. He hadn't the instantaneous reflexes of the best athletes. They'd been impatient with him, sneering.

After a few yards the wall ended in a pile of rubble. Inga jumped down with a girlish squeal. If she'd expected him to catch her, to soften the jolt of her feet against the ground, she had to be disappointed.

Such thin arms and legs!—yet, Inga had something of a gymnast's poise.

"It's like a living thing, isn't it?"—Inga was asking.

The creek, she meant. The rushing white-water rapids.

Slipping her hand into his, another time. Her small-boned breakable hand, clasped in his.

5.

Large ungainly clumsy moths batting against streetlamps. Mesmerized by the dim bland warmth of *lights*.

Something had gone wrong in their lives. Some error, blunder, stumble not their fault.

He dreaded being one of them after all. A Sargasso Sea of the *derailed, formerly promising. Dropout.*

Those who'd completed PhDs but declined to accept jobs not commensurate with their visions of themselves. Those who'd completed coursework but not dissertations. Those who'd quarreled with their dissertation advisors. Those who'd been betrayed by their dissertation advisors. Those who were continuing with their work—their life's work—regardless of rejection. A few were "geniuses"—unrecognized, unappreciated. Quite a few were bewhiskered, with long straggly hair. Some might actually have been homeless, living on the street. Many were *just a few credits short of graduation.* Many had not set foot on the university campus in years yet could not bring themselves to leave the university town as (it's said) laboratory animals are reluctant to leave their cages if their doors are opened.

Mesmerized, hypnotized. Paralyzed.

He didn't consider himself one of these. No more than he considered himself one of the street people, junkies and drug dealers. He avoided them all, he was superior. He was known to them as *Romulus,* no one could recall or had ever known his actual name.

His face was (still) a young raw handsome face. He'd grown a soft, downy beard, to appear older; one day soon, as his hairline receded, he would let the beard grow longer, fuller.

Approaching a former philosophy professor's office, knocking hesitantly at the (opened) door. The professor was seated at his desk, speaking with another person. A student—of course.

He was no longer in that category. And he understood that, though his former professor thought well of him, had graded him (reasonably) highly, the fact that he was no longer a student, no longer enrolled in the institution that was a *university*, made a profound difference.

You could see it in the face of the other. In the eyes.

You? Who are you? Go away, don't take up my time. You no longer exist.

"Tell me something you've never told anyone else. Something 'forbidden.'"

They were in his room. In his bed amid rumpled sheets, no longer fresh-laundered.

In this place, venetian blind drawn to the windowsill, light dim, they told each other stories of their lives; but he was more interested in the stories Inga wasn't telling him.

He teased her, cajoled her: what she'd done, what had happened to her, about which she'd never told anyone out of embarrassment or shame.

"But then—you won't like me." Inga spoke hesitantly.

Like, not *love.* Inga understood, she had better not risk uttering the word *love.*

"Don't be ridiculous, Inga. I'm crazy for you, you can see that."

Crazy for you, that was fatuous. That was (maybe) a joke. How much harder for him to stammer *Look: I love you.*

He'd never asked anyone else this question, which he was asking Inga. Evidently, he'd never cared so much for anyone else.

Or, was he testing Inga? Was *he* performing for *her?*

He told her of awkward incidents in his earlier life. Accidents he'd had, blunders he'd made. How embarrassed he'd been in a high school English class when the teacher, meaning to be flattering, or meaning to be funny, remarked that he resembled a young Tom Cruise—which had been true, sort of. At the time.

His fumbling efforts playing baseball, basketball, soccer. Hoping to try out for the junior varsity football team but the coach advised him *No, son. Not for you.*

None of these incidents cast blame upon him. He was circling a confession of absolute shame. But he was hesitant to tell Inga his "most forbidden" memory unless she promised to tell him hers.

Inga was reluctant to fall in with the game, if it was a game. She wasn't laughing quite as much as usual.

He heard himself telling Inga of his (shameful, unforgivable) failure to visit his (dying) grandmother in the hospital. He was fifteen. He was a sophomore in high school. He hadn't exactly realized how seriously ill his grandmother was, or maybe he had but hadn't wanted to acknowledge it. His grandmother loved him, he had always loved her. He had loved his grandmother more than he'd loved his parents because his grandmother had loved him without qualification while his parents had loved him provisionally, if that. He could trust her, he could not trust them.

She'd expressed the wish that he would come to see her but he'd stayed away. Unforgivably, stupidly, selfishly he'd stayed away. Telling himself that he would see his grandmother when she came home as if it had been impossible for him to comprehend that his grandmother might not come home.

Telling Inga, his voice choked, that a part of his mind knew very well that his grandmother was dying, how terrible it was, how strange, that he wasn't visiting her with his parents. Not once. Not once in three and a half weeks.

His mother had said, "You know Grandma loves you so much, Ronnie. No one else loves you so much."

Quite a confession! His mother hadn't realized what she'd said, he supposed.

It had been an emotional time. A small boat violently rocking in waves. No one at the helm.

Still, he'd stayed away. Why, he could not now comprehend.

Inga sympathized with him, comforted him. But he wasn't telling her the worst: that he hadn't gone to see his grandmother even in her final days because he'd preferred to hang out with a friend playing video games after school. Nothing he hadn't done many times. He hadn't even liked the friend, much. Yet, he'd stayed away from the hospital. *Shame.*

Awkwardly Inga said, she was sure that his grandmother understood. He was only fifteen at the time . . .

As if *fifteen* were *five.*

It was annoying to him, that Inga was so glibly consoling. He didn't need this girl to assure him that he hadn't behaved like a shit to his grandmother, he knew that he had.

Yes, and to others he'd behaved badly, selfishly. Except they hadn't mattered to him as his grandmother had.

He swiped at his eyes, irritably. Angrily.

Now, he urged Inga to confess to him. She couldn't have lived to be twenty years old without having done *something* . . .

But Inga was reluctant. Telling him maybe another time.

When he pressed her she said wistfully: "But you won't love me."

Love. A kick in the gut. When had he told Inga he'd loved her? Possibly he had, in an unguarded moment, making love to her in this bed; for afterward, he seemed to forget what had passed between them.

"No. I'll love you *more.*"

Still, Inga resisted. He sensed her restlessness, her wish to leave.

"I can't really think that you have anything to hide from me, Inga! Not *you.*"

He laughed at her, he was amused by her. She seemed to him very young, of limited interest to a person like himself who was so much more mature.

He made love with her less gently than usual. He wasn't going to hold back. Desire swept over him in a rush. A wish to take his own pleasure from her, to thwart her.

He risked hurting her—though (he was sure) not much, there would be no visible bruises or welts.

Just pressure, leveraging his body as a weight, a force, thrusting himself into her, not waiting for her to establish any sort of rhythm with him; more forcibly than usual, less accommodating. There can come a time when a lover becomes a stranger, lovemaking becomes abrupt, unfamiliar, not comforting and not affectionate. He held that in reserve. He held that as a threat. He withheld his usual tenderness, or his mimicry of tenderness, knowing that she would miss it and feel the loss. She would understand that he was disappointed in her. He was angry with her. Irony in his manner, potent as a drop of anthrax.

But he walked her back to her residence. He would not allow her to walk by herself. There was an awkward silence between them.

It went on like that, a week, two weeks. It was clear that he was punishing her. Until finally she gave in saying *All right*.

All right she would tell him. The most shameful thing in her life, no one in her family knew.

But he had to promise her, she said. That he wouldn't hold it against her . . .

He laughed at her. "Of course. I promise."

Wondering what on earth this naive girl could possibly have done, that loomed so large in her imagination. His curiosity was stirred.

It happened before she'd met him, she said nervously.

The summer before her first year at the university, she'd been working as a waitress in Lake Placid, in the Adirondacks. She was staying with an older cousin who worked at the Lake Placid Club, which was considered a classy place.

But as soon as she arrived in Lake Placid, rooming with her cousin Glenda, she discovered that Glenda wasn't working at the Lake Placid Club but at a strip bar outside town, called Blue Heaven.

Glenda told her that there was more money, lots more money, waitressing at the strip club, than in the family restaurant in which she was employed. So Inga got a job waitressing at the strip club. She wasn't a performer, she was a waitress. She helped at the bar. There, she met men. She went out with these men. They were older, they were married. It was no great secret, that they were married. Guys in their forties, fifties. Old enough to be her father.

As she explained hesitantly, she tried to avoid doing *anything much* with these men. They were, like, regular dates—to a degree. They took her to restaurants, they went bowling. They took her out on their speedboats, by moonlight. She drew the line at sailboats, she was afraid of sailboats on Lake Placid. Drinking and sailboats were a bad combination, she was sure.

Mostly, the men were grateful for just her company. Her and Glenda both. There were a lot of laughs. In fact, Glenda had a fiancé, back home.

Inga assured him: it wasn't always what you might think. The men were grateful for their company. There were *alternatives*, things they could do for the men. What she called their *needs* were easily satisfied. They weren't fussy, they weren't expecting all that much. They did pay well. The more they drank, the more they paid. They were embarrassed, awkward. They usually had a lot to drink, to be relaxed with her and Glenda.

Yes, she took money from them. She accepted money. Of course. Would she have spent five minutes with them otherwise?—*no*.

Telling him it was a kind of a *wild time* in her life. When she'd broken up with a guy back home. Hard for her to believe, now.

Shaking her head, marveling at her own behavior. Not meeting his eye.

He'd gone quiet, hearing this. He had not expected anything like this.

"It was a kind of a, a weird time in my life. I can't believe it now, exactly."

Still, he was silent, speechless. The way of philosophy is to be skeptical, to question but in the moment he had no idea what to say.

Inga had always seemed to him shy. They had been together here in his room, in his bed, no more than four or five times, and each time had been an effort on her part, a performance of a kind, or at least it had seemed so to him. He'd had no clear idea if she had had sexual relations with anyone before. He'd tried to ask her, she'd been too embarrassed to reply. Maybe a high school boy friend? He had to concede, he didn't really understand the female body. If he fantasized about the female body it was not an actual person, only just a body. That, he could imagine. But the person inside the body, a person not unlike himself, with an interest in some of the intellectual subjects in which he was interested, was baffling to him, and not at all sexually arousing.

He had not suspected Inga of being anything other than a naive, innocent girl. You wouldn't call her a *young woman*, this was a *girl*.

In their relationship he was the dominant party, in the urgency of his desire he was violating *her*—she consented to the violation out of love, or adoration, for him.

Even now, as she stammered this astonishing confession, he was disbelieving. He laughed—"That's ridiculous. Don't tell me you were a—like, a—prostitute. That's a joke, right?"

Inga shuddered. Her skin looked so thin, so translucent, he imagined he could see the pulsing blood beneath.

"You're joking, right? You don't mean it."

Inga said slowly, yes, she'd been joking. She'd just made her story up.

"Some kind of tall tale, huh? You and, who's it—'Glenda.'"

Inga acknowledged, she didn't really have a secret. Not any kind of real secret. She'd just wanted to seem *interesting* to him.

She didn't want to disappoint him, she said.

He'd brought a six-pack of beer back to the room. Inga didn't like the taste of beer but was trying to drink it, swallow it, because he'd urged it upon her, hell she needed to relax, she was too uptight, she took everything too seriously.

Following this he didn't see Inga for a day and a night and another day. Measuring the hours, methodically.

He was thinking: he'd heard that persons afflicted with *albinoism* sometimes had shorter life expectancies than normal.

But of course he scorned *normal.* If what was meant was *average, ordinary.*

He didn't call her. He would not call her. But then, suddenly he had to see her.

They met at the Chinese restaurant. There was a booth near the back—*theirs.*

He hadn't been able to sleep, he told her. He wasn't accusing her, exactly.

She was looking repentant, waiflike. She said, "Why did you ask me, if you didn't want to know? You made me tell you." She began to cry.

He said, "Don't be ridiculous, it's nothing. You're an adult, I'm an adult. I didn't know you then. I've been thinking it over, it's the past. 'Where is the past? It doesn't exist. We live now. We can't remember the past.'" Who had said these words?—Ted Bundy, he recalled. What a joke! Life, life was the joke. Fuck life. He was shivering, for it was true. The past was a place no one could visit. We all came from that country but we can't return.

He left her in the booth in the Chinese restaurant. Damned if he would tolerate *crying.*

Bitterly he resented her power over him. In fact, she *had no power.*

He would leave town without telling her. Fuck the university, he was never going to save enough money to pay his debts. Even the fucking interest on the fucking student loans, he wasn't repaying. He was on bad terms with the bookstore manager, a female who'd seemed to like him, for sure she'd been coming on to him, a few years older than he and a married woman, sweet-talking initially but a bitch accusing him of stealing from the bookstore. (Which she had no way of proving.)

He packed his backpack. He had few possessions. His journal, in which he wrote in longhand. The clunky old Dell laptop, that weighed a ton. A change of clothes or two, socks and shoes. He would take a bus out of Sparta. Any destination. Random, chance! Or he might backpack along the Flint Kill trail, downstream this time, all the way to Lake Ontario. This prospect excited him.

As if something tough and sinewy he'd been chewing without being able to swallow had finally been swallowed, without his choking. That Inga would look for him in the bookstore, in the lecture class, at his rooming house, and he'd be gone.

6.

But outside his window there was pelting rain. Within a few hours, gale-force winds.

A heavy rainstorm, lightning and deafening thunder. A hurricane that had begun in the Caribbean was ravaging the Atlantic coast, as far inland as central New York State. Abruptly his lights were extinguished, he had to grope in the dark.

This was no weather for backpacking. The earth would be saturated with water for many days, storm damage would block wilderness trails.

Badly he wanted to flee Oriskany. Needing to get outside, out of his room.

Flint Kill Creek would be overflowing its banks, he yearned to see this.

After a day and a half the storm passed. Electricity was restored. He called Inga not knowing what he was going to say but when he heard her soft-quavering voice, in an instant he was in a mood to forgive.

In a mood to apologize but could not find the words.

Would she meet him? Walk with him? Along the creek? The confinement of his room was stifling to him, he could not bear it another hour.

He ran to meet her, at the edge of campus. They kissed, grasped hands. She was wearing dark glasses, the sky was glowering-white. He saw in her face an abject plea—*Will you forgive me? I love you.*

How fresh, razor-clear the air following the storm! Sun flashing like a scimitar. The sky was washed-blue glass, that made his eyes ache with its beauty. Everywhere molecules of moisture glittered tremulous and scintillant on tree limbs, the smallest twigs.

On all sides, storm damage. Fallen and broken tree limbs, fissures in tree trunks showing ghastly white like bone marrow. Deep puddles in the trail. And the creek swollen from rain, rich-mud-colored, propelling debris and spilling over its banks.

Inga had never seen the creek so high. She stared, fascinated.

Difficult to look away from a rushing stream. As if contorted shapes—animal, human—were rushing past, ever-changing. Broken things, clotted vegetation, bloated corpses of small animals.

A malevolent energy seemed to exude from the water, as if it might be radioactive to the touch.

Inga wasn't wearing proper footwear for a hike, only sneakers that were soon soaked through. A hooded jacket, jeans. He was wearing waterproof hiking boots. A khaki jacket with many pockets. It was a cold morning in early November, the deciduous trees were near leafless.

At the Rapids the creek had risen to within eighteen inches of the bridge floor, where usually it was several feet. The current was more turbulent here, the wind stronger.

He was surprised to see how with the rapidly rising water there had emerged a "spill" over a rock formation of about thirty feet in height, above the creek. He had noticed this rock shaped like a humpback whale and had meant to explore it sometime.

Ordinarily water trickled thinly across this rock face to drip into the creek below but now the shallow streams had converged into a single stream rushing over the rock face to spill into the creek in a cascade of spray, froth.

Like a living thing, Inga had said, with a shiver of dread.

As daylight waned the sky was becoming overcast once again. A few hours' sunshine, now it was ending. Hulking cloud-galleons were blown from the Great Lakes. They should turn back soon, there would be more rain. But his heart beat in exaltation, a kind of triumph.

They were crossing the bridge, he was walking quickly. Beneath the rusted grid of the bridge floor, a dizzying churn of muddy water.

Inga's hand brushed against his as if accidentally; he eluded her. Enough! Not just yet.

Not that he was punishing her, he *was not*. He wasn't childish, vindictive. *She* was the child, behaving recklessly. Daring him not to be shocked by her account of Lake Placid, repelled.

Why had he been surprised?—really, he had not been surprised. Inga's sexual passivity, her willingness to yield to him, a certain coy detachment from her own body—this suggested a perverse sort of sexual experience, devoid of authentic feeling.

Midway on the bridge Inga seemed to panic, staring down at the rushing water beneath her feet. The sight was mesmerizing, paralyzing. He seized her wrist as if to wake her. She shook off his hand but followed dazedly after him, descending the bridge ramp.

On this side of the bridge waves lapped against the embankment at the base of the crumbling concrete wall. There lifted to the hikers' nostrils a stench of garbagy water, rot; the particular stench of rotting meat.

In surges, skeins of filth. Little inlets of erosion, puckered waves at the base of the bridge where, even in the denser water, you could make out concrete rubble, rusted pipes, that must have been left beneath the bridge when it was constructed decades before.

Strange, he'd hiked to the Rapids many times but hadn't noticed the debris beneath the bridge before, that looked like broken and abandoned bodies.

Slow-moving traffic over the narrow bridge, that was barely two lanes. In the roadway, deep puddles through which vehicles made their way with caution.

He was recalling Niagara Falls, which he'd seen as a young boy. Hypnotized by the thunderous falls. That thrumming, that struck a chord deep within, annihilating the spirit. There could be no *I, I* beside the thunderous falls. He'd learned subsequently that the riverbed was eroding under the terrific pressure of the waterfall, approximately one meter a year; over twelve thousand years, approximately seven miles. No waterway without erosion, no waterway not altered by time.

Inga was speaking to him. He'd been listening to the rushing water, he hadn't heard.

". . . told you," she said wistfully. "I told you, you didn't listen."

No idea what she was talking about. Her face appeared swollen, wounded. He felt a fierce love for her, and a wish to punish her.

"You don't love me now, do you. You lied to me. It's what I thought would happen—you *promised me*, and you lied."

"Don't be ridiculous," he said. "I've already forgotten it."

"No. You haven't."

"I don't even know what you mean."

"You know exactly what I mean."

Impulsively, Inga pulled away from him and climbed up on to the concrete wall as she had on a previous hike. It was several inches wide, wide enough for her to walk on safely, except it was wet, had to be slippery. But damned if he was going to pull her down.

She meant to be playful not willful. She *meant* to be capricious, extending her arms like a tightrope walker. A pale blue vein pulsed at her temple.

She was angry with him, was she?—he wasn't going to humor her. He'd forgiven her, that was enough. He wasn't going to grovel.

He disliked needy people. He feared needy people. Weakness in himself, as well as in others, he feared. He refused to succumb to her whims. Damned if he would plead with her to get down.

Turning from her, to walk ahead along the trail. As she called to him, or he thought she'd called to him, and in confusion he turned back, now irritated, frankly annoyed, in a lunge grabbing for her arm, intending to pull her down to safety after all, but she resisted, slapping at his face; now with both hands he meant to grab her, with brute strength he meant to swing her down onto the ground, she gave a little cry as her foot slipped, and part of the crumbling wall fell away. Panic in Inga's face, she'd lost her balance, was falling—he reached out for her but couldn't prevent her falling into the rushing water only a few feet below.

So swiftly it happened! He stared, incredulous as Inga was borne away beneath the bridge, her arms flailing in the muddy water.

Calling her name, running along the creek bank, that was dense with underbrush partly submerged in water. He tried to keep her in sight, the flailing arms, the pale-blond hair, turned from him, borne swiftly downstream with the current. Desperately he waded into the water, to his knees. He was shaken, near to losing his balance. He shouted after her, his throat was raw. He couldn't dive into the water to swim after her, he'd never been a strong swimmer. Among his friends he'd been the weakest swimmer, his limbs poorly coordinated. He could not risk drowning now. He had not the strength to save her. He had not the skill to save her. He had not the courage to save her. Already he'd lost sight of her.

It was not to be believed, it would become a memory cloaked in the most profound disbelief, how quickly Inga had disappeared from his sight. He clambered up onto the roadway shouting for help. A stunned voice in his head—*Is this happening? This, is this happening—to me?*

Gusts of cold wind, rain, spray from the rapids—his stunned face was wet, glistening. All that was happening seemed to be happening outside him, beyond his control, like a film running rapidly, silently at a little distance.

A vehicle was making its way across the bridge. He stood on the ramp waving his arms wildly. The driver of the vehicle braked to a stop. He tried to explain to the middle-aged man what had happened, a girl had fallen into the creek just below the rapids, on the other side of the bridge, she'd been swept downstream, he had lost sight of her . . .

The driver promised to call 911, he had a cell phone. Not sure if there was reception here but he would try once he got off the bridge.

He left the man fumbling with his cell phone, he returned to the creek.

If the cell phone didn't have reception, the man would drive to a nearby house, he would make the call from the house. *He* returned to the trail, where he was needed. Searching for Inga in the rushing water. It wasn't too late, he still might be able to save her, she could not have drowned so quickly.

In the rushing water, broken tree limbs, boards. Bits of plastic, newspaper. He could see a human figure nowhere. The figure of the slender white-skinned girl, nowhere. His eyes filled with moisture, his vision was impaired. A premature dusk seemed to be lifting from the earth, the rushing water.

Ran, until dense underbrush prevented him. His hands, his face were bleeding from brambles, thorns. Panting, near fainting. His heart was hurting in his chest. He was a quarter mile from the bridge, he was a half mile from the bridge. Soon, he would be too far away to hear the siren of the rescue vehicle when it arrived at the Rapids.

He would persevere, he would not give up. That would be an argument in his favor—he had not given up. Stumbling along the creek bank, pushing through underbrush. In case he sighted Inga, and would wade out, and swim to her, and save her.

Calling her name—*Inga, Inga!* But there was only the rushing water, with no name he could recall.

THE PHLEBOTOMIST

Outside the medical clinic, a soft explosion of (blinding) light. The sky had been overcast when she'd entered the building two hours before, now she fumbled to put on dark glasses. Her eyes felt raw and moist as newly cracked eggs.

For a moment she was disoriented. As if she'd been inside the featureless beige brick building for an incalculable period of time. Had she left something behind in the waiting room? In the oncologist's office? She rummaged in her handbag, had she lost her keys? Her cell phone?

As so often in this past year she searched frantically in her handbag to reassure herself that she hadn't misplaced keys, cell phone, wallet . . . No: she had not.

But had she driven to the medical center? Alone?

And where had she parked their car?

No one in sight, no one awaiting her. Evidently she'd driven herself.

It should not have felt strange, to be alone here. For after all, she was *alone*; and *alone* is a state of being you carry everywhere with you.

Seeing now, on a walkway leading to the parking lot, a lone figure, male, in dark green scrubs, smoking a cigarette in quick urgent puffs. His hair would have been shoulder length and straggling but was tied in a loose rakish knot at the back of his head.

A medical worker, smoking! Just outside his place of employment.

The man had to be defiant, she was thinking. Or just brash. Or—oblivious.

She was pondering how she might avoid this person without attracting his attention when, as if aware of her thoughts, the man with the tied-back hair turned, his eyes moving swiftly onto her.

Did he recognize her? She recognized *him*.

The phlebotomist who'd drawn her blood earlier that morning after two phlebotomists, both women, had failed to tap into a usable vein. She recalled his plastic ID badge, his name began with *M*.

Has he been waiting for me?—the naive thought came to her like an arrow shot at random.

Such thoughts came to her from time to time. Rarely logical thoughts, more often implausible, improbable. Arrows shot at random in her direction.

She was hesitant to approach the phlebotomist. She wasn't in a mood to encounter anyone just now, even casually, impersonally, in passing.

She recalled, too: this medical worker had been the one to call her name from the doorway of the oncology waiting room, summoning her to the blood lab which was preliminary before seeing her oncologist. Reading from a clipboard he'd mispronounced her name—"Matt-son"—with an equal stress on both syllables—while her name was "Matheson"—stress on the first syllable.

So that, when he'd first pronounced the name, she'd allowed herself a childish moment of relief—*No*—*not me!*

Frowning, the (masked) phlebotomist had glanced about the waiting room, in a louder voice repeating: "Matt-son."

She'd risen to her feet. Of course. Had to be *her*, escape isn't so easy.

Now, outside the clinic, without the sturdy white surgical mask he'd been wearing M__ appeared older, coarser skinned than she would have expected. Attractive in a sulky-sullen way; a spoiled prince, humbled in dark green scrubs like an ordinary worker. His jaws were heavy, his dark eyebrows met bristling at the bridge of his nose. The rakish tied-back hair was smoke-colored, beginning to recede at the uneven hairline.

His eyes were liquidy-dark, warmly alert. Striking eyes, beautiful eyes. She'd noticed those eyes as he'd leaned close to her knotting a tourniquet tight around her upper arm, instructing her to make a fist.

She'd noticed, but had looked quickly away. Closed her eyes. Not wanting to see the needle sinking into the vein at the crook of her arm, and not wanting to meet the gaze of the phlebotomist, at such close range.

She was not sure if it was distressing, or if it was flattering, how readily the phlebotomist recognized her outside the clinic. She'd removed her mask as soon as she'd stepped outdoors and was wearing oversized dark glasses now, which obscured half her face. But she supposed that her face—ivory-pale, with high cheekbones, a full lower lip—was striking, at a casual glance. If one didn't look too closely at the fine white lines at the corners of her eyes and bracketing her mouth.

She did dress with care in subdued, yet expensive clothing, when she saw her oncologist at the medical center at six-month intervals. Recalling the end of Kafka's *The Trial*, that the condemned are advised to try everything, must leave no effort, however futile, untried, to forestall the inevitable.

Still, she'd have liked to think that, in the blood lab if not the oncologist's examination room, she was anonymous: invisible.

And that, outside the blood lab, a kind of protocol was observed: a medical worker didn't "recognize" a patient.

"Hey: h'lo!"—the phlebotomist lifted his hand in a jaunty greeting.

Too late to turn aside. "Hello . . ."

Wanly she smiled. It wasn't within her power to be rude to another person, for such rudeness required a stronger will than she possessed.

"So—how's it going?"—daring to put this cliché-question to her. As if they were old friends and such familiarity was natural between them.

She resented it, this intrusion. Tall looming male, all but blocking her way to the parking lot. But if she left the sidewalk to cross the lawn that would look very odd, indeed.

For essentially, the phlebotomist's question was in code. He knew she'd had an appointment with her oncologist after the blood lab so he was asking her—*Good news today, or not-so-good?*

Liquidy-dark eyes brimming with sympathy. Or something like sympathy.

It wasn't likely that she was going to tell a stranger intimate medical facts. And if she did, to what purpose? She'd avoided confiding in even close relatives, even her husband when he'd been alive, the details of her long-term condition.

Stiffly she murmured what sounded like a grudging *All right.*

"Okay. *Good.*" He nodded, gravely.

These were mere clichés, lazy habits of speech. She knew. Yet the phlebotomist smiled at her as if her reply was a genuine relief to him.

She had to concede, M __ had drawn her blood with exceptional skill. With her small veins she'd become a connoisseur of phlebotomy over the past seventeen years. Though he was a large man, bearish, with large hands, and might have been clumsy. Though she didn't really feel comfortable with a male phlebotomist, and had been dismayed by the sight of him. Where the first two phlebotomists had caused her to wince with pain, and left the soft insides of her arms bruised, M __ had found a usable vein in his first try.

No real reason to be fearful of this man. Not in bright daylight like this, the medical clinic just a few steps away.

Other patients would surely be leaving the clinic. New patients would be arriving.

"Cigarette?"—the phlebotomist held out his pack to her.

"No, thank you!"—she had to laugh, the offer was so brash, ridiculous.

But then, the medical worker in his dark green scrubs didn't hesitate to smoke just outside the medical clinic.

"You're thinking—what? Cancer patients don't smoke?"

You could see that M __ was an affable fellow who enjoyed laughter and appreciated the opportunity to laugh. Yet, M __ was also the sort of fellow who enjoyed correcting others.

"Or, you disapprove of smoking?"

She felt her face blush, M __ was looking at her so intently. As if inviting her to acknowledge he'd entangled her here against her will; he'd maneuvered her into an awkward and aimless exchange, and that *was* funny; for it was clear, she wanted only to push past him, and escape.

"Smoking isn't a good idea for anyone, I think." Disliking the primness of her voice, wishing that M __ could know that this voice wasn't essentially *her*.

"So true, ma'am!"

Ma'am. She was experiencing that frisson of something like dread or panic associated with medical situations in which a stranger, in clothing indicating a subordinate status, leaned very close to her, to take her hand or her arm, to inject something into a vein, or to affix electrodes to her chest, abdomen, ankles, or to insert her bare shivering breast between the metal plates of the mammograph machine, in anticipation of sudden, speechless pressure/pain.

Cannot help how you steel yourself for pain. The surprise of pain, and the fear.

"Anyway, Ms. 'Matt-son,' you're not such a cancer patient. You're not scheduled for chemo or radiation."

Oh, how did M __ know *that*? What else did he know about her, if he knew that?

No idea how to reply. No idea if M __ was—literally—harassing her; or whether she should be touched that a stranger seemed to care for her well-being.

It was something of a flirtatious gesture, not entirely intended: shaking her head in exasperated disapproval that he was *going too far*. Must know that he was *going too far*. Violating medical ethics or at least the likely conditions of his employment at the medical clinic.

All this while M __ had been following close beside her, into the parking lot. A large shambling affable dog that has attached itself to a naively friendly stranger.

Had she been over-friendly to M __? Had M __ misinterpreted her response? She had a habit of nervous laughter in situations like this, in which the perimeters of acceptable behavior were unclear.

Wishing to be defined as a *sensible, not excitable person* and not an *easily frightened, inclined-to-paranoia female.*

It was a very public place. Not far away was a suburban roadway. The parking lot was two-thirds filled with vehicles.

At her car, M __ lingered. She'd unlocked the doors with the remote device but was hesitant to climb into the driver's seat as M __ stood close beside her, peering down at her with the small terse smile of a medical worker uncertain of his patient's mood. She knew that, if she opened the car door and climbed inside, M __ would insinuate himself between the car door and her, and stoop to speak to her; and she did not want this. Still, M __ 's smile could hardly be said to be threatening.

Clearly, the phlebotomist had something to say to her. Yet, he seemed not to know what it was, exactly. His manner was headlong, improvisational; he might have been an actor who has misplaced his script and was waiting for cues from her, of which she herself had little awareness.

Again, the random thought came to her—*Of course he has been waiting. He'd called your name to summon you.*

Her heart had begun to beat absurdly, she had no idea what this sudden intimacy with a stranger might mean, if it meant anything. Of course as a woman she'd had encounters with men—as a girl, with young men and boys—who'd approached her with an unmistakable erotic interest; but these encounters had been in specific places, at specific times, in which the rules of conduct were more or less prescribed. She had been free to respond or to not-respond as she'd wished. Now she was an older woman, as she'd come to think of herself, though only in her early forties; such encounters were rare, more to her relief than her disappointment.

Until her husband's (unexpected) death the previous year she'd been a married woman for more than half her life.

M __ asks her if she's feeling all right? She is looking a little pale . . .
Hurriedly she assures him of course, she is *all right*.

But a sensation of faintness rises in her, catching at her throat.
She fears a sudden weakness, her knees dissolving to water.

Unobtrusively, with the deftness with which he'd sunk a
needle into her vein, the phlebotomist steadies her. Gentle but
firm hand at her elbow where, inside the sleeve of her cashmere
jacket, there's a tight-wound adhesive strip, securing a patch
of white gauze, the phlebotomist himself fastened around her
arm after he'd finished drawing her blood earlier that morning.

In his kindly-concerned way, the way of an experienced medical
worker, M __ asks her if she has been coming to the medical center
for very long—(as if, if M __ has access to her medical records, he
wouldn't already know the answer to this question)—and she hears
herself tell him *yes*, but then *no*, for she doesn't want this man to
think that she is a chronically ill person, she never identifies herself
in such a way, her closest friends, even her relatives and even her
husband, have never known. For her condition is such, incurable,
chronic, only just mildly symptomatic, there has never been any
reason for them to know.

Also, in her vanity she doesn't want the phlebotomist, who is an
attractive man, not so very much younger than she is, to consider
her weak, sickly.

Politely she asks him if he has worked very long at the medical
center?—and he shrugs his shoulders negligently, as if the question irks him; confides in her that he'd wanted to be a doctor, a
specialist in something obscure like colon cancer that metastasizes
to the kidneys, or glioblastomas, but all that was "out of my league."
Even if his science grades had been high enough and he could have
transferred from community college to a four-year university, he
couldn't have afforded medical school.

Speaking of himself, his lost, younger self, with an air of bemusement. Exhaling smoke luxuriantly, wanting her to know that he isn't *bitter.*

"More, like, what you'd call 'enlightened.'"

He tells her of his training as a certified medical assistant. They'd learned to take vital signs, perform EKGs, draw blood from computerized mannequins. He's also certified as an EMT—Emergency Medical Technician.

"We're the people who save lives," M __ says, affably, "—we arrive in ambulances when you call us, we have defibrillators, we perform CPR, we do tourniquets. We haul you out on stretchers no matter how heavy you are, and some of you are damn fucking *heavy.* We're also the lowest paid of all medical workers, d'you know that?"

Actually, no. She does not know that.

"During the worst of the pandemic, a lot of us got sick. *I* got sick—sick as a dog. But I wasn't hospitalized, I managed to keep breathing on my own. Overtime pay was worth it, for me at least."

He tells her that several coworkers contracted COVID at the clinic, and two of them died.

She tells him that this is very—very sad. She knows several people, too, older people, who'd died of COVID in the early chaotic months before the vaccine . . .

"It's still with us. It won't ever go away. It's smarter than we are. This will be a century of 'plague'—we have to learn to live with it."

She concurs *yes.* That is probably so.

"Some say that we deserve it. 'We'—the overcivilized, affluent West. Punishment for despoiling nature."

His words are grim but his tone is somewhat light, insouciant. He has been staring at her hands, her rings. She would hide her hands beneath her armpits as a child might do except she is holding her handbag.

"Hey: beautiful rings. Is that an opal?"

"Y-yes . . ."

"Is that, what d'you call it, a 'diamond cluster'?"

"I'm not sure."

He asks if she is married and she tells him *no.*

"Not now."

"Same with me. Not now."

The thought comes to her—*Is he the one? To drain my blood.*

It's absurd, it's purely fanciful, she has long had a childish fantasy of her blood being drawn by a stranger not unlike the phlebotomist in his medical scrubs. Calmly, methodically, patiently drawing her blood in a slow but ceaseless stream, as numbness rose in her, and coursed through her body; pints, quarts, gallons of thick dark blood passing out of her body as her heart, the source of much agitation, pain, dread gradually slowed, to a stop; the phlebotomist sworn to remain with her until the very last ounce of her blood is gone and her body is left waxy-white, smooth and pristine as marble and her eyes open, clear, and unseeing.

Even the word is intriguing: *exsanguination.*

As if to dispel her somber mood M__ asks lightheartedly if she'd like to have an "overpriced latte" with him. At the Starbucks in the medical center . . .

Quickly she tells him *No thank you!*

"Or we could go somewhere else. For a drink. But that would have to be later, since I have just fifteen minutes left of my break."

She hears herself laugh nervously. Oh, this is a *girlish laughter,* not appropriate for a woman in her early forties . . .

"I—I have to go home now. My husband is expecting me . . ."

"Is he!"

M __ smiles indulgently as if knowing full well that this isn't true. But M __ is too gentlemanly to express overt skepticism.

"Let me ask again, I think I've misspoken. *Would* you like to take just a few minutes to have coffee with me, or a drink?—just to continue our conversation. Not at the Starbucks here where people might recognize us but maybe—somewhere else."

Is this a reasonable next step? She isn't sure.

While her husband had been alive she'd known who she was. As a child and teenager living with her parents she'd never had a doubt.

But now, in this altered state of being, bathed in blinding light, she is often unsure. Each day is an unrolling scroll, unpredictable. She is afraid of losing something—worse, she is afraid that she has already lost something crucial and cannot remember what it is.

"You could come to my house. That way, no one would know us."

She hears herself say these words, with a kind of bravado. *He* didn't expect her to say this, she is sure.

"I suppose I could do that," M __ says, uncertainly. "Is that a better plan?"

"I—I'm not sure. Is that something you do?"

"Something that I *do*? D'you mean, as a person—or—as a phlebotomist?"

"But you are both . . ."

"Even if it wasn't, ma'am, I could make an exception. For you."

She feels a flutter of gratitude, the phlebotomist speaks so warmly.

"You could follow me in my car. . . . I live about three miles away on Mount Holly Road."

"I saw that. 'Fifty-one Mount Holly.' You have a view of the town, you could probably see the medical center from your house. You could see *us*, if you had a telescope."

"I don't think so. There are too many trees . . ."

"I mean, if you were at your house now, standing at a window. If you had a telescope."

She tries to think: could she see such a distance? With a telescope? But does she have a telescope? It doesn't seem likely.

"Ms. Matt-son: I could explain to my supervisor that I have to leave, there's been an 'emergency' that requires my participation. She'll be pissed as hell but what can she do? I'm her best phlebotomist and she knows it. And the lab is understaffed."

"If that's the case—if patients need you . . . Maybe you could come to me another time."

"What would you like, ma'am? Now, or later? I don't want to disappoint you."

"I don't want to behave unethically. I mean—I don't want you to behave unethically."

"Well, I've taken an oath. I'm a certified phlebotomist in the state of New Jersey. However I behave, it can't be 'unethical.'"

She is relieved to hear this, though she isn't sure that she understands. She is about to suggest that they postpone their appointment to another, more convenient time, since this is such late notice for him, but M __ says grandiloquently, tossing away his smoldering cigarette: "There's no time like the present, ma'am. In fact, there *is* only the present."

He will follow her in his van. He has decided that he won't notify the lab supervisor, for *she* is more important. If he returns to work—and she drives to her home—he might never see her again; she will have changed her mind, it often happens that patients change their minds at crucial junctures, when they have (temporarily) lost their resolve.

This possibility—that she might drive away, and never see the phlebotomist with the tied-back hair again—fills her with panic.

She clutches at his arm, at the coarse synthetic texture of the lab coat; he covers her hand with his, to comfort.

Just as a precaution he asks her to provide her address for him, on his cell phone. Her fingers are clumsy, trying to type on the unfamiliar phone which appears to be a much more recent model than hers, a smooth silver device scarcely larger or thicker than a playing card.

"You know, I'm thinking that maybe I should drive *you*. Drive you to your house. That way, we're in the same vehicle—mine. I can bring you back later for your car. Vehicles can stay in this lot overnight, no one will ticket you. What d'you think, is that a plan?"

"Y-yes. I think so."

"Is that a *yes*? Definitely?"

She is feeling decidedly lightheaded. But the sensation seems to be airy, uplifting; as if helium were filling her lungs with elation, an almost unbearable joy.

Whatever she'd believed she had lost, in fact she has found.

Or indeed, *it has found her.*

"Y'know, Ms. Matt-son: you sent a signal to me. Really, you can't rescind it."

"What—what signal? What do you mean?"

"This morning I called a name for bloodwork that wasn't your name. It resembled your name but wasn't. That was a test. You listened—you decided to answer to that name. Why did you do that, ma'am?"

"I—I assumed that that was me . . . You were calling my name."

"Maybe another person was expected, and it wasn't you? But because you came when I summoned her, that person became you."

"I don't understand . . . What person?"

"'Matt-son.' 'Ms. Matt-son.' That is now *you*."

He laughs. She wonders—*Is he teasing?* His laughter isn't cruel, malicious.

Laughter that follows us through our lives. Beginning when we are children. Is it cruel, is it malicious, is it kindly, is it *loving*? Desperately we search for clues.

In a voice exuding patience the phlebotomist explains.

"Like I said, it was a test. You'd be surprised how many people fail the test. They hear a name that isn't theirs, they know that it isn't theirs, yet—they don't object. They're thrown into doubt. They think—*Is that me?* I'm standing in the doorway with my clipboard, I scrutinize the room, there are always a few individuals who look nervously at me. I pronounce the name again and they—*you*—think *It must be me.* And so they—*you*—rise to your feet and come with me."

This, he recounts in a jovial voice. She has no reason to distrust him, the phlebotomist is a medical worker, one whose occupation is to serve persons like her. One of those *on her side.*

As he speaks he has been leading her to his vehicle, a rust-splotched dull-white van with paneled sides, in the employees' corner of the parking lot. There, she hesitates. Her legs seem to have gone numb.

"Ma'am?"—he nudges her, helps her climb into the van, which is awkwardly high for a woman of her height to navigate. Firmly he shuts the van door and lopes around the front of the van to hoist himself into the driver's seat with a grunt of satisfaction.

On the seat behind them is the phlebotomist's emergency kit in a backpack—which, the phlebotomist explains to his passenger, consists of disposable plastic syringes, transparent plastic tubes for the drawing of blood, adhesive tape to wind tightly about the upper arm. Plus (slightly soiled) cotton swipes and an eight-ounce bottle of alcohol that seems to have overturned and leaked pungent-smelling liquid onto the frayed seat.

The phlebotomist turns on the ignition, backs the van around deftly and heads for the exit. Is she expected to give directions?— for a moment the woman is confused, uncertain which direction to turn for Mount Holly Road but the phlebotomist doesn't hesitate: "This way, ma'am?—Okay."

THE HEIRESS. THE HIRELING.

(in memoriam Julio C.)

She has begun to sleep more soundly in the new place at the edge of the lake large as an inland sea. She has begun to sleep with more passion hearing waves in the night like great tongues lapping. Her dreams thrill her even as they exhaust her. Her dreams caress her even as they batter her. Her dreams are a source of intense love-sensations for her even as they cause her to weep in the luxury of guilt for she is a (new) widow and a (new) heiress and the fact is *the elderly husband had chosen her, she had not chosen him; the elderly husband had loved her, and wanted her, and it had made him very happy, the elderly husband had died of sheer happiness, and the madness of such happiness, marrying her.*

In the throes of such dreams finding herself sprawled in the vast bed but negligently covered as if charges hurtled against her—*slut, whore!*—have made her careless, defiant. Bedsheets scrunched up beneath her haunches and naked arms and legs outspread if she has fallen from a great height. Not a new bed, in fact a very old bed with hard horsehair mattress and carved mahogany headboard but so new to her it has no identity to her except as *the vast bed in the new place.* Fallen in sleep not into blunt dull death but into a languorous swoon. Fallen in sleep in all confidence that softness would enclose her like a cocoon, and break her fall. In this vast bed called *king-sized.* Yet, it seems larger than *king-sized.* At least—*graveyard-sized.* Sprawled in the center of the bed equidistant from either side she cannot stretch her arms from one side to the other thinking *But I am missing him: the other.* The elderly husband had been her husband less than three months dying just twelve days before his one hundredth birthday.

——

Sinking slowly into dreams that do not spring from anything so mundane as the present circumstances of her (celibate, bereaved) life which are, even to her, banal and ordinary but from a mysterious source of which she knows little: a singular root like spokes from a wheel. That the elderly husband died so soon after they were married was less of an astonishment to her, the (new) widow, than the fact that, to the mortification of the elderly husband's adult children, the elderly husband had fallen in love with her just five months before. Aggrieved, wrathful, and bent upon vengeance the elderly husband's adult children glared at her out of faces contorted with rage like the faces of those sculpted beings in Rodin's *Gates of Hell.*

——

Feverishly she sleeps through the delirious hours of the night in this place new to her at the northern shore of Lake George in the Adirondack Mountains approximately 1,300 miles from the granite mausoleum in the Palm Beach Memorial Cemetery in which the elderly husband's ashes are interred. Well into the windswept morning she sleeps. Her brain aches pleasurably with such sleep. Her lungs are full to bursting with the joy of such sleep. For something is coming to her in this sleep. For someone is coming to her in this sleep. *You will not even need to know him when you see him, it is enough that he will know you.*

No household staff to interrupt her sleep. No lawn crew with roaring motors to interrupt her sleep. She is the sole proprietor of the large brown-shingled house at the end of the quarter-mile graveled driveway as she is the sole owner of two hundred eighty acres north of Lake George, New York. Giving herself up lavishly to dreams so much more potent than anything in waking life which has become for her a dully anesthetized life, muted and routine, cocooned by immediate wealth and the possibility of further wealth when the last of the lawsuits is finally settled. For in the wake of the death of the elderly husband has come a succession of lawsuits challenging his will with the avidity of filth bobbing at the edge of a stagnant lake.

In these dreams she observes in unnerving close-up (as she'd been spared in life) the bitter resentment, revulsion, repugnance in the faces of the elderly husband's adult children who, so long as he was alive, contrived to maintain a steely-eyed affability in her company however in private they might have pleaded with him to send her away, begged him not to marry her, a woman nearly fifty years younger than he, and looking younger still. In these dreams like rolling, rocking waves in a hilarity of drunken glee she laughs openly at them as a defiant child might laugh *Catch me if you can! You fools, you can't.*

Claiming that she'd seduced, cajoled, manipulated *an elderly delusional ninety-nine-year-old man* into marrying her, with the intention of inheriting his estate upon his (imminent) death when in fact she'd married her husband for love. *For the sake of his love for her.* Sleeping now in the vast canopied four-poster bed in the master bedroom of the new place recalling how he'd begged her to marry him. *He, her.* Secure in the knowledge that this place to which she has fled, exhausted and battered by the protracted legal battles that have persisted longer than the marriage preceding it, is her rightful inheritance, though but a portion of that inheritance; that it is her reward, though she had not demanded such a reward, nor even been aware that such a reward might be hers; she had not declined a prenuptial contract for no such contract was required of her by the adoring elderly husband; shocking to her, yet gratifying, how the elderly husband defied his adult children for her sake; even as in elderly naivete he'd abandoned her to their fury slow-gathering like thunderhead clouds in the perpetually ravaged sky above the Adirondack Mountains.

Sleeping ever more soundly, deeply. Sleeping with such passion, her heart threatens to burst. (Yes: she does rouse herself to shakily cross the hardwood floor to the adjoining bathroom when required. She does rouse herself to descend the staircase, rummage in the enormous refrigerator for something edible she has caused to be delivered from the grocery store in the Village of Lake George with the Visa card shared with the late elderly husband.) Not thinking of any future for the intense pleasure of sleep is *now*, not *then*. As in the intense pleasure of *he*, not *her*. For if the final lawsuit initiated by the vindictive adult children winding its way through probate court with the peristaltic obstinacy of goat-sized prey winding its way through the guts of a boa constrictor is decided in the widow's favor the widow will be even wealthier than she is now; and how strange to her that in the midpoint of her life she has become an heiress of such an estate even as she is the sole survivor of her own family; even as she'd been a devastated widow years before having lost an earlier husband who survives in her memory like tender scar tissue on a part of the body not visible to the mourner as it is not visible to others. And since she'd had no children from that long-ago marriage she finds herself the sole survivor of her lineage and thus the end of that lineage.

Shuddering in the throes of sleep. Entranced, mesmerized. In this new place in this vast bed beneath the ravaged Adirondack sky each morning more reluctant to open her eyelids still less to *get up! get dressed!* for why should she rouse herself to mere wakefulness, consciousness out of languorous sleep, heavy-limbed as Rodin statuary, her soft-muscled heart beating slowly and calmly in the wake of swooning dreams that leave her sweetly exhausted, satiated yet with a longing to return to sleep where there has begun to be visible, framed as in a tunnel emblazoned with light, a dramatic silhouetted figure lacking a precise face: tawny panther eyes glimmering in darkness fastened upon her as the *widow, the heiress, the target.*

Giving herself up to the dream and the elusive figure within the dream she finds herself romantically drawn to this individual guessing him to be *male, a young relative of the elderly husband, grandson, great-grandson, or great-nephew or (more sordidly) a hireling of the adult children whose identity will remain forever unknown to her and so prescribed to exact a revenge on their behalf no more personal than surgery.* This morning following a night of tumultuous dreams like rolling thunder in the sky above the wave-choppy lake she succumbs to further sleep, deeper sleep; sleep pressing down upon her like warm soft suffocating gauze; no will to force herself to rise from bed any more than the elderly husband after the terrible blow of the massive heart attack had the will to rise from his final bed in the intensive care wing of the Palm Beach hospital and cast off the blue plastic tube jammed between his (undentured) gums, tear out the IV lines from the atrophied veins of his bone-thin bruised forearms attached to pole hooks and backfilled with now useless frothy-pink blood. Thrumming machines and monitors had been allowed to continue for some minutes following the event decreed as *death* until these too were disconnected, disabled by the time the (new) widow could be summoned by cell phone to hurry to the hospital breathless and stunned and too late by twenty minutes.

And so, weeks later at the edge of the dark-rippling lake she has
not the will to rouse herself to full wakefulness, to force herself to
place the soles of her (bare) feet on the thin carpet on the hardwood
floor and rise to her full height (five feet eight inches: taller than
the ninety-nine-year-old husband by several inches) for how heavily
and snugly the bedclothes weigh upon her, how warmly, like a great
cocoon; and so entranced she sees with avid interest the figure of
the young man emerging with more clarity as in a film in which
the camera moves slowly, unhurriedly yet inexorably forward as
if by caprice singling out a fated individual, a particular *being* out
of an immense landscape; a young man frowning in concentration as he drives a vehicle along a winding mountain road; this
vehicle, a steel-colored Land Rover with four-wheel drive ideal for
rough terrain. Slow caress of a narrow barely paved road winding
like a meandering stream in the heavily wooded foothills of the
Adirondacks north of the Village of Lake George.

In the depths of sleep marveling that the (yet faceless) driver of the
Land Rover has, like the widow, traveled more than 1,300 miles
from the stucco-white oceanside enclave amid tall palm trees in
South Florida where she'd first met the elderly man whose name
meant nothing to her—(truly! no idea who he was! or maybe
almost no idea for admittedly the surname has associations of some
magnitude and especially in South Florida)—who would become
her second, and final husband; and where this husband, reduced
to ashes, remains in an elegant onyx urn in a granite mausoleum
in the Palm Beach Cemetery; in a trance of concentration seeing
the young driver leaning forward to peer through the windshield
of the Land Rover for a ghostly mist has been rising, drifting

over the road winding sinuously as a snake, scarcely a glimmer of moonlight, only the headlights of the vehicle beaming ahead little more than twenty feet into darkness. Nowhere to stop on this road, so the driver cannot stop. Nowhere to turn around on this road so the driver cannot turn around.

In her sleep feeling the throb of the driver's mounting excitement indistinguishable from dread for he is fated to continue to his destination. *She* is his destination.

He would protest he is not a killer. He has killed iguanas, yes!—but he has never killed a human being. He has never enjoyed killing iguanas, it has been solely at the bequest of (white) employers that he has killed iguanas with a tire iron, with a machete, with poison. He has disposed of their lurid-mangled bodies. He has washed, scrubbed pavement where iguanas have died in crazed struggles not to die. This mission in the North is different. This mission has taken him to New York State which has been for him only a name, indeed a rare, remote name. This mission has taken him into the mountains whose name he would be hesitant to pronounce aloud. This mission is something of an accident, it will sink without a ripple into his life like a stone tossed into the vast dark lake he has been approaching. This mission he has been (reluctantly) cajoled into as a favor for his employer whom he respects and fears, of course he is being paid but he is being paid *also*, primarily it is doing a favor for the person whose oceanfront property in Palm Beach he has helped maintain since the age of eighteen; if he happens to be stopped by local police he will arouse their suspicions at once, he is of an ethnic minority not much represented in upstate New York, he is olive-dark-skinned, with shoulder-length luster-less black hair, jaws stubbled with a three-day beard, capillaries broken in sleep-deprived eyes giving those eyes a demonic glow. In her dream the (new) widow sees him with sudden fatal clarity, she does not recognize him except understanding immediately who he is, why he is, he *is* a hireling of the family, possibly she has glimpsed him tending to her husband's property in Palm Beach, difficult to recognize individuals when they look so much alike in their drab lawn-crew attire, always long work trousers despite the heat, wide-brimmed straw hats protecting their heads against the Florida sun, eyes lowered in sullen respect in the presence of (wealthy) (white) employers.

In her sleep mesmerized by this unnamed individual even as she is beginning to be fearful of him knowing that it is a sordid and shameful task he has undertaken but he will not turn back for he has no choice, and he *will be well paid.* In her dreams she has colluded with him as if she has herself set him upon his journey in her most delirious and delicious dreams discovering belatedly that it is not within her power to stop him. *It is within our power to summon but not to nullify.*

In her sleep the suddenly startling sound of a vehicle making its way along the graveled driveway. In her sleep the vision, seen through the windshield of the Land Rover, of the vast dark lake stretching out of sight and the sprawling shingle-board house on an incline above the lake in which there is but a solitary room illuminated, on the second floor; and in that room the dreamer lies asleep; as wielding a flashlight the driver of the Land Rover climbs down from the parked vehicle, makes his way to the heavy oak front door of the house as he has been instructed; he has slipped on tight-fitting latex gloves as instructed, these are not the looser cloth gloves he wears when he is working. As the stairs are carpeted, and the second-floor hall is carpeted, he makes his way in silence; like a black panther of the Florida Everglades he is hard-muscled, stealthy, and deadly; his heart is a hard fist beating in anticipation, in the thrill of apprehension, yet in shame that he has no volition except to move forward in this house of a size that would be intimidating to him if he allowed himself to consider it, still more the vast mountainous landscape beyond the house—a chaos of fir trees, poplars, birches, furtive paths crackling underfoot with desiccated leaves of a kind unknown in South Florida. *Push open the door, it won't be locked. Don't be squeamish. Don't be deterred if there is resistance. Muffle the screams if the screams hurt your ears but know: there will be no one except you to hear.*

Glittering like a nest of pale snakes the sleeping woman's naked arms and legs are visible outside the disheveled bedclothes. She is breathing deeply as one might try to breathe underwater, enormous effort for the merest sliver of oxygen, but there is no oxygen underwater, she is drowning in the dark lake's waves lapping now like eager tongues as quickly he advances upon her—*The predator does not own the prey time to escape.* Tawny panther eyes exude only the slightest twinge of pity for her whom he is ordained to kill, he is hired to kill such vermin and is determined not to be squeamish seizing a pillow from many pillows strewn about the bed (so many fancy pillows, he's offended seeing so many, infuriated) and deftly lowers it onto the sleeping face, the slack mouth will shape itself into a rictus of a scream but too late, the sleeping woman will wake from her besotted trance but too late; she will fight like a crazed animal, as she has never fought before in her life but too late, he will overpower her—of course: he is much stronger than she is, he outweighs her by thirty pounds, he is younger than she by twenty-three years. Harden your heart against the enemy, he has learned to despise this woman as his employers despise her: *gold-digger bitch, slut. Whore.* As he has killed iguanas fighting for their lives like demons so he will kill this woman who is a stranger to him, it will be a hellish struggle but he is prepared, he will not be deterred, he is a man of his word, it will be over soon (he tells himself) and he will begin at once the 1,300-mile journey south to be paid the remainder of what is owed him.

WEEKDAY

It's a weekday, Thursday in September. Early morning following
(yet another) insomniac night. Bright sunshine hurting his eyes,
his pupils shrink to the size of caraway seeds. Tracy has promised
to drive a friend to her colonoscopy exam and feels obliged to wait
at the clinic to drive the (anxious, exasperating) woman home
again and so it falls to Howard to drop the baby at Lilliput Day
Care on his way to the lab, that's to say it falls to Howard to drive
approximately five miles out of his way to drop Krissie at day care,
plus two or three other stops at Tracy's request, not that he minds,
he doesn't, freely acknowledging it's *the least he can do* considering
that Tracy is the adult who stumbles from their bed in the night
if/when Krissie frets in the room next to theirs needing (no doubt)
her night diaper changed.

Except (mildly) resenting Tracy's rapid-fire instructions to him
as she secures Krissie in the baby seat in the rear of the Subaru
Outback, Howard nodding in the affable-husband way he has

cultivated, half listening, half-distracted in the dull-headache aftermath of a long twitchy sweaty night riddled like buckshot with flashes of dreams in which he's at his computer in the lab scrolling through endless databases dreading to think how close he'd come to a colossal blunder the other day collating six-month research reports to send to his supervisor late at night when his eyesight had begun to fade, only just thought to double-check before clicking *send*; as Tracy is re-reminding him to stop at the ATM at the Wells Fargo on his way home, they need cash badly, five hundred dollars in fifty- and twenty-dollar bills, *is he listening?*—as Howard stifles a jaw-wrenching yawn, nodding *Yes! I am.* Of course Tracy has an additional penciled list to hand him at which he won't glance confident he'll remember: ATM, Walgreens (prescription refill, mouthwash, toilet paper), the Italian grocer (Sichuan pepper, half pound of Pecorino, parsley, watercress, garlic, that special "special virgin" Italian olive oil), no need to pick up Krissie since *she* will do that on her way home at four P.M., as usual. Howard prides himself on his particular sort of photographic memory, a high point of his academic career (about which Tracy has been hearing for the entirety of their life together), a perfect score on a final exam in organic chemistry at Penn when he was a junior, premed at the time, nothing like such a feat before or after in his life which (he acknowledges, nonjudgmentally) is still in the process of developing, far from complete. Tracy repeats: ATM, Walgreens, grocer, and remember the mouthwash she wants is Scope not Listerine and "original" not "mint" and if Howard makes that mistake again he'll have to use up the mint mouthwash himself, plus remember also: the toilet paper should be the thicker kind not the thinner, that's practically tissue paper and useless.

In yoga tights and ancient faded Dartmouth T-shirt Tracy stands in the driveway waving at Krissie, making funny-mommy faces barefoot on the asphalt as Howard backs out with a salute wave he isn't sure Tracy has seen, or has acknowledged, a stab of frank relief, elation just to press down on the gas pedal, feel the sturdy vehicle accelerate, stitched smile on his face fading as Tracy disappears in the rearview mirror and he's thinking how grating his wife's once velvety voice has become more Velcro now, scratchy-rough, but this feels disloyal, this is misrepresenting Howard's exasperated affection for his wife and he feels guilty at the thought, certainly a petty thought, trivial and inconsequential, unworthy, fact is he's jealous of Tracy and Krissie, knowing how Tracy wouldn't hesitate for a nanosecond if she had to choose between her husband and their daughter; the mother-baby bond is so strong, nine months in the belly, all that nursing, noisy swooning smacking sucking, sure he's just a little jealous, what man isn't, even as he understands how stupid it is, how stupid he is, he's thirty-six years old for Chrissake not an immature kid and so distracted by such thoughts he realizes that he has turned left on Ventnor, should've turned right (he realizes immediately) since he isn't going south to the Nichols Labs campus just yet but north to Drummond Road, Lilliput Day Care at the intersection with Seven Mile Road, and having turned left he has the option of an (illegal) U-turn on Ventnor which he doesn't want to risk, this hour of morning, traffic cops are out in their white cruisers like bloated albino ticks amid the bloodstream of traffic, and so much traffic at rush hour and Krissie's in the back seat chattering excitedly, can't take a chance on something happening with his daughter in the vehicle, Jesus!—certainly not. That would be the end of his life, absolutely.

So continuing at precisely the speed limit south to Tyndale Road where he can make a left safely onto Meridian, intending to circle the block (in fact: two blocks) back to northbound Ventnor but at this hour of morning there is no left turn allowed which he should've remembered, no left turn onto Meridian between 7 A.M. and 9 A.M. weekdays, one of those local traffic regulations you'd know if you've driven this route ten thousand times which Howard has, more or less, yet: he forgot.

"Asshole!"

And the sun rising over the skyline, blurred and blinding. Another scary-hot day promised, one in a succession of unspeakably depressing record-breaking mid-September days (and nights) with a promise of a high of ninety-seven degrees Fahrenheit by two P.M. and the AC in the Subaru slow to kick in, Howard is reluctant to turn it up higher because the fierce cold drafts will make Krissie shudder with cold trapped in the kiddy seat in the back, just shorts and a light cotton T-shirt and no sleeves for her, what was Tracy thinking?—but better for him to suffer than Krissie whose chattering is a source of delight to her parents, like a bright-feathered bird somehow snatching language out of the air, at an age to be asking questions which Daddy answers in his affable-distracted Daddy way (half) hoping Krissie will lose interest and doze off as she does sometimes in such circumstances, secured in a kiddy seat, he and Tracy marvel at how quickly their daughter can fall asleep at three years even when there's noise and commotion around her. *His* brain is a sort of ravaged sponge impervious to tiredness, normal exhaustion not enough to guarantee anything like a full night of sleep, a few beers before bed make him woozy but if he falls asleep he wakes up with a jolt within an hour or so, now he's feeling dazed, dazzled from sleep or rather the rude awakening from sleep, another area in which he's jealous of Tracy, too. In this hungover state his eyes feel more than usually opaque, there's a scummy scrim over most things giving the world a faint sepia cast like a faded Polaroid. Or is it exhaust from a diesel rig just ahead?— still on Ventnor headed south he sights a Wells Fargo ATM in the next block, on the right, not their branch bank but another, more convenient actually since he can make the withdrawal now instead of on the way home, seeing a vehicle just pulling out of a parking space, time on the meter, always a good omen, he leaves the motor running, AC on low, tells Krissie that Daddy will be right back and sprints to the ATM thirty feet away, withdraws—how much did Tracy ask for? five hundred? three hundred?—cash flowing through their fingers like water, Jesus. His brain *is* actually aching, his eyes, he'd had (maybe) two hours sleep in total the night before, broken into fragments like froth on a polluted river, recalls Tracy twitching and sighing in her sleep, sudden coughing fit (hers) waking him just when he'd finally gotten to sleep, which Tracy won't recall. Sleeping with another person is so weirdly *horizontal.* He'd wrestled in high school, not too seriously. Instead of a gym mat, a bed mattress. Not natural to be *horizontal* in combat. But of course you aren't *horizontal* wrestling, you start off vertical. Oldest competitive sport, originated with the Greeks, not for Howie, you have to be mildly crazy, obsessed with diet: fasting, bingeing, bile threatening to rise into his mouth, the abuse of the body by the mind, his back breaking out in red pustules, no thanks. If he'd done better maybe, but he hadn't. Face flaring with heat, recalling. And recalling Tracy leaning into the rear of the station wagon to buckle Krissie into the kiddy seat, swath of a thick thigh inside black spandex pants, the startling heft of his wife, daunting to him, the husband; during the pregnancy she'd steadily gained weight, swelling, ballooning, rubbery-spongy flesh always warm to the touch, arousing to him, intimidating, he'd teased her initially at becoming "chubby" but soon ceased, overcome, outdone. Not one of those husbands to comment dryly on their wives' bodies, masking dismay with good-natured humor, his wife's body is hers and no damn business of *his.*

She'd been the one to bear the child, he isn't going to forget, not that she'd be likely to let him forget, anyway he *isn't*.

Back in the Subaru careful to ease out into traffic on Ventnor. Vaguely he recalls he's looking for a U-turn, left turn, a part of his brain tugging at him reminding him he should be headed north, not south, at a traffic light the cell phone rings, he feels a frisson of something like dread when Tracy calls him, God damn she knows better than to call him when he's driving, what is so fucking urgent, so soon after he has seen her but this is typical of his wife, impulsive without thinking, the emergency can't involve the baby, instinctively his eyes move to the rearview mirror, seeing Krissie in the back, looks like she's asleep, shouldn't answer the phone with a child in the car (if an accident, if the child dies *involuntary manslaughter*: he's protesting he had not meant it, he had not meant to risk his daughter's life, acting without thinking, acting impulsively which is a kind of *selfishly*)—but what the hell answers the phone keeping the device out of sight if a traffic cop should happen to glance into the Subaru, talking on a cell phone while driving is illegal in the state, could mean points on his driver's license even if there's no accident but fuck it, fuck Tracy calling him the way she has a habit of calling him when he's in the car not unlike letting a dog run to the end of his leash then yanking him back hard *show you who's boss* but he manages to answer unobtrusively and even quietly considering how irritated he's feeling—*Yeh, what?*—and Tracy informs him she'd forgotten *batteries for the remote, get them at the drugstore, AA8*. Howard grunts, makes a mental note: *AA8*.

Why's he so annoyed at Tracy these days, not good for him. A husband's feelings for his wife wax, wane, wax and wane and wax, but his feelings for his children are *steadfast*.

Sunshine glaring off the hood of the station wagon: his damned sunglasses are in the door pocket beside him, awkward to get them out and onto his face. But this he manages, too. Switches on the radio, it's NPR, barrage of upsetting news, politics, like filth pellets flung against his face yet fascinating, hard to resist. Passing a Walgreens he wonders if he should stop now—before he forgets: *AA8*—otherwise he'll have to wait until he drives home, not sure when that will be, could be after 6 P.M., he'll have to exit on the east side, traveling south; if he stops here (he thinks) he might not be able to get Tracy's prescription filled, this isn't their Walgreens, but possibly since it's a Walgreens their computers must be all connected, he has never tried but that makes sense, then he realizes that he doesn't know if Tracy has called in the refill or if she has forgotten, possibly she *has* forgotten for this has happened in the past when she'd asked him to stop at the drugstore, he'd wound up waiting forty minutes once, pissed as hell and feeling now a twinge of mild anxiety, apprehension, Tracy's carelessness will put him in a rotten mood, already he's feeling like shit about the NIH proposal, has avoided telling Tracy about the layoffs among the lab techs, if she asks about his friend Tarek, his friend Anushka he will make up some excuse, temporary leave of absence, the double-blind coagulant trial postponed, which is more or less true. There's a nagging doubt about the NIH grant, he'd spent so much time already on it like throwing money down a rathole, an expression his Maine grandfather used to utter with grim glee, his brain feels clogged with cobwebs, he'll need a couple espressos to wake the hell up. How close he'd come to a blunder of the kind that would torpedo his slow-ascending career. Conflating two files. Or maybe (maybe!) it was a glitch in the software. Damned department too cheap to provide the database tools that would make his life easier. No need to tell Tracy. Cold sweat oozing in his armpits. No intention of telling Tracy how he'd vetted the proposal but totally missed this crucial blunder except (reminds himself) he'd caught it in time, he had not clicked *send*. PhD in cognitive psychology, more educated than most lab technicians but now most lab technicians are female post-docs, young Asian women, he's one of the few "straight white males" remaining, a grim joke. But it's no joke. But it *is* a joke, Howard has a PhD, from Rensselaer, his supervisor tells him not to worry. Rejected for Harvard Med he'd reacted in anger deciding to continue in graduate school for a PhD, he'd do research science at a top university, top research labs like Nichols, clinical medicine was a dead end anyway. His brain has prompted him to take the expressway ramp at Merrimack Avenue, he's been in the right lane as if dragged by gravity and this way he can exit at Van Buren and drive west on Five Mile, to State Road and the Nichols campus, good luck that traffic is lighter here, he's feeling better already, elated, as if he has made a decision, vaguely he'd have said it was the decision not to stop at the Walgreens now but wait for *their* Walgreens, on his way home, so he will have time to check about the prescription, also the Italian grocer, recalling the first time he'd ground Sichuan pepper onto a meal Tracy had prepared, the strange acrid heat flaring up into his nostrils. A throb of panic at Van Buren when it looks as if there's construction blocking the roadway but it's okay, there's a lane open, STOP and then SLOW, crawling along in a slow procession of vehicles, good he'd managed to get the sunglasses adjusted, Goddamned sun is so bright. He isn't running too late (yet) but doesn't have time to spare daring to pass slower-moving vehicles on the right, on Five Mile, probably this is illegal but he's a skilled driver, hasn't had a "moving violation" in years.

Approaching the sprawling Nichols campus he begins to feel a cloudscape lowering over him like a concrete ceiling, familiar obsessive thoughts like returning to a cave, crawling into a cave, sickening-familiar, sees himself in the Subaru glinting in bright-morning sun like the armor of a beetle scuttling into a cave but the immediate worry is finding a Goddamned parking space amid a sea of vehicles, should know better by now than to arrive after eight-thirty A.M., of course Howard has a lot assignment but the lot is oversubscribed, can't find a space large enough for the Subaru, some of the spaces reserved for compacts, an entire row reserved for handicapped, feels a stab of fury, most of the row is empty but at last he finds a space a quarter mile (at least) from his building, muttering to himself, pulses beating hotly in his head but he's grateful for the space, yanks out the ignition key and already on the run locks the Subaru with the remote, sickish-smoggy air in his lungs like frayed tungsten wires but as soon as he steps into the cool-conditioned air he's feels reprieved, *in place*; the air is a balm to his abraded soul, his skin smarting like sunburn, like mortified pride but anyway it's *his* secret, no one else knows. Sends his assistant for two espressos, already he's feeling hopeful, this will be okay: promises himself. He will work through the day, he has worked through similar days in the past, an undertow you just step into, take a deep breath and step through, no reason for panic or alarm, telling himself *You have been here before.* Which is true. Rejected at Harvard, also at Penn (graduate school), but acceptances at Drexel, Rutgers (New Brunswick), Rensselaer Polytech. Eventually you are okay, you find a parking space, your application is accepted, the grant proposal will be completed in time for the NIH deadline. Grateful for the first hot swallow of espresso, quick jolt of caffeine in his veins, he's anxious to log back into the project, his fingers type in the password without the (evident) intervention of his brain, suddenly opening before his eyes like one of those gigantic tropical flowers that effloresce at rare intervals, of a beauty and intricacy unfathomable at which you stare and stare enthralled and in dread you will be sucked inside, devoured. But no: he's comfortable at the computer, in the swivel chair shaped to his buttocks. Immersed in numbers and the frank elemental pleasure of typing on the ergonomic keyboard that feels shaped to his hands in IMAK smart gloves, only rarely feeling twinges of pain, carpal tunnel syndrome so-called. Hours passing in an oblivion of concentration interrupted only by a hastily devoured late lunch at the worktable, his assistant brings the usual Asian salad, also two Diet Cokes, at the edge of his brain there's something nagging for (probably) he has forgotten something, batteries for the TV remote, AA8, or is it AAA8?—he will purchase both, he knows. Or is it to call the drugstore, to check on Tracy's prescription?—though he has (he thinks) the little plastic container that contains the pills, small white anti-inflammatory pills he can show the pharmacist, if needed; or is it the Italian grocery but (he thinks) he has a list for that, Tracy gave him the list, it's in his pocket, probably the shirt pocket, he's making a mental note to check even as his cell phone rings, annoyed to be interrupted at this crucial time, by late-midafternoon after a headachy-lethargic start he has acquired a certain momentum of energy, purpose, concentration, surprised/vexed to see it's Tracy (again!) and there's a voice in his ear he has never heard before raw and frightened—*Where is Krissie? I'm at the day care, she isn't here, Howard?—where is Krissie?*

***

"God *damn*."

He has marked *** in red ink on his calendar for the following Monday, June 11, but now he can't remember why. He has always been the most methodical of men but evidently forgot to annotate the three-pronged red asterisk with an explanation, even a time of day.

Routine appointments he marks on his calendar with a single * in red. More important appointments, ** in red. It is rare that any appointment is important enough to merit *** but rarer still that he'd forget to include details for such an important event.

In the days of marriage he might've summoned his wife to peer at the calendar, help him recall. Could've checked the wife's calendar to see if it might yield a clue.

Now, no one he can summon. He will have to figure this out for himself.

*** means an occasion of significance. Nothing routine or optional. Not a professional meeting, he's sure. Business dinner, no. Medical appointment, no. Not a dental appointment, not a meeting with lawyer or accountant. Not a concert, film, play, or dinner with friends, which would merit but a single *.

Nothing to do with the children, he's sure. Last weekend he'd taken them, the younger ones, alternately quarrelsome and sulky-passive, to the ridiculously overpriced "safari" theme park—he won't have visitation rights for a while.

Not another court date. Thank God, he's finished forever with *that*.

Medical test? This is a possibility except he'd marked June 15 and also June 23 for (unrelated) tests, with ** in red but including, as he usually did, the time, doctor's name, even the address to save him the effort of looking it up on the day of the appointment.

Glancing back through May, April, March he sees a scattering of red-inked asterisks. Some of these were medical appointments, some were professional, some were social and some, the most dreaded, were court dates.

One was his ten-year-old's birthday which in a surge of emotion he'd marked **.

Each of these dates had been carefully annotated so that he'd known exactly what it was. And each day, accomplished, was crossed out with a neat X.

Sometimes it happens that he has more than one appointment on a single day. These are neatly listed in sequential order. He'd have guessed: on the average, each month, about 15 percent of his appointments are special enough to merit **. *** is so rare, months pass without one.

The last *** occasion was back in February, a crucial medical procedure that had gone well, or well enough.

Negative is all you need to know of a biopsy. All else is a bonus.

June 11 is a most annoying mystery: marked *** for special attention, yet blank.

Hates to waste time but he has little choice if he wants to know what his important appointment is on Monday. Examining his calendar frowning, perplexed.

All his adult life he has kept a calendar atop his desk where he can see it easily. He has only to glance up to see if a day is marked or free—no need for an electronic screen, scrolling.

An old-fashioned calendar, of thick glossy paper. Handsome calendar commemorating American national parks, this month's park is Yosemite, gorgeous color photo of mountains, frothy falling stream, impossibly blue sky.

Never has he been to Yosemite. But maybe—someday . . .

An old-fashioned calendar means that you write in details, in pen. Your calendar is your diary, sharply edited. A man's calendar is a part of his identity, he would be lost without it.

He considers it a sign of a weak character, the failure to mark dates. A serious person never trusts his memory—of course. He is deeply hurt, and deeply angered, if someone misses an engagement with him, with the excuse that they'd forgotten to mark it on their calendar.

Oh Christ! I'm so sorry, must've forgotten to mark it, totally forgot . . .

No excuse. *He* never forgets.

Women he has known—women with whom he has been what's called *intimate*—(including both ex-wives)—had kept similar calendars except were never trustworthy with dates.

Stricken with embarrassment he can feel to this day, when he'd missed an important social engagement since K. in her careless way had forgotten to mark her calendar, following a telephone call invitation.

Clenched fist of rage in the pit of his chest. Taste of black bile, this woman who'd been his second wife, from whom he is newly divorced, so infuriated him.

Patiently he'd explained to K.: mark the date on a calendar immediately. Jot down as much information as you can right there, on the calendar.

Don't trust memory.

As a kid he'd known that. Keep a calendar, keep a record, make sure the calendar is large enough, don't abbreviate or scribble, and above all—*don't trust memory.*

Otherwise, life slips from you. Swirls down a drain, unreclaimable.

The women, the wives, had never listened to him. Or rather, they'd pretended to listen. As soon as love fades, indifference, like a blank stone wall, intercedes. The most devastating deafness.

All he can imagine is: he'd been on the phone, he'd been distracted or upset, marked June 11 *** on the calendar absentmindedly intending to fill in details later but forgot.

It's true, he has had some crucial exchanges lately. Since January. Health issues, medical concerns, court dates, severing ties with the second wife, he vows will be the *final wife.*

Staring at the blank rectangle as into an open hole dug in the ground—*** June 11.

What? Where? Who? Why? What time?—no idea.

———

In the past he'd have had more numbers to call, or email addresses to contact, to track down this mysterious date.

Friends, acquaintances, business associates, relatives of his own or his wife's whom he might casually call without embarrassing himself—*Excuse me but did we make a date for next Monday? My calendar is marked but . . .*

When he'd played squash, tennis. Before his back had gone all to hell. His old friend Bill Strauss.

Hey Bill—did we make a date for—is it Monday?

He is about to call Bill, knows the phone number by heart, when he remembers with a jolt of dismay . . .

No. Not Bill. No longer.

Then he thinks: is it with that woman he has just met, what's her name, introduced to her by a friend—*Laura, Lauren, Lorrie, Lorna?* (Half the women he meets these days are some variant of *Laura!*) But he has misplaced her name, phone number, email address.

Like his kids, the new woman prefers to communicate with texting. Which isn't exactly his thing.

Then he realizes: it isn't the new woman, more likely it's his old friend Sandra Stratton. He has been meaning to call Sandra but has procrastinated for months. Anxiously, guiltily.

H'lo Sandy? So sorry I haven't called, we seem to be out of contact, hoping you are okay. This is bizarre I know, please excuse me but—do we have a date on Monday? On my calendar I've marked something very important . . .

Tries to recall what terms they are on. Years of friendship, and more than friendship. Not such good memories, recently.

He calls Sandra, leaves a message on her answering machine which sounds mechanical, inhuman. (Something new? He doesn't remember this message on Sandra's machine.) He means to sound expansive, hearty, but instead his voice falters.

With Sandra Stratton he'd always been the dominant one. In a couple, one is dominant, the other dominated. Law of nature.

No games. He'd appreciated that, and Sandra had seemed to appreciate it too. Except there'd been a misunderstanding between them, exactly what he can't recall.

Not related to his unraveling marriage. Not related to anyone else in his life. He is sure.

Sandy? I've been missing you. I've been thinking about you a lot and sorry that I didn't call, if I failed to call, if I disappointed you, I am sorry, I apologize, anyway I am hoping to see you—Monday? Did we set a time? Please can you call me back tonight?

"Christ!"—he's sweating, leaving such a lame message. Wishes he could erase it somehow on the woman's answering machine but there it is, irrevocable.

Realizing too late that the date on Monday can't be with Sandra Stratton, he'd heard that Sandra has moved to the West Coast, has decided to change her life and return to—whatever . . . He hates to think he has made a fool of himself for nothing.

Maybe—R.M., his accountant?

Maybe there's a crucial decision he has to make and has been forestalling, having to do with finances? Income tax? His will?

Well beyond the age when he should have made out his will. He knows. No need to remind him, *he knows.*

But what good timing, he'd have to change his will (again) if he'd had one. He'd have left most of his estate to K., obviously he'd have to change his will, now at least there is no will to change, that's a relief but not much of a relief since drawing up a will lies before him, he will need a lawyer, every atom in his being resists engaging a lawyer, every atom in his being resists drawing up a will, he has no intention of dying anytime soon.

Now that he examines the earlier months of the calendar he sees that it's riddled with appointments with R.M. like (red) lice. At least R.M. drops by the house with documents to be signed, he doesn't have to drive to the accountant's office downtown.

Hates driving into the inner city, as it's called. Graffiti, shuttered houses, abandoned cars, *high crime area.*

A law-abiding person, an unarmed person, a decent person, a person like himself risks his life driving into any *inner city* in America today.

He doesn't own a gun. He doesn't believe in civilians with guns. He is one of those who imagines, if he holds a gun in his hand, he will be fair game for a shooter to kill.

But R.M. comes to him, fortunately!

Possibly it's that time of year already, time moves swiftly now. Since his fiftieth birthday, he has noticed. Quarterly tax payments, checks which R.M. has made out for him to sign, to US and New York State treasuries.

Last time he'd made out a check for $87,000 to the US treasury, he'd made an error and the check bounced though he'd had at least $80,000 in the account, an honest mistake attributable to the distractions of his life at that time.

R.M. had called, to explain. Or, R.M. had said he had.

Can you actually call the IRS? Can you make excuses, plead a client's inadvertent mistake, with the IRS?

No avoiding it, he has to call R.M. Leaves a message with R.M.'s secretary just to make sure. Sounding matter-of-fact and not harassed or embarrassed: *H'lo Rich? I'm just calling to confirm if we have an appointment coming up? Monday* P.M.*? Just discovered on my calendar. . . .*

Then he happens to see, June 27 is marked ** 5 P.M./*R.M.* So June 11 wouldn't also be R.M. Fuck!

If there's anything he hates it's giving the impression of not knowing what the hell he's doing. Especially you do not want lackeys like R.M. or assorted moneymen or lawyers thinking he doesn't know what the hell he's doing.

If there's anything he wants said about himself, like an epitaph on a grave marker, it's *Here is a man who knows what the hell he is doing.*

Especially, he wants his children to know that. And the ex-wives. And their Goddamned blood-leeching attorneys. And his brother Mel who always lorded it over him, just three years older but acting so superior.

He has a sudden impulse; he'll call Jamie.

First-born son, oldest kid, first marriage. So long ago, if he isn't thinking clearly he will confuse Jamie with his own young self, just twenty-six when Jamie was born.

In his address book there are several numbers for Jamie, all but one crossed out. Last address, San Francisco, Jamie had been commuting to Palo Alto, years ago, doing well, or maybe not doing so well, some sort of start-up company. He misses Jamie.

Vaguely he recalls, it was a misunderstanding about the Visa card.

Except he makes the call and there's a recording: *Sorry that number has been disconnected.*

Feels a touch of panic, he's not sure where Jamie is now.

Jamie's mother would know. But he's forbidden to contact that woman ever again. Injunction, court. Not that he wants to give her the opportunity to gloat over him another time.

Just leave us alone. Go away—die.

Hours later, 2 A.M. Unbelievable! Hours he has been lying sleepless in bed.

Trying to recall what the hell June 11 might be. An appointment with—whom? What?

Gets up, stumbles in the dark, light switch. Goes downstairs.

Pours a glass of whisky for himself. His brain feels fractured. Returns to his home office, examines the calendar again.

Just—*** in red ink on June 11. No other information.

"Some kind of riddle. Is it?"

If so, it's *his riddle.* His own fault, no wife to blame.

In a deep desk drawer he keeps calendars from previous years. His old, past life. The key to the *** mystery may be in these calendars which he saves out of a fear of discarding something important he might need to know someday.

Dates, years. He'd lived these calendar days singly, some of them long, interminable; others had passed swiftly. But now—all are gone.

Unsurprisingly, most appointments are marked with a single asterisk—*. Others, **. But very few are marked ***.

He is perplexed that most of the *** appointments are inexplicable to him now. He only vaguely recalls details. A person, persons—important to him for some reason, but why? Initials, names. Place names. Milestones of a life, evidently. But—gone.

And what was never marked on the calendar has ceased to exist entirely.

One consistency over the years is that each of his calendars has been large, and beautiful. American West, Antarctica, Audubon Birds of America, Impressionist Art. Several were gifts, as he recalls. But he can't recall from whom.

Practically speaking, he rarely glances at the color plate photographs. There isn't enough room on his desk to open the calendars fully, he has to keep the photographs folded over.

"The answer is in here. Must be."

Must be? He isn't sure. But for the remainder of the night compulsively he cross-checks the calendars hoping to detect a pattern.

What were his appointments in previous years, in June? Some of the initials he has forgotten—must've been important at the time if marked with an asterisk. But there are many repetitions: tax lawyer, divorce lawyer, R.M. Radiology lab, Dr. F., Dr. B. Court dates. Woman he'd met on Martha's Vineyard—S. (Stacey?)

Surprising to see that he'd had the kids three weeks in succession in 2019. Must've been when K. was traveling with her "friend."

Feels a sensation of vertigo, staring at the calendars. It's his habit to cross out days, so there's a sense of encroaching annihilation, oblivion—never noticed this before but there it is.

When did happy smiling kids turn into sullen brats leaving him hieroglyphic messages on his cell phone like marks in mud?—he'd like to know.

If he could do it over not sure what he'd do differently—that's the hell of it.

"Let It Be." Favorite Beatles song he'd hear in his head like a kind of brain Muzak. Sometimes what he was hearing was "Let It Bleed."

The oldest calendar in the drawer is 2013. Before that he must've thrown the calendars away. (Too bad! Gone forever now.) Checking 2013 (which appears to be more annotated than the current calendar) to see what he was doing on June 11 of that year.

Not a special day evidently, no red-inked asterisk, only the faded word *Mel.*

Just—*Mel.* Now he remembers.

Some sort of coincidence, is it? No?

Such short notice, he hadn't been able to get to the funeral. Which was why he hadn't troubled to write down time, place—he'd known that he couldn't get there. His first thought was that it was in Cleveland but that was wrong, Mel hadn't lived in Cleveland for years.

Somewhere unexpected—had it been Atlanta? He'd never understood why in hell Mel had ended up in Atlanta.

Business, maybe a marriage. Or both.

Mel wouldn't have wanted him at the funeral, anyway. He could imagine his brother's sneering aside just for him to hear—*What the hell are* you *doing here? Who invited* you?

Since their mother's death, hostility. Some things you can't forgive.

"God *damn*."

Obsessive thoughts. Mounting anxiety. If only he'd noted the time for June 11 . . . Or a single initial. All he'd need, he is sure, to bring back the memory.

Strange, how memory can be jogged by a single detail. But it must be the singular detail.

"Clancy."

One of his best friends from high school. Basketball JV. Mike Clancy.

But Mike moved to Atlanta. Yes, that was Mike in Atlanta—not Mel.

Lost touch. Not sure why. Must be—how long?—twenty years? Not likely it's Mike Clancy he's meeting on Monday.

Feels a yearning to call Mike. Misses Mike like hell. But—better not . . .

Let it be.

Let it bleed.

Daylight, he's feeling a little less anxious.

Any insomniac night you get through, you feel good to have survived. He thinks he'd fallen asleep toward dawn, for a while. Infinitely better than nothing.

A normal day, weekday. Receives emails as usual, takes calls. He is more edgy than usual, distracted. Hoping that someone will provide information for him, casually: *Looking forward to seeing you on Monday, I've made a reservation at ___.*

No one says this, however. Nor does he ask. No one seems to notice how distractedly he speaks with them, how his mind is elsewhere.

Possibly, it's they who are distracted. It's he who is *here.*

Until finally, it is Saturday. No more weekdays. And then, it is Sunday. Less than twenty-four hours until Monday morning. In the past several days he has slept fitfully and that sleep has been suet-thin, unnourishing.

His heart feels strange. He hears himself panting after minimal exertion. Jittery sensation he'd had taking steroids for bronchitis, he'd vowed never to repeat. *Christ!*

New idea: he will tabulate all the red-inked asterisk days from all of the calendars in the desk drawer, measure these against the first six months of the current year, determine which appointments overlap significantly. One of these might be identical to the appointment in the near future.

But he's too restless to sit still. Keeps losing his place in the calendars. His fingers are icy cold, clumsy. His extremities feel—remote. He wastes precious time reading through the calendars as if he is reading the diary of a stranger, lost days, years.

Where *is* the past?—he'd used to wonder as a kid.

Later, you cease wondering. *Let it be.*

Obsessed with the damned appointment, but why?—if he has an actual date with someone that person will contact him when he doesn't show up. This has rarely happened in his lifetime but yes, it has happened.

Might be a restaurant. Might be an office, a medical clinic. He will soon learn.

···

Twelve hours now to midnight and June 11. No doubt, the appointment is after nine A.M. at the earliest so he has another night to endure.

Then: impulsively he decides to fly to Cleveland. Hasn't been back for years even to see the old house. Old neighborhood, school. Church, churchyard.

He makes a call, secures a flight. Easy to arrange if you have money.

Takes an Uber to the airport. Wild! What you'd imagine an adult doing if you were a kid. When you were a kid.

Usually he plans trips methodically, weeks beforehand. Calendar marked, plans printed out. He has fantasized how one might simply arrive at an airport and purchase a ticket for—wherever.

Cleveland is an easy flight. No trouble getting a first-class ticket in the commuter plane.

Shaky in the air, wind buffeted. He'd be uneasy but doesn't feel his usual trepidation at air turbulence since it's still June 10, he has hours ahead.

If he misses the appointment he will receive a message. He will explain, apologize.

Had to fly to Cleveland. Family emergency. Will get back to you.
Postpone our date, okay?

In Cleveland he rents a car: more freedom. The airport is smaller than he recalls, he is accustomed to larger airports. Railway shuttles, airport hotels. Familiar sights as he approaches the city on the expressway.

New construction, yet areas of abandoned properties. Blight of inner-city America. Whose fault? Not *his*.

He takes care to drive at just the speed limit. Not too fast, not too slow. He will avoid road rage. Natives of the city, high crime area, gun ownership, homicides. Drug trade.

Exits at Euclid Avenue. Then to Adams, then Reservoir Street. He feels his pulse quickening. It has been years.

No one he knows any longer in Cleveland. Where once he'd known so many.

No one with whom he has kept in touch.

Long-dead family, relatives. Poor Mel!

Make your grave, now lie in it.

Or is it "bed"? Lie in your bed you've made.

He sees that the old neighborhood has changed. Worse than he'd expected.

Deteriorated. Dereliction.

Staring appalled at what he sees. Rundown buildings, graffiti-streaked walls, half-collapsed houses amid rubble . . . *He is not a racist but.*

"Like another world. Not this world."

Faces glimpsed on the street. Not faces of his childhood. Stretches of pavement commandeered by homeless persons in sleeping bags, some in makeshift tents like an occupying army. Grizzled heads, bewhiskered jaws. At a curb what looks a ghastly wizened female squatting, grinning at him as he drives past.

Not a matter of race, he thinks. Some of the occupying army are dark-skinned, but many are white. Sickly white, legion of the damned.

He is beginning to regret having returned. Is this a mistake?

Stubbornly he continues on Reservoir Street. He is not going to turn back. He is not afraid.

He is not armed. He is not paranoid. He will not be scared off.

There!—his old house. The house of his childhood.

He sees with relief that it isn't so rundown as neighboring houses. A brick duplex, color of wet sand. Dark green shutters at the windows, slightly aslant. The front stoop needs repair. Steps crumbling. Sidewalk badly cracked.

Does he imagine—*an outline in white chalk* on the sidewalk? *White outline, body, crime scene?*

Deliberately he drives past the house. His heartbeat is quickened, alert. All his senses alert. Imagines himself in the sight of a rifle—X marks the spot that is *him*.

As he recalls there is a liquor store on the avenue. The front window is protected by bars, iron-grated, but the store is open. Day-Glo graffiti streaking the grating. Ring bell to be admitted.

He's white, he's respectable looking. Well-dressed. Stands tall, smiling. Purchases the most expensive whisky in the store: Johnnie Walker.

The shopkeeper is an old (white) guy. Crosshatched face, unsmiling. Flicker of recognition?

Almost eagerly he asks, *D'you know me? Remember me?*

The shopkeeper doesn't seem to hear. Doesn't understand. Maybe he's deaf. Maybe he's foreign, doesn't know English.

There's some problem, the shopkeeper can't change a fifty-dollar bill. He's looking vexed, impatient.

Stony-faced bastard, probably has a shotgun under the counter. Surveillance cameras recording. At the ceiling there's a TV monitor in which the customer's tall shadowy figure appears ghostlike, faceless.

He tells the shopkeeper it's okay. Keep the change.

Tries to think of a joke to make. Sharing a moment of levity. Two (white) guys in the old neighborhood. Maybe the old man had known his father. His brain is blank.

When he leaves the liquor store with the bottle in a paper bag the heavy door shuts firmly behind him. Locked.

Anyone on the street? Watching?

A few pedestrians, or street people. Not many. What are called "youths"—loud brash voices shouting words unintelligible as if in a foreign language.

Vehicles passing in the street. Faces of drivers, passengers. Blank as small moons, staring as the well-dressed middle-aged (white) man approached a rental BMW carrying a paper bag with a bottle inside.

Returns to the car he'd left unlocked. Hadn't meant to leave it unlocked but he'd only been gone for five minutes. But no risk, he has the key of course.

Drives back to the old house. Again, his heartbeat quickens.

Decides not to park near the house for there are already vehicles at the curb. Rust-streaked, derelict-looking. There is room for the BMW but he doesn't want to make the effort of parallel parking, might draw attention to himself and the shiny car.

More room on an adjacent street called Derby. Long swath of vacant lot, rubble. Tries to recall what was there? Row houses?

Crosses Derby on a pedestrian walkway beside the old railroad bridge. Railings defaced with Day-Glo graffiti like angry grunts and shouts.

In the distance, what sounds like gunshots. He freezes, listens.

Possibly just thunder. The sky is bruise-colored, layered in cloud.

Old memories, he'd been a kid on this walkway. Often running toward home, short of breath.

He has opened the bottle of whisky, this is a rare act for him, in public. But no one is observing, it's fine.

Might as well *steel one's nerves*.

Whisky will stop the tremorous hands, also will help him sleep. He has a vague plan to sleep in his old room beneath the eaves tonight.

*

Smiling to recall Momma boasting of him to relatives—*Ronnie is the deep one! See in his eyes. He's quiet, he listens hard. Takes it all in.*

He is relieved, the house at 338 Reservoir hasn't really changed very much. Something like pride he feels. His mother had kept things so clean. *Aching-clean*, the kitchen counters and linoleum floor.

But the neighborhood is so *cramped*. All the houses are built close to the curb, no front lawns, concrete steps leading directly to the sidewalk.

Small distinctions between the houses, that had meant so much at the time. Their house had seemed wider, more attractive than the others. The sand-colored brick had seemed more elegant. Momma put potted geraniums on the front stoop, kept the sidewalk swept clean.

He is very excited. Yet, he is feeling almost sleepy—fatigued. Standing uncertain in front of the familiar house.

It seems that no one is inside. A dim light in the vestibule. No lights elsewhere in the house. Dusk is thickening in corners, alleys. The sky is a strange iridescent dark, a shiny wing descending.

Should he ascend the concrete steps, ring the doorbell? It was so very startling when the doorbell rang, Momma would always give a little cry *Oh! Who is that!*

Whoever answers, he will explain himself to her.

On the front door there is a tinselly wreath, leftover from Christmas. It has been months since Christmas.

Is no one watching him? (No one is watching him.)

A block away on Derby Avenue teenaged boys are shouting to one another. Up the street, a pedestrian or two. No one sees him, he is sure. He is invisible.

As if returning home he turns up the alley, beside the house.

Somehow he knows the back door to the house will be unlocked. Momma would keep it unlocked for him, and for Mel. After school.

His hand is trembling, reaching out. Nonetheless, he opens it. *Hello? Hello? Hello . . .*

He hears a sharp voice. He ducks, stoops to get inside before there's a shot.

But of course no one has seen him. If there's a shot, a second shot, another shot it's *cross fire*, nothing to do with him.

He has slipped through the barrier, he is safe inside. Panting, short of breath. But home.

Recalling from childhood in this house how something he'd worried about, agonized over, turned out all right. Many times, his fears were unfounded. Once he stepped into this house.

Boys who'd threatened him, older boys from the high school, cruel smiles breaking over their faces as they've sighted him cowering in an alley and he's trapped, can't escape. . . .

It's all right, sweetie! You're safe. Safe with me.

No one has been stalking him, he should have known that. Ridiculous to be frightened.

A sudden explosion close beside his head. Something wet envelopes him, chill pelting rain. He stumbles, loses his balance but doesn't fall.

Or, if falling, so slowly falling his mother stoops beside him, to hold him in her arms.

Weak-legged, as a little boy. You learn to walk by staggering, falling, and getting up again. Lifted, held.

Momma's voice is just slightly chiding. It is Momma's way of loving.

He understands: Momma doesn't want to reveal how much she loves him, prefers him to his rude older brother, doesn't want Dad to know she prefers one of their sons to *him*. It's the family tug of war, invisible currents, forgotten until now.

Sweetie! There you are.

Momma stoops to hug him. Momma is exasperated with him because he has been hiding somewhere but of course Momma loves him. To love is always to forgive. He is forgiven, he knows. He is laughing, breathless. Losing his balance and would fall but Momma holds him upright in her strong arms.

No matter what you do, how old you've become, how many wicked things you've done in the sprawl of your life, Momma will love you.

And how beautiful Momma is!—flushed cheeks, reddened mouth. Eyes crinkled at the corners with love of him. He has almost forgotten how luminous Momma's face was when he'd been young.

. . . on earth have you been? I've been looking everywhere for you . . .

Momma tells stories about him. All Momma's stories are about him.

You would not believe where this child was hiding!

Momma rarely tells stories about Mel for Mel is not deserving of stories. He is so happy that Mel is gone. He does not want to share Momma with Mel, all that is over.

Seeing with a twinge of dread that Momma has laid out fresh-laundered clothes on his bed, including underwear.

Gently Momma reminds him: *Yes today is the day but I will be with you all the time and it will soon be over and when you come home you can have all the ice cream you want.*

An appointment at Children's Hospital. On the calendar marked for weeks. *That* is what it is: the calendar date! For weeks he has been staring at the date marked in red on the kitchen calendar. For weeks he has been frightened.

Surgery scheduled. Tonsils and adenoids removed.

He cannot believe that this is going to happen to *him*.

His brother Mel is gloating: *Some people they* put to sleep *never wake up.*

Laughing meanly. He tries not to hear.

(Where is Momma to stop Mel? He doesn't want to call for Momma, that would only make things worse.)

Mel says, *Then know what?—you're dead.*

They do an autopsy *on you. Know what that is?*

He thinks he knows. He shuts his eyes tight. If he says nothing and doesn't cry but just seems sad Mel will lose interest in teasing.

Mel chortles, *Cut you open like a chicken.*

But Momma isn't taking Mel to the hospital with them. Mel has to stay home. Maybe Mel will die, someone will come into the house and slash Mel's throat, Mel will die while they are gone and maybe they will never see Mel again.

Momma scolds, *Mel, just stop!*

To him Momma says, *Don't pay attention to him, sweetie. Your brother is just trying to be funny and not succeeding.*

Trying to be funny and not succeeding. He will remember these words of his mother's, so sharp and succinct, for the remainder of his life.

In the car Momma says that Mel loves him very much, it's just the age Mel is, eleven years old. Just how he is.

Wish he would die. Before I get back.

For a moment anxious wondering if he has said these words aloud? But Momma doesn't seem to have heard.

At the hospital Momma speaks in her special voice for strangers.

Our name is ___. We have an appointment with Dr. ___.

A smiling nurse comes to escort them. Momma is holding his hand tight, he cannot lose his balance and fall. They are brought into a room where there are children's books on a table, a stuffed animal. Coldly he looks away, he is not a baby to be so fooled.

Momma is not going to leave him, she has promised. He knows that he can trust Momma.

A needle sinks into the soft crook of his arm, so fast he hasn't time to cry. He hasn't time to scream. Momma grips his hand hard staring into his eyes so he can't look down at what the nurse is doing to his arm with a needle.

Momma is talking with the anesthesiologist—he will remember that word for the remainder of his life: *anes-thes-i-ol-ogist*.

The *anesthesiologist* is smiling at him but he doesn't see the man's face clearly. He is instructed to count back from one hundred but he loses the way like tripping on the stairs, he is falling and only Momma can save him.

A bullet has ravaged his chest. A bullet has ravaged an artery leading into his heart. Another bullet has ripped through his neck. But Momma is holding him close—as she has promised. He is in a little bed, a bed with wheels. He is bleeding profusely but Momma can staunch the bleeding with her fingers pinching. Momma leans close to him, he sees only Momma's face. It is the fullest moon, it is a moon that has expanded to fill the entire sky. He is beginning to feel sleepy. It is a very pleasant sensation, soothing and warm. His mouth has gone dry. There is no moisture in his mouth even as a chill rainfall envelops him. Momma is saying she is here, he is safe with her, she is never leaving him, not ever.

Just be brave, sweetie! You will be asleep, and then—afterward—it will all be over.

He knows. He doesn't doubt. He believes Momma. As Momma is smiling at him, kisses his forehead that is beginning to feel numb, he begins to melt into parts. His neck, his upper chest, his left shoulder. It is all so wet, he is melting away. But Momma says, *I am so proud of you, sweetie! Wait until you see what we have for you, what your present will be for being such a good boy.* His small cold hand in Momma's warm hands, cupped in both Momma's warm hands as with a soft sliding exhalation of breath he sinks into the happiest sleep.

FRIEND OF MY HEART

And now, after thirty-two years, seven months, three weeks, and a scattering of days we will meet again.

Hel-lo! Do you remember me?

Or maybe, in my voice of velvety dignity: *Hel-lo Professor K__! Do I look familiar to you?*

For weeks I have been rehearsing my greeting. My approach to you. For weeks, what I must summon my courage to do publicly, before witnesses, to *you*.

However: I am undecided whether I should announce myself so explicitly. If you recognize me, and recall what happened between us, how you have harmed me, how you have irrevocably damaged my life, you might panic and call for help, or manage to get someone (innocent) between us, or flee the stage, and I might be restrained before I can execute my plan; but if I don't identify myself so that you understand the reason for my action, there is hardly any point to my action at all.

For what is *revenge* if it is not registered in the brain of the Other?

Like the proverbial tree that falls in the forest with no creature to hear it, *revenge* that is not made unambiguously clear to the subject is hardly *revenge* but mere catastrophe, that might happen to anyone, innocently/accidentally, to no purpose.

———

Or maybe I will say, simply—*Hello, Erica. Are you surprised that I'm still alive?*

———

"Excuse me. These seats are reserved for faculty."

"Excuse *me*. I am faculty."

A dramatic moment. I had not intended to call attention to myself at your lecture but somehow it has happened, and I cannot respond otherwise to such an insult.

The insipid blond girl-usher stares at me in my rumpled khakis, denim jacket worn at the elbows, baseball cap pulled low over my forehead, water-stained hiking boots. She is likely mistaking me for someone who doesn't belong in what is so quaintly called the *college community* but might be a hostile townie, or a homeless person, with an oversized backpack, stringy thistle-colored hair, and truculent manner; she is uncertain how to behave with me—whether to back off, or call for reinforcements to prevent me sitting in a so-called "reserved" seat at the front of the auditorium.

She isn't one of my students—ever. I would remember her, and definitely she would remember *me*.

"Y-You are—faculty?"

"Indeed yes. And I am sitting here."

Another girl-usher comes tripping down the aisle to assist the first, who is perceived to be having difficulty with an interloper. I am trying not to be angry at being treated disrespectfully, explaining to the dolts that I am a longtime member of the English Department faculty.

"It's undemocratic and elitist to reserve so many seats. Not all these 'VIPs' will show up for this meretricious lecture, I guarantee."

My voice is icy, calm. If the silly girl-ushers had any doubt that I am a faculty member they should be convinced now.

By this time I am sitting in defiance of the ushers, backpack on my knees. And I am not going to budge. In the very center of the first row in the choicest seat in Hill Auditorium directly below the podium where you will be giving your much-ballyhooed and pretentiously titled lecture "Gender/Language/Sexuality" in twenty minutes.

The girl-ushers are at a loss what to say to me. Certainly, they are not about to touch me. Summon a security guard? To remove me?

It's gratifying, to see that they are, just a bit, just slightly, marginally, frightened of *me*.

You would be amused by this scene, I suppose. *You*, the most celebrated academic feminist of our generation, a shameless plagiarist/charlatan who has concocted a career out of the labor of others whom you've used, sucked dry, and discarded.

The insults hurtled at me in the ordinary course of my life would be a joke to you!—the illustrious E__ K___.

Fortunately, one of the English Department faculty arrives to assure the ushers that yes, the eccentric person who has seated herself in the reserved seats is indeed a *faculty member*.

It's a pleasure to see the blond girl-ushers' faces clot with chagrin. Not that they will apologize to me of course.

Though I have been an adjunct instructor in English and Communication Arts at the college for eleven years it is strange how no one seems to know my name. Or will acknowledge my name. That is the pretense.

Should I be insulted?—I will not be insulted. Not by pygmies.

Should I be wounded?—I will not be wounded. I will not be *disrespected.*

There is nothing shameful in being an *adjunct instructor.* There is nothing shameful in having no car, in being obliged to bicycle to campus from (rented) quarters three miles away, even in rainy or snowy weather. There is shame only in the elitists who have denied me a permanent position at the college even as they have given themselves such positions, with tenure, and raises, and every kind of benefit denied to adjuncts; even as they are well aware of my superiority over them, as a scholar, and as a writer, and as a teacher, and as a *thinker.*

Elitists who misuse their power to offer exorbitant lecture fees to individuals like *you.*

(No, it is not fair, it is not just: that you will be receiving, for a fifty-minute talk you've given before *ad nauseam,* as much payment as an adjunct instructor receives for a twelve-week course. Outrageous!)

With my baseball cap pulled low over my forehead I turn to glance about the auditorium. I might have wished that few would turn out for your lecture yet I feel a twinge of something like pride, that so many have: the place is buzzing like a hornet hive. The largest crowd for the annual endowed lecture since Oliver Sacks. Undergraduate women—girls, really—silly, insipid girls!—clutching copies of your newest, most trendy compilation of others' ideas—*Masks of Gender: Language, Sexual Deceit, and Subterfuge*—which they will ask you to sign, breathless and eager as children.

Gradually the reserved section is filling too. Colleagues of mine in the English Department to whom I am invisible, nameless. Initially they avoid me as the tenured avoids the untenured, if it is humanly possible, without being explicitly rude. (The élites need us, after all. Or rather, the college needs us to work for a fraction of the salary at which the permanent faculty works.) No one sits beside me until those are the only remaining seats.

Murmuring *Hello* to me, without exactly looking at me. As I grunt what sounds like *H'lo*.

Though they affect not to know my name, they certainly know me. A plebeian, a prole, a wage-slave in their midst. A leper. Yet a valuable *worker-leper*. Daring to sit amid the reserved for the fancy endowed lecture as if we are all equals.

But no need to worry. I am very well-behaved. For the time being.

As you noted, thirty-two years ago. *Still waters run very deep. Still waters mined with explosives, deeper still.* (How shrewdly you knew my soul, dear Erica, though we were not yet twenty years old!)

Just sitting here innocently, backpack on my knees. This somewhat bulky black nylon backpack with zippered compartments which I am not going to set down on the floor but keep very carefully on my knees with my clasped hands securing it.

(Close-up: in a film the camera would linger lewdly on this backpack and the stubby-fingered hands securing it.)

(Close-up: an impassive masklike face, all but hidden by the baseball cap. Glimpse of agate eyes, thin-lipped resolve as on the sexless face of an Inuit soapstone carving.)

When I'd learned last May that you, of all people, had been invited to give an endowed lecture at our quaint old "historic" New England college, immediately I'd sent out a barrage of email protests: it's my belief that one should protest against the misuse of college funds, especially for outlandishly high fees paid to ill-qualified academics. Then, when I was told that the invitation had been accepted, and could not be rescinded, I volunteered to introduce you on the grounds that I am "prominent" in your field, and I know your work "thoroughly"—of course.

Though I did not emphasize this fact, for I am not a shameless name-dropper, I noted that I had been a classmate of yours at Champlain College, indeed we'd been friends, for a while near roommates.

I was unsurprised when my request was denied. Yet somewhat surprised that the request was denied so rudely, in a chilly email from the dean.

Thank you for your suggestion. However, other plans are in place.

It was at that moment that something like a shiny blade entered my heart. *Plans are in place.*

At that moment, I saw what might be done. What must be done.

Revenge is a dish best served cold.

Thirty-two years, a dish grown very cold.

And so, I am seated in the reserved seats, directly in front of the podium. Exactly where, if you glance out into the audience, you will see *me*.

(Close-up: *What does she have in the backpack? A weapon?*)

(If so, it would be the kind of low-tech weapon that must be used at close quarters. Not a weapon to be operated at a distance like an AK-15—a large, bulky, military-style automatic weapon of the kind favored by homicidal maniacs.)

(For intimacy is the point of the assault. Something small, concise but deft, unerring of the size of, for instance, a Swiss army knife.)

(Aristotle's *anagnorisis*—recognition.)

Waves of applause. Thunderous applause.

Must resist the impulse to press my hands over my ears.

For at last—E__ K__ has appeared on stage—yet, this person is not *you*.

Walking with a cane? Your head shaved? In a bright, showy, kimono-like costume? *You?*

Twelve minutes after the hour, escorted onto the stage by an apparatchik from Gender Studies, a former PhD student of yours from Stanford, who will introduce you—E__ K__ has entered the bright, blinding lights of acclaim from which there can be no retreat.

Shocking to me—how you have changed. Older—*other.*

I must admit, I am stunned. My mouth has gone dry. My stubby fingers clutch at the backpack on my knees.

Who is this?

Is this—you?

Seated on the stage looking short of breath. Smiling like a fat old eunuch Buddha with a bald-shaved head. A greedy look in your face as you listen to the fatuous introducer praise you with every sort of cliché, absurd unwarranted hype, lists of books, awards, and honors, visiting professorships, MacArthur "Genius" Award—*Bold, original, outspoken, defiant. Bringing women's rights issues to a totally new plateau. Feminism as confrontational theater. Gender as deconstruction. Female speech / guerilla speech. Politics of a New Radicalism. Courageous, pioneering . . .*

Shrewdly you are wearing oversized dark-tinted glasses so the audience can't see the crepey skin beneath your eyes—can't see your shiny little pig-eyes darting about bemused by such comically inflated praise.

Must be pancake makeup slathered on your face. Not that makeup can disguise the jowly sag, creases, crow's-feet bracketing your eyes. Eyebrows penciled in dark and given a curious antic "arch"—ridiculous. Square-jutting jaw like Gertrude Stein, and with the heft of Stein's (sexless) body, in the famous Picasso portrait. How different from the beautiful girl you'd been!

For yes, you were *beautiful*. Must admit.

Then, you'd have shuddered at the sight you are now. You, who were so intolerant of *fat*.

Not that you are *fat*—not exactly. Overweight by thirty pounds, perhaps thirty-five pounds, but you are a tall woman, large-boned, and you carry yourself like an Amazon warrior, still. Though both your face and body exude soft middle-age flaccidity yet (as I stare, I see this) you are not unattractive, in fact (one might say) you are exotic-looking, weirdly seductive.

For that has been a paradoxical cornerstone of E__ K__'s doctrine of "perverse" feminism: the pansexual body is not neglected or repudiated but rather celebrated. Even pornography in which women are objectified is celebrated by a devious logic unacceptable to an earlier, more puritanical generation of feminists. Cunningly you'd calculated that you could not build a career upon agreeing with the older, liberal pioneer-feminists who'd preceded you, who'd been your mentors when you were a graduate student; you could not build a career of any substance by acquiescence or compromise. And so E__ K__ made a career out of the inflammatory and provocative. *Sex is not political. Desire is not containable. What is, is not what should be.*

Ideas you'd swiped from me, long ago when we were undergraduates. Papers I'd "vetted" for you for psychology, philosophy, linguistics, feminist studies.

A strange costume you are wearing for an academic setting: gold-spangled, quilted, a kimono with exaggerated shoulders, falling loosely over silky black trousers flared like pajamas. A crafty way of disguising your fifty-three-year-old body from the sharp eyes of the young.

(*Fifty-three!* Difficult to believe.)

(Fortunately, my lean, rangy, flat-chested and flat-hipped body has aged very differently from yours; indeed, along with my mostly unlined face, it seems that I have scarcely aged at all and no one would guess me to be your almost-exact age.)

On your feet (that had once embarrassed you, so *big, broad, flat*—size ten EEE) are square-toed black shoes graceless as cudgels, orthopedic shoes in disguise; seeping over the sides of the shoes are (puffy, swollen) ankles mostly hidden by the flaring pajama-legs, which is a good thing.

And yet—amid thunderous applause you have heaved yourself to your feet. You walk with a slight limp, favoring your left side, but you maneuver your black-shellacked cane like a plaything.

"Thank you! I am very honored to be here . . ."

A sugary voice! A ghastly smile! Fat, wetted lips like a sexual organ, distasteful to see.

Unctuous words. Clichés like faux pearls on a string. And so many pearls, and such a long string. How skilled in hypocrisy you've become, like a lyre you've learned to stroke in your sleep, designed to draw predictable responses from your credulous audience.

What a fraud you are—but a very clever fraud. Making a career out of exploiting the anxieties of *females* in a world of *patriarchal males.* Pretending to believe that there is a *radical female speech* inaccessible to the enemy, i.e., the *male,* that might unite us.

And then, I see that, for just an instant, you have glanced down into the front row of the audience—at me.

Yes, I am sure—at *me.*

For alone of the crowd I have not been applauding. Just sitting here with arms tight-folded and my backpack on my knees. And my hiking-booted feet flat on the floor. And my baseball cap, rudely you might think, pulled low on my forehead, so that I can peer out at others without their seeing me.

You are startled by the sight of me, for a moment thrown off-stride. Can't quite recall who I am—is that it? Or is it the intransigence of my being, my refusal to applaud you like the others?

And so, I allow myself a smile like a scissors flashing.

Yes. It is I, your closest friend Adra you'd imagined you had outlived.

Kirkland, Erica A.

Leeuwen, Adra M.

Alphabetical destiny: abutting each other on lists in our freshman residence at Champlain College, Vermont. In a large psychology lecture in which seats in the steeply banked auditorium were assigned and attendance assiduously taken.

Not destined to be friends, obviously. For you were "popular"—drew friends like a magnet. When you walked into a room all eyes swerved onto you, conversations faded, as if you'd strode onto a lighted stage; within a few days of the first semester everyone knew your name. *Erica! Erica Kirkland.*

Of course, I took little notice of you. At first.

Vaguely aware of the tall swaggering girl in our freshman residence with long thick streaked-blond hair, shrill laughter, restless eyes and a face that "lit up" a room. Aggressively you recruited admirers, foolish girls trailed in your wake for you did not like ever to be alone but rather surrounded by a circle of witnesses like handmaids holding mirrors to reflect your face.

Did I even know your name?—I'm sure that I did not. At first.

As a work-scholarship girl I had neither the time nor the inclination to linger in the dining hall after meals; I did not seek conversations, as I did not seek friends; I had a spare, single room on the top floor of the residence which meant that I could work through the night if I wished, with no roommate to complain or distract me. I could not comprehend how others in the residence could so happily drift from room to room, smoking their perpetual cigarettes, laughing loudly, wasting hours of precious and irretrievable time in chatter. Fifteen hours a week I worked at the college library. My fitful, brief, self-punishing hikes in the pine woods above the college left me exhilarated and primed to return to my work. I cared only for my courses, my books, and my own writing efforts; the vicissitudes of my interior life—moods ever shifting like the sky above Lake Champlain.

Yet, our names sounded alike. Our names abutted each other on lists.

"Adra—Erica. Separated at birth."

The first thing you said to me, with familiarity startling as a nudge in the ribs.

No one at the college had spoken to me with such intimacy, that suggested a kind of teasing; even my relatives didn't speak to me in such a way, for I never encouraged them.

I didn't know how to answer. I didn't know if I was offended by you smiling into my face as you were, or whether your attention was flattering.

"It's like we're twins—you know—'separated at birth.'"

You must have thought that I was slow-witted, you had to explain your remark.

You laughed, the twin-notion was so extravagant. For obviously Adra and Erica hardly looked like twins: one so strapping-blond, gorgeous and the other—well, not-so.

I remember that we were in the residence hall, on the first floor by a stairway. I remember that you were standing discomfortingly close to me, and I stepped back. A hot blush had come into my face.

My eyes swerved aside, I would not look at you. Shrugged and murmured a vague *Yes. Maybe*—as you'd murmur to humor someone who has tried to be clever but the effort has fallen flat.

Later, I would wonder if you'd meant to be cruel, ironic. And it was that intention that had fallen flat.

"D'you smoke, Adra? No?"

"No."

"Not ever?"

"Of course not! Not *ever.*"

Hard to believe, that had been an era in which everyone smoked. In our residence hall, in classrooms. Seminars in which our professors smoked, dropping ashes into Styrofoam coffee cups.

Your brand was Tareytons.

"You should try, Ad. It's like caffeine—it gives you a *charge*."

With time, you began to call me "Ad"—familiar as a nudge in the ribs.

With time, shyly, I began to speak your name—"Erica." The sound—the three quite sharp, distinctive syllables—felt strange on my lips.

Yes, I did begin to smoke. But only in your presence, at first, with cigarettes you gave me—"Here, Ad. You look like you could use a cigarette." Casually you'd hold out your pack of Tareytons to me, giving it a little shake.

It makes me faint to recall that gesture. I think that I don't want to recall that gesture, which was often made in the presence of other girls, as if to signal a special connection between Erica and Adra that excluded them.

(Eventually, I began to smoke alone. In time, by the end of college, and through the protracted misery of my twenties, I was smoking two to three packs of cigarettes a day, which I could not afford; each time I lit a cigarette I felt a wave of faintness, recalling *you*. Cursing *you*.)

(But I am over that now. It has been decades since I've thought that inhaling toxic fumes into my lungs has been "romantic"—that anything passed from you to me might have been "romantic.")

"'Shy.' You wear 'shyness' like armor, Ad."

Your strategy was to observe, to analyze. You were not being *critical*, you claimed. As a feminist, you were utilizing tools of *deconstruction*.

Where Adra was *shy*, Erica was *bold*.

Or rather, Adra was *shy-seeming*.

Together we read the early feminists. Mary Wollstonecraft, Charlotte Perkins Gilman, Virginia Woolf. Simone de Beauvoir, spoiled for us by our discovery that she was in thrall to her long-time lover Jean-Paul Sartre, a walleyed gnome/womanizer whose infidelities de Beauvoir too readily forgave.

"If I'd caught Sartre unfaithful to me, with someone young enough to be his daughter, I'd have stabbed the bastard. Right in the groin."

Like a child you spoke savagely. Others who were listening were taken aback by your vehemence but I just laughed.

"Would you do the same, Adra?"

"No."

"Why not?"

"Because I don't give a damn about men. Where men stick their penises is of no concern to me."

You laughed, startled. You were impressed by such words. Though you were a brash, bold, outspoken young woman you were yourself in thrall to men, or rather to sex; to the allure of sex that was a part of the air we breathed. You wouldn't have thought of dismissing, as I had, what seemed to mean so much to the human species.

For it was true, I didn't give a damn about men. I was tall, lanky-limbed, with a plain, fierce white-skinned face and a prepubescent body (at age eighteen), uninterested in attracting the attention of others except by way of my writing, and then it was only the attention of my professors that meant anything to me. And then, only a very few of my professors, for the faculty at Champlain College was not much distinguished.

You said, staring at me, "Of course. You're right, Adra. Only another female knows what a female wants, by instinct."

You could not have spoken more jubilantly if you'd made this discovery entirely by yourself.

———

Still waters run deep. Still waters mined by explosives, deeper still.

It seemed natural to me, to prefer my own company to the company of others. In high school I had mastered the art of *icy calm detachment, indifference.*

For I did not trust you. Any of you.

Though most of the girls in our college residence had been afflicted with homesickness virulent as flu for the first week or two of the first semester, soon a bizarre change came over them, a rabid need to be together much of the time, to walk in braying packs to the dining hall and to gather in one another's rooms late into the night. Homesickness was forgotten in a compulsion to confide in one another, to talk wildly about things that should have been kept private, and to laugh at things that were not remotely funny, like getting drunk—("wasted") and throwing up at a fraternity party— "making out" with some guy they scarcely knew—"flunking" an exam. And of course they talked about one another ceaselessly, with relish, with pity, with a pretense of outrage, with the most lurid and unapologetic curiosity—*My God have you heard!*

What they said of me, I could imagine. Or maybe it was mostly pity they felt for what they perceived as my *aloneness*.

. . .*wouldn't be bad looking if she wasn't so sour.*

. . . *if she'd just* smile.

(But why would I smile at them? It was enough that, by degrees, I was learning to smile at *you*.)

You liked to quote Sylvia Plath (whom with your blond hair and manic ambition you resembled, to a degree)—"'I eat men like air.'"

Dropping by my room on the fourth floor of our residence when I was working late on a weekend night, in the aftermath of a fraternity party or a "date." Eyes dilated and mouth swollen, hair in a tangle, smelling of beer, male sweat, and (I imagined) semen—"Hi, Adra! Can I interrupt?"

You were very funny, very wicked complaining of the guys you went out with. Wanting me to know both how popular you were, how every guy who saw you desired you, some of them even fought over you, and yet how bemused you were by them, their clumsiness and stupidity, how disdainful you were even of sex, unless it was *the very best sex.*

Did I want to hear this? No.

Did I want to hear—some of this? *No.*

And so one night when you came to my door to rap lightly with your knuckles and push it open and ask *Can I interrupt* quickly I stammered that I was busy, I had no time. *Not at the moment*, I did not want to be interrupted. *No.*

Seeing in your face a look of faint incredulity. That anyone would rebuff *you.*

But you went away. You did not insist. You laughed, you went away, gracious if a little drunk, a good sport. Never one to push yourself on another but rather one who calculates a new point of entry, a new strategy of triumph and revenge at another time.

—

(It was true, I worked late into the night, in a kind of fever. I believed that I did my most inspired work after midnight and I did not want to waste my waning energy listening to your droll tales told to impress me, to make me envious and jealous and yearning to be like you. *No.*)

—

How did I come to know your secret. One of your secrets.

I did not ever actually *know*, I think. But by accident hearing you in one of the bathrooms and knowing it had to be you, exiting at once when I heard what it seemed I was hearing and not wanting to know anything further . . . Quickly disappearing into my room, and the door shut.

But soon, others knew. Began to know something. How you starved yourself, bloated your stomach with Diet Cokes. And then, how you ate—ravenous as an animal. At the worst of times you hid away to eat. Campaigning for vice president of our class. Posters with your face everywhere on campus. (And some of us, over-zealous on your behalf, having put up your posters returned after dark to deface or tear down the less attractive posters of your rivals.) It began to be whispered how you crept away to vomit—to force yourself to vomit. Sticking a finger down your throat, quickly the reaction came, a nervous reflex, deftly executed. *Just this one time. I haven't done it in—months . . . Just the pressure right now. Stuffed myself like a disgusting pig.* You could make a joke of it, almost.

Why are you telling me. Why, I don't want to know.

Embarrassed and ashamed for you. Stricken with concern for you.

Though we did not—yet—know the clinical term *bulimia*. Though we had heard—(some of us)—of *anorexia*.

(*Anorexia*: aversion to food. Fear of food, fear of "getting fat"—developing hips, breasts. Aversion to menstruating. How well I understood!)

But I don't want to share these secrets with you. Not with anyone. Even you.

Also: I have work to do. Always, I have work to do. Like saying a rosary, *work to do.*

Please don't knock at my door. Please don't interrupt.

Please don't make me feel sorry for you, fear for you, it is a way of seduction, I am not strong enough to resist.

And so: a girl in the residence was speaking of you, meanly, maliciously, and I overheard and came up to her and told her to shut her mouth—"It's none of your business, what any of us do." The girl—her name was Beverly Whitty—one of those who'd adored you and followed you around and was rebuffed by you—was shocked, and the expression in her face so inane, fatuous in alarm, I shoved her back against the wall as I'd never done before in my life to anyone—as I'd never imagined doing. *And yet it was easy!*

All who witnessed this were shocked. But no one dared protest as I strode away, tingling with righteousness, my blood beating in my veins as rapidly, happily, I ascended the stairs to my room on the fourth floor.

How easy, to shove another. What a surge of pleasure, one could become addicted.

It was at this time that fear of Adra Leeuwen began in the residence where before there'd been only a kind of wary disdain. I did not trouble to discourage it.

Our residence advisor Miss Tull (as we called her) summoned me to speak with her. She was a nervous woman with a tenuous air of authority and a permanent strained smile (she knew how flighty, fickle, febrile girls our age were, how swiftly they could turn upon even someone they claimed to adore). Of course, the silly frightened girls had reported me, but it was not clear that they'd reported the reason for my having behaved as I had, my defense of *you*.

In Miss Tull's sitting room I was stony-faced, unyielding. By the age of nineteen I had attained my full height of five feet ten but I was still lean, flat-hipped as a boy, with close-cropped hair like a boy's, and a pale, somewhat sallow skin that was the very expression of adolescent *sulk*. My reputation in the residence was of a high intelligence linked to a sharp, sarcastic tongue. (But why was this? I rarely exchanged remarks with anyone in the residence except you; and I was never sarcastic with you.) I have no doubt I intimidated poor Miss Tull, who clasped her hands tightly together to disguise their shaking. This was not yet an era in which psychological counseling was recommended for students displaying the slightest "aberrant" behavior, so Miss Tull simply spoke to me, with a pretense of calm, drawing upon tactics very likely provided for resident advisors by their supervisors—("You are a very intelligent young woman, Adra. It is just surprising—it is unexpected—that you would behave as you did . . .") Frowning and silent and staring at the carpet I let Miss Tull speak for some minutes before I said, "What I did to—her—was morally justified. I would not have acted as I did to halt a malicious slander if it had not been justified."

"But we are hoping it won't happen again, Adra . . ."

I had to smile. With Adra Leeuwen there is no *we*.

However, I didn't contradict Miss Tull. As a young child I'd learned the strategy of allowing my elders to think what they wanted to think while I did what I wanted to do as soon as their backs were turned.

When you found out, you squeezed my hand, and said, with rapidly blinking eyes, not quite looking at me, laughing—"Look, I don't know what the hell it was, what it's about, all I heard was—you stuck up for me. Thank you, Adra! Anybody else, they'd have said nothing. They'd just—wouldn't—have stuck up for me." Your words were halting, uncertain. Still you could not look at me. A hot blush came into your face and seemed to spread to mine, to my chill sallow cheeks.

All that I could think to say was: "Well, I'm not 'anybody else.'"

Stiff, trembling. Needing to run away.

"Well, I just wanted to—thank you . . ."

"We don't have to talk about it. Okay?"

"Well—okay."

Stiffly walking away. Feeling your eyes on the back of my head, quizzical, grateful.

Next time I saw you, in a public place, you were flushed with triumph. You were looking gorgeous—not like a girl who has been sticking a finger down her throat. Your friends crowded around you, to congratulate you for having won the "hotly contested" election for vice president of our class by a narrow margin—something like fourteen votes.

———

(Yes, it was a rumor that you'd cheated somehow in the election. Supporters of yours had rigged ballots. For you aroused such adulation, such loyalty. I did not wish to compete with these friends of yours, I kept my distance aloof and uninvolved.)

———

"Friend of My Heart." The sentimental Irish song one of the girls in the residence played on the battered old piano in a corner of the living room. Unbidden the melody comes back to me sometimes. Very ordinary, you'd have to say banal, yet the song had the power of burrowing into my brain.

Friend of my heart, where have you gone.
Friend of my heart, I am so alone.

Driving my shuddering Honda Civic rarely less than one hundred miles a week when I was commuting to teach at two other colleges beside this college. And during these hours, it was "Friend of My Heart" that echoed in my brain.

To live as an adjunct instructor is to commute—if you are lucky enough to have more than one job. Because this college will not employ me as a full-time instructor, still less give me tenure, until my car broke down last year I was obliged to drive seventy miles to the state university at Troy, to teach a course that meets on Monday and Thursday evenings for ninety minutes; here, I teach on Tuesday and Thursday mornings. Fortunately, I can bicycle to my classes here; I can take a train to Troy. An adjunct instructor lives by her schedule, and the "schedule" is whimsical and wind-driven as fate.

You would not understand. *You* who earns in a single cobbled-together lecture an adjunct's salary for an entire term.

Where have you gone. I am alone.

It was genuine, my indifference to you. At the start.

A giant icicle, a stalactite, strikingly disfigured, that begins to melt, and to drip, and by degrees loses even its disfigured shape. Melting, bleeding away.

For you were so very friendly to me. Waving to me, calling to me, inviting me to sit with you and your companions in the dining hall, and blinking in surprise when I declined. For truly, I had thoughts of my own to think, which I did not want scattered and broken.

Not thinking—*No! I will not be seduced by you, and dropped. I am not that lonely, and I am not that stupid.*

Yet, we became friends. Somehow that happened.

By degrees it happened, in the winter months of our freshman year. Hiking together in the pine woods above the college—just Erica and Adra. Brisk, exhilarating walks along snowy trails. You kept up a stream of excited chatter, your plans for a "fantastic future" to which I murmured assent, half humoring, half-impressed. And so by spring a change had occurred between us. A quickening of my pulse when I saw you on campus, and an undertow of apprehension, dread.

"Adra! Hey. Wait. Walk with me."

I was a tall girl. Invariably I'd been the tallest girl in my class even in high school. One of the tallest persons in the class.

Yet, beside you, at Champlain College, I was not taller: we were of a height. (Though you wore heels, often high-heeled boots on your large, broad feet to boost your height; you did not shrink to make yourself smaller.)

Wanting to trust you. Wanting to believe you when you told me how special I was, like no other person you'd ever met before.

And how grateful you were, when I took time to help you with your classwork. So very—flattering . . .

"Ad! Thank you *so much*."

And, "Addie! You're my *heart*."

In such ways, my indifference melted. My resistance. An icy little puddle at my feet was all that remained of my pride.

In our Introduction to Psychology class of one hundred thirty students it was our destiny to be seated side by side—*Kirkland, Leeuwen*. And so naturally you might ask me to explain, for instance, the distinction between Pavlovian and Skinnerian conditioning (a distinction you never could recall); you might ask me to help you prepare for quizzes, midterm, and final, and your term paper on an overambitious subject ("Is there a 'female speech'?") which with your numerous campuses activities you didn't have time to adequately research.

That first paper for which you received a stellar grade—A+.

And how funny it seemed to us, that my grade for my paper, at least as solid as yours, received only an A.

Over a period of time it came to be that I "helped" you with virtually all your academic work. Under the pretext of our studying together, working together, earnestly discussing issues together, your exploitation of me flourished. I am not claiming that it was systematic—it was spontaneous, opportunistic. For you were a very bright individual, for one who was so gregarious: quick-witted, agile, and resourceful as any predator. Ideas flashed from your brain, half-cracked, half-inspired—few of them original, or even plausible—but the many distractions in your life made it impossible for you to sit still long enough to actually—(what is the plebeian word?)—*work*.

To explore an idea, to research and present an idea, to do the drudgery of footnotes, a bibliography—to write, write, and rewrite—that is *work*.

As I am an adjunct instructor seemingly by fate, so, by fate, am I obliged to *work*. While you—your inane "research"—is supported by a ceaseless succession of grants and appointments. Are you not ashamed to be so blessed while others, your peers, your superiors, are accursed?

Of course, it was flattering to me as an undergraduate that you so appreciated my help. And truly you did not ask of me that I contribute so much to your undergraduate papers as I did; you'd only asked me to "skim"—to "make suggestions." But being generous as I was, that's to say besotted and foolish, I could not resist pouring out my brain, that's to say my heart.

Papers in feminist theory, literary theory, the philosophy of language, "gender studies" (new and revolutionary at the time, a bold anthropology of sexual identity)—how many times you'd squeezed my hand, or hugged me as no one had ever hugged me—*You are just so, so brilliant, Ad! Oh God what would I do without you.*

Strange that, beside yours, my own work seemed dull. Those papers that bore the name "Erica Kirkland" seemed (somehow) more exciting, more glamorous, than those bearing the name "Adra Leeuwen."

In our classes, you spoke frequently. Bold, assertive, and seductive.

I was apt to brood in silence, bent over a notebook in which (it would appear) I was taking notes earnestly. My face was stiff, impassive. It was not clear (even to me) if I was stricken with shyness in class, or with stubbornness.

Gnawing at my lower lip until it bled.

There are no new ideas. Only new appropriations.

This has been the cornerstone of your career. How convenient, for a plagiarist to proclaim! An ideal way of obscuring the fact that you've stolen your ideas from others.

J'accuse: The core of *Masks of Gender: Language, Sexual Deceit, and Subterfuge* was stolen from one of my papers, itself a masterwork of undergraduate pretentiousness—an application of Hegelian principles to ideas of intentionality in consciousness originally developed by Edmund Husserl, and all of it imposed upon the *female voice.*

Have you forgotten, this idea was originally *mine*? And how lavishly you'd thanked me for it, and praised me for it . . . Yet in the Acknowledgments to your "seminal" book there is no "Adra Leeuwen."

In none of your books. In none of your footnotes. Nowhere!—in more than thirty years.

The heartbreak of looking for my name. The futility.

(At least I don't buy your books. It is enough for me to stand in a bookstore and leaf through them checking the index, checking footnotes for my name and hoping no one will discover me at this humiliating task.)

I did not want to acknowledge how shallow you were, enrolling in courses that would assure you high grades; avoiding the most rigorous courses, which, with typical recklessness I never hesitated to take—symbolic logic, phenomenology, cognitive psychology, Saussurean linguistics, Husserl and Heidegger, Lacan and Foucault. Which was why, at the time I withdrew from college in the spring of our junior year, my grade-point average was almost exactly the same as yours.

To you, appearances were all. Impressions were all. Whatever you wrote, or handed in as your writing, was a stratagem to be admired and an appeal for a high grade. Anything less than an A was distressing to you, and required emergency conferences with professors; if a professor did not appear to be utterly charmed by you, you dropped the course. *Look at me, admire me, are you impressed with me, love me. Surrender to me! Die for me.*

Later, I would learn that I wasn't the only person you flattered in this way. I wasn't the only naive "friend" you exploited. But I was the one who did the most for you, over a period of more than three years.

Stupidly, I was the *friend of your heart.*

—————

"Adra? Can I say something—personal? You won't be offended."

Won't be offended. Of course not.

It was a giddy prospect—not being offended. Dizzying, like standing at the edge of a deep ravine.

Out of your smiling mouth, these words: "What I really, really admire about you, Adra—(I guess I'm envious!)—is how you don't give a damn how you appear to other people—what they think of you. Like, guys."

A shrug of my shoulders. As if what you were going to tell me would not be wounding as it would be to another, ordinary girl.

"It's so cool, Adra. You don't even *try.* You let your hair go, sometimes you don't wash it for days. Looks like you barely comb it.

You never wear makeup—of course. (You don't even own makeup, I'm sure.) Your face could be a boy's face, almost. A handsome boy's face."

You dared to touch my face, with your fingertips. For a long moment I did not flinch away.

Nearing the end of sophomore year you said, casually: "We should room together, Ad. Next year? Okay?"

Like a blade these words cut into me. Thrilling, with an undertone of dread.

"No. I don't think so."

"What d'you mean—*no*? Why not?"

"I don't—want—to room with anyone."

You stared at me, wounded. *With anyone!* But how was Erica Kirkland—*anyone*?

The prospect of sharing a room in a residence hall with you filled me with panic. Like being pushed close to a mirror, so close that I could not see the reflection in the mirror, in this way blinded, suffocated. *No thank you. No.*

You went away, wounded. Furious. You were not so forgiving now for you had offered yourself, with rare openness. And in my shyness, in my fear of our intimacy, I had rebuffed you. It is likely that you were thinking *She will pay for this insult.* Though I could not have guessed at the time.

And then, in our junior year, the scales tipped away from me, I had no idea why.

No longer did you call out—*Ad! Sit with us.*

Or—*Ad? Save me a seat at dinner.*

Your invitations to accompany you to lectures, receptions, parties began to diminish. You dropped by my room to visit me less frequently.

At a distance I would see you, swaying-drunk, giddy and your face lit with merriment that excluded me, that seemed to me vulgar and foolish, shameful. And I retreated from you, and shut my door and locked it.

Rarely you invited me to walk with you in the woods above the college, that had been our special place.

(Did this mean that, elsewhere, another individual was being favored? Another very special unique brilliant *girl friend*?)

You won an award for "outstanding citizenship," and others crowded around you to congratulate you. You published an essay in the school literary magazine, which you'd never shown me.

Were others "vetting" your work now? Trying not to be sick with jealousy.

At a little distance I watched you. I was edgy, anxious for your attention. Though I did not seek it. When you needed help with a paper on normative philosophy, the news came to me through another girl, a network of girls, each of them passing on the request—*Erica is worried to death, she is going to flunk this course. But she doesn't want to ask you to help her, she feels that she has taken up too much of your time as it is.*

"That's silly. That's just ridiculous. Tell her to bring it to me. Of course I'll be happy to help her."

And this was so. I was happy to help you.

That paper, we received an A. Both of us quite proud!

Weekends when I was not working at the library, I had time to myself. Too much time, perhaps. I had time for my own work, for my "creative" writing, and I had time for your work, which had begun to be more daring now, more original and imaginative, in ways I could not have foreseen. *As if you had swallowed me whole, and had grown around me.* I did not mind providing footnotes, combing research materials in the library while you were at fraternity parties, attending a conference in New York City. I took pleasure in knowing how it would surprise you, that I'd expanded your sparsely argued fifteen-page paper into a thirty-page paper, richly footnoted, brilliantly argued. One of your "pioneering" papers.

I did not "stalk" you—the very notion would have been repugnant to me. But sometimes it happened (by chance) that we were walking in the same direction, onto the hilly campus, you in the lead, and me trailing behind, like a dog that is dragging one of its feet, reluctant to be seen, and yet hopeful.

And you would see me, and wave to me. "Adra? C'mon, catch up and walk with me."

You laughed at me. (Did you?)

You took pity on me. You were pitiless.

With the innocence of the most profound cruelty you inspired others to laugh at your lanky-limbed disheveled friend. Your friend who was indeed "special" yet deeply unhappy.

Of course it was not stalking. "Stalking" had not been invented.

And one day on the steps of Lyman Hall you said, "Look. I'm tired of you following me, Adra. It's boring. You're boring."

But it was a joke. (Was it?) I was shocked, but managed to laugh. Tears flooded my eyes, which often happens when I am taken by surprise, I cannot seem to *see* or even to *hear* for my senses are blocked by the surprise.

"I'm not 'following' you. That's—that's ridiculous."

"You're acting like a damn *girl*."

"You! You're the damn *girl*." Suddenly stammering, "You—you bleach your *hair. You're the girl*."

Hated you! Could have flung myself at you and scratched and gouged your eyes you'd outlined in dark brown eye pencil and darkened with mascara that gave your lashes a stiff look like the legs of long-legged spiders.

You laughed at me, seeing the fury and misery in my face, that you knew I dared not express. Turning away, with a negligent gesture of your hand as if you were waving away an annoying fly—"Oh, go away. I'll see you later, Adra."

There are the exploited, and there are those that exploit.

The predator, and the prey.

The parasite, and the host.

It was a time when I walked often—alone—in the woods above the college. I did not really hike any longer—I did not have the time.

I had a fear, too, of getting lost in the trails for I did not have a strong sense of direction. The area of the brain that monitors spatial relations had not developed in my brain as it develops in others.

Walking with you, for the last time, in the fresh pine-sharp air, all my senses alert to the point almost of pain, and my heart running rapid as a mountain stream, and you are breathing deeply and humming under your breath which (you know) is distracting and annoying to me and suddenly you say, quizzing me, "Which way is the college, Adra? Just checking." And I am jolted from my thoughts and not immediately able to comprehend our location. For it is not a simple fact, that the college must be behind us; the trail has been curving, twisting, turning back upon itself, indeed we have turned onto several trails, and a panic comes over me that we are lost . . .

"Don't be silly, Adra. Nobody gets lost *here*."

You'd hiked long miles, five or six hours, seven hours in the Adirondacks. You'd belonged to a hiking club. Your leg muscles were hard and thick, stronger than mine. It was natural for you to become impatient with me, who had so poor a sense of direction.

In hiking boots your feet were large as a man's. The only feature of yours that truly embarrassed you, you'd said you *hated*.

But you liked it that my feet were the same size as yours, in length. In width, my feet were narrower than yours.

We sat on a fallen log. We noted how tiny ants swarmed beneath the bark which we lazily picked off. Dreamily you said, "There are trillions of ants and no leader. No 'queen' as in a bee-hive. Ants in a colony are like neurons in a great brain, but they are brainless."

Some of this I knew also, from our psychology lecture. In fact, I had been reading in the subject, and must have told you, in my fascination with the mysteries of evolution, and now you were quoting me back to myself, in a way that was impressive to me as if what I was hearing was entirely new.

With a shudder I said that it was terrible to think of ants—

"What they represent."

"What they 'represent'? What's that?"

"Ourselves. They are like ourselves."

"Oh, I don't think so. Ants are just *ants*."

You laughed at me. At times you found my seriousness charming but at other times you found my seriousness very boring.

Stubbornly I said, "Nothing is just what it is. It is also what it represents."

"No! An ant is an ant, and five ants are a single ant. A trillion ants are just one ant."

"That's what I meant. They are terrifying." I didn't know what we were talking about but I was feeling uneasy, disoriented.

"Oh, I think they're wonderful as they are. Just—ants."

I doubted this, in any case. Amid a mound of teeming ants, surely some ants were *more special* than others. Alpha ants? Egg-laying queens, as in bee colonies? Asexual worker ants, lesser female and males? Not egalitarian at all.

But you were never much interested in *facts*. Biology, botany, history—you took what you wished, superficially.

Grinding the heel of your boot into a small ant hill, crushing as many scurrying ants as you could. The look in your face!—murderous, grinning.

Saying suddenly, quietly: "You know, Adra—I think we should keep some distance between us, for a while."

This was not a great surprise. It should not have been a great surprise.

I did not wince, or cry—*Oh but why?*

You told me just to "sit"—"think your deep boring thoughts"—and you would return in a half hour. But you did not return, as I knew you would not.

At the edge of a steep ravine I was sitting. By the ravaged ant hill, about which hundreds of ants now scurried in a paroxysm of panic. I was afraid to stand for my legs would tremble if I did. All that day, on the hiking trail, I had been feeling lightheaded, uneasy. I was wanting to cry, and clutch at your hand. Hoping that you would ask me to room with you next year—our senior year.

Why, when I had rejected your offer to be roommates, did I now want so badly to be your roommate?

Unknowing, a participant in a game. When I'd been the stronger and more independent, you had pursued me; when our positions were reversed, and my strength was revealed as mere weakness, you lost interest.

The irony was, I had become a more interesting person, through my friendship with you. More mature, less childish. Unfortunately, more vulnerable.

In my backpack I always carried supplies, for both of us—water in a plastic container, plenty of tissues (Erica's eyes and nose watered badly in the cold air), a Swiss Army knife of classic red stainless steel.

The Swiss Army knife had originally belonged to an older relative in my family. It had been purchased from an Army-Navy discount store in my hometown. Just the look of the knife, its practicality, concision, sexy red hue, had made Erica smile when she'd first seen it.

Now, the knife seemed particularly valuable should I want to slash my wrists, or my throat. Or, better yet, slash another's throat on a remote trail.

(Yes, this is a joke.)

(As Freud said, There are no jokes.)

In fact, I didn't take the knife out of my backpack just then. I thought of it, yes—but did not touch it.

After forty minutes I managed to stand, shakily. I could not see clearly—my eyes flooded with tears. Groping for the log, sitting heavily on it, weakly.

I had not cried in such a way since childhood. My vain, frayed life like a ratty old unraveled sweater passed before me as in a poorly executed film of jerky and frayed images.

Shame! You are not even brave enough to die here.

She wants you to die, so she can be rid of you. So that she can mourn her "deeply troubled" friend and write about you.

And accept condolences, for the loss of you.

But you are a coward, you will let her down. You can only return to the husk of a person you were, and will be.

⸻

But I did not return to what I'd been. Five days, five wretched nights later, I departed forever from Champlain College.

Nor had you returned that day to find me as you'd promised. Where I was sitting dazed by the edge of the ravine. Where I wept, abashed and exhausted. Instead you would claim—(to my very face, brazenly)—that I'd taken another trail down the mountain, after we'd agreed to "each go our separate way"—for this was something we'd done "many times before."

Your lies were both brazen and melodic. For you took pleasure in lying, in the very face of the one you had betrayed.

Soul-murder. You committed *soul-murder*, deliberately. I was your victim, though not your only victim.

⸻

"And now, in conclusion . . ."

For the past fifty minutes I have been staring at you. We have all been staring at you. Stunned by the horror of you.

Few know, as I know, how you'd once looked. How vile you are now that your (ugly) soul has emerged. Your coarse, showy blond beauty has faded as if it had never been and now you are revealed as a middle-aged woman who has let her body go and has become sexless, graceless. Over the years I'd observed your official photographs change with glacial slowness (for a feminist, you were certainly loath to acknowledge your aging); yet now, exposed on

127

the bright-lit stage in your ridiculous tent-kimono, head hairless as soapstone and face sagging, you appear much older than your calendar age so that I am thinking—(gloating?)—that you must have a medical condition, or you'd had one; cancer, probably. (I wonder: do you still smoke? Do Tareytons still exist?) Chemotherapy has ravaged you, face, throat, body, and scalp. Perhaps you'd lost weight and have more recently packed on weight as a warrior might pack on armor for self-protection.

Oh—it is upsetting to me, to see the change in you, who'd once been so—seductive . . .

Especially I do not want to imagine what your ruin of a body looks like, hidden inside those silly clothes.

Friend of my heart—this is what you deserve.

". . . thanking you all for your kindness, and hospitality, and your warmth on this beautiful campus . . ."

Each of your words, uttered with breathy insincerity, is a banality, a cliché. Yet, strung together, like cheap pearls on a cheap string, they bring to mind a memory of beauty. I shut my eyes so that I see only narrowly through my eyelashes, that shimmer with tears, and I scarcely see *you*—fat old woman with a Buddha face.

Instead I see that other. The girl you'd been.

When greed and ambition had not (yet) shone in your face.

Boring. You are boring. Go away, Adra.

I'd withdrawn from college in March of our junior year. With only eight weeks to go before the end of classes. A straight-A average, abandoned!

But that is what *breakdown* is. Nothing to joke about, as real as a broken limb. Broken back.

Returned home, so weak I could not get out of bed some days but lay in a half sleep of fever and dread. It was diagnosed that I had infectious mononucleosis which I'd thought was a mythical illness but turned out to be real. The transcript of my grades came to the house, a column of Is—*Incompletes.*

These would change automatically to Fs if I did not return to complete the courses within a semester. But I did/could not return.

In this initial skirmish, you won. In subsequent skirmishes in the long battle, you have won. But your victories have been predicated on victims not fighting back.

Giving up. *But I did not give up.*

After I left Champlain College, broken and ashamed, we lost contact. I did not write to you, and out of shame and guilt you would not have written to me. Perhaps you forgot me: for I was but one of those unwitting participants in your cruel game. Those whom you'd exploited, for all we could give you, that you might forget us as one of those carnivorous insects that sucks frogs dry and leaves behind the frog-husk, would forget its succession of victims.

For several years I would live at home as one might live underground. For a while I stopped reading entirely—the "life of the mind" had nearly destroyed me. I would work at low-paying jobs including public school substitute teaching. In my midtwenties I dared to return to college. This was not elite Champlain College where my tuition had been paid for me but one of the State University of New York branches, functional and charmless as an automat. Working days, attending classes at night, I eked out a beggarly master's degree in English and communication arts; eventually my PhD was earned with labor like the labor of one breaking rocks with a sledgehammer. But it was too late, I'd missed my time. Older than others on the job market by five, six years and soon then condemned to a lifetime of adjunct teaching—for which I learned to be grateful if at the same time spiteful.

Grateful? Spiteful.

(One of William Blake's lesser-known rhymes, you are speculating.)

Yet I did not ever give up my intellectual aspirations—I will never give up . . .

All the while I was keenly aware of *you*—who'd gone to Duke on a fellowship, then a first-rate department of stellar feminist scholars and critics. You were never a scholar, you hadn't the patience. You were never a true critic, you hadn't the taste. You were no kind of intellectual, for you hadn't the intelligence. But you had the seductive manner that, in academic circles, is a most effective substitute. Soon, you became the protégée of a famous feminist, coeditor of a massively successful anthology of women's literature from Sappho to the present time. You'd assisted in this project, one of the great curatorial projects in American feminist literary history—*you!*

From there, so launched, you were hired at Princeton, and then hired away to Columbia; then, in a dizzying coup, you were summoned to Stanford where you received a half-time appointment in gender studies and a half-time appointment at the Stanford Institute of Research. There, you cobbled together—(you did not *write*: you are too wonderful for mere *writing*)—the fandango of purloined material that would become *Masks of Gender*. Your star ascended, brightly glaring with sparks, while mine smoldered, and nearly went out. (Indeed my star was hardly a star, rather an ember.)

Many times, pride swallowed like phlegm, I wrote to you—in appeal, in accusation, bemused, furious, matter-of-fact, and "nostalgic." Of course you did not answer—why would you answer? These were the days of (typed or handwritten) letters in envelopes, sealed and stamped, that shifted by degrees to email, so fluid, so seemingly (though not actually) bodiless, anonymous. I would write emails to the editors of journals in which your work appeared, and to your publishers; I would write to the dean of the faculty at

Stanford, and to your departmental chairs; I would write to femi-
nist colleagues enclosing photocopied material that condemned
you, often with zestful wit. Some of these colleagues were kind
enough to respond to my appeals, but most were not. And those
who were initially kind soon ceased communicating with me
when I sent them more material, heavy packets of photocopied
material, and demanded that they join with me in a "class-action
suit" against you.

Every friend, I have come to see, is a fair-weather friend.

For years, as possibly you know, I have been publishing reviews
of your work in quasi-academic journals, the most public being
The Women's Review of Books; it has been my solemn task to evis-
cerate your (insipid, bestselling) books, your shoddy scholarship
and questionable theories. Boldly I have dared to attack you as a
plagiarist and thief—a betrayer of the heart. A *faux feminist* who
sells out women.

You have won many awards, however undeserving. That is a
matter of (shameful) historic fact. I have won no awards—I am not
ashamed but, in a way, proud. *For I do not conform to the expectations
of others*. My threadbare life does not make a striking resume for a
book jacket—(I have yet to publish my first book)—yet I am stub-
born in resilience, I believe in myself—one day, my contribution
to cultural studies will be appreciated.

Each semester it seems that I open my veins, and bleed. And
I bleed, and I bleed. I teach the great texts—the *pre*texts of
our debased era: Freud, Nietzsche, Dostoyevsky, Kafka, Sartre,
Camus. And one or two students, perhaps, will appreciate me—in
their student evaluations they will write *Ms. Leeuwen is an excellent
teacher I think. She is very well knowledgeable and her tests are hard
but not unfair. When I did not get a high grade like I thought I should,
I went to talk to her and she went over my paper with me, and took*

time. She is not like some teachers that are resentful of you when you come to their offices and the first minute you are there, they are waiting for you to leave.

I feel sorry for Ms. Leeuwen, there is something sad about her. But she is excellent reading to us passages from Jean-Paul Sartre on disgust.

Other people in the class do not feel this way. They do not like Ms. Leeuwen because of her hard grades and how she does not flatter us. One of my friends said she would slash her wrists if she turned out like Ms. Leeuwen but I do not feel this way. My thinking has been sharpened by Ms. Leeuwen and I would take more courses from her if these existed.

Other evaluations, cruder, frankly stupid, scribbled by persons to whom I gave grades lower than A, I do not dignify by reading. Quickly shoving the forms into the unwieldy envelopes, and "filing" them in the trash.

At the start of my career at this college I was not so marginal a figure. I was not shunned. Indeed, I was admired by many in the tenured ranks and by the dean of the college. Often I was complimented on something I had written, published in an obscure journal; I believe that these were sincere compliments. But, at departmental meetings, I could not resist raising my hand to question, to comment, sometimes to disagree, which was not what an adjunct instructor should do; this, I knew, but could not resist for that is my nature—*to speak truth, not to flatter.*

In this way, though some colleagues continued to like me, and some to be amused by me, gradually the majority became weary of me, after eleven years—the *plain dealer* in their midst who says aloud what they should say but dare not.

Shamefully, though I am the most experienced, the most published, and the most intelligent of the small army of adjuncts that helps keep the college afloat, like galley slaves hidden from the upper deck of the élites, there was a small cadre of colleagues who'd tried to terminate my contract last year. Only my reasoned appeal, and my threat of bringing a lawsuit against the college, with a likelihood of sensational repercussions in local media as in *The Chronicle of Higher Education*, thwarted this attempt to destroy me. But I do not trust anyone here now.

All this, I would like to tell you. But there is not time.

At last—you have finished your overpriced lecture. You have concluded with a poem by Elizabeth Bishop (of such exquisite beauty, you do not deserve to utter it aloud in your honeyed voice) and now you are peering coquettishly over the rims of dark-tinted glasses at the credulous audience exploding in applause.

It is deafening—such applause!

And now—a standing ovation.

Stubbornly, I remain sitting. I am sure that some of my tenured colleagues will remain seated as well, for not all of them can have been persuaded by you, yet, by quick degrees, as if shamed by the younger persons behind them, my hypocrite colleagues rise to their feet, smiling and abashed like Chinese elders routed by the cudgels of the Red Guard.

At the podium you have the grace to remain standing, somewhat surprised-looking, or so it seems, at the waves of warm applause washing over you; now, you are leaning your bulky body pointedly on your cane, and a look of fatigue has come into your face. Quickly the Gender Studies apparatchik comes to your side, to escort you from the stage.

Another time, your gaze drifts onto me—I think. As I sit here in the choicest seat in Hill Auditorium, stubbornly refusing to stand, arms crossed over my backpack as if to secure it.

And then, the unexpected occurs.

Though I have prepared tirelessly for the next stage of my confrontation with E__ K___, steeling myself for the most demanding performance of my life, all is—suddenly, capriciously—changed; and what was to be, by my vow, is not to be after all.

At the conclusion of the program, there is to be a book signing. Many, many students have lined up in the foyer, awaiting your arrival there; but I do not intend to be one of them.

Instead, matter-of-factly I leave my seat, and make my way up onto the stage. No one takes notice of me—the performance is over, people are milling about in the aisles, making their way to the exits. A stagehand is pushing the podium into the wings. In my most pleasant voice I call your name—"Erica! Hello"—as I follow you and the woman who is escorting you off stage as if this were the most natural thing in the world and not an act of trespass and daring; and without hesitation, certainly without suspicion you turn to me, with a smile, as if anticipating something pleasant, and not catastrophe; and adrenaline rushes to my heart, so powerfully I nearly faint.

First glance, you must think that I might be a graduate student—straggly hair, cap pulled low over my forehead, bulky backpack I am struggling to unzip, out of which I will probably (you assume!) tug a dog-eared copy of *Masks of Gender* to ask you to sign; your escort will frown in annoyance, but you, in your mode of noblesse oblige, will say *Why of course! How shall I inscribe it?*

Second glance, you will see that I am not so young. Probably not a graduate student, and given the state of my attire probably not a (full-time) faculty member.

Third glance, if there is time for a third glance, you will see that I am middle-aged, as you are; with a face less obviously ravaged, and a body still lean, if perhaps too thin, and my skin papery pale, no longer the resilient skin of youth.

"Is it—Adrienne? Is it you?"

Almost, I can't *see*—you are so dazzling in the gold-glittering kimono.

And you are staring at me. An expression in your face of wariness, warmth—surprise . . .

"Adrienne? It's you?"

On your cane you hobble toward me. This is so unexpected, I am unable to respond.

Your lips are parted, glistening. Your eyes inside the dark-tinted lenses are indeed pouched with tiredness, yet alert fixed upon my face.

I murmur that I am not Adrienne—"Not exactly."

"You were my dissertation student at—Columbia?"

I don't correct you. At this moment my name seems laughably insignificant—*Adrienne, Adra.* How could it matter?

The shock is, you have recognized me. You have identified me—*friend.*

The black nylon backpack has slipped from my hands. It falls at my feet, forgotten.

With seductive boldness you dare to take my hands, that are cold, and warm them between your palms, that feel almost hot, moistly hot, and comforting.

Is this real? Can this be real? Through a buzzing in my ears I hear your honeyed voice, and the affection in your voice. *Friend. Here is a friend.*

You seem delighted to see me. Unless it is just a performance for several of my colleagues who have hurried to surround you—but I don't think so, I believe it is genuine, you are not pretending now that the lecture is over and the audience has departed.

As one would to an old friend not seen in years you are complaining dryly of your "wreck of a knee"—the "mostly futile" surgery you've had to correct it. With startling familiarity you say you've decided just to "flaunt my ugly baldy-head—why not?"

I am standing numb, speechless. Is it possible—the impossible is happening? *My friend is returned to me?*

"So—you're teaching here, Adrienne? They're lucky to have you. You're coming to dinner with us, I assume . . ."

Glances among my colleagues. Eyes avoiding my eyes.

"I—I don't think that I've been invited . . ."

"Of course you are invited! I insist."

You turn to the others with an imperial look. Still you are grasping my hands, so strangely. Is it possible—(I will think this later, sleepless that night and in subsequent nights in the throes of an enormous burgeoning love like a great snake that has forced itself down my throat)—that you do, in fact, recognize me?—Adra Leeuwen?

But no, this is not so clear. While recognizing me, my face, this look of yearning in my eyes, perhaps you have conflated me with another yearning girl, enough like me to be a substitute for me?— but this does not invalidate the warmth with which you address *me.*

How sad it is, you are no longer beautiful. You have morphed into an eccentric middle-aged woman, a "celebrity"—one who means well, who is not sardonic or malicious. You are leaning on me, instead of on your cane; I feel something like a tremor in your hands. I sense that you are exhilarated by the warm applause but you are also fatigued, and not well.

The kimono is a brave, silly choice; the black slacks are more practical, hiding fat, quivery legs. You smell of perspiration—your underarms are damp. You are making a fuss over me as—what is this?—lights flash, for a girl photographer from the student newspaper is taking pictures, and a professional photographer from the college development office.

Flashing lights! I am too confused to smile—overwhelmed—for no one has taken my photograph in a very long time.

My colleagues are tugging at you. Casting icy glances at me. Come with us, Erica!

Time for you, distinguished guest lecturer, to sign books in the foyer. Then there is a dinner to follow at a local restaurant, and so with dogged persistence, that steeliness that underlies your gregarious social manner, you repeat to your hosts that you assume I've been invited. My face burns with a hurtful sort of pleasure. It is up to me to say graciously *Oh no, I'm very tired, I wasn't intending to come to dinner—but thank you so much*; yet, as my colleagues stare at me glowering I do not stammer these words.

"Adrienne? You're coming to dinner, yes?"

"Yes . . ."

"I'll see you at dinner, then. Save me a seat!"

Your eyes are damp with—can it be *tears*? Remorse, regret? Affection born of loneliness?

Save me a seat. These words echo in my head: so sweet of you, if ridiculous, hypocritical—you must know very well that as the guest of honor you will have a seat, in fact it is the seat of the guest of honor; and if *you* want someone to sit close beside you, if *you* want someone, an old, dear friend, to clasp your hand, to drink with you, and reminisce with you, and laugh with you, it is your prerogative, and no one is likely to deny *you* who have been paid, for a fifty-minute lecture, in excess of an adjunct's salary for an entire semester.

In my soiled and ill-fitting khakis, in my hiking boots, worn denim jacket, baseball cap over straggly hair, with my wan, pale, truculent face I am not exactly dressed for the quasi-elegance of either of our "good" restaurants; but it seems that I am invited, and that you will insist that I sit beside you, to the consternation of your hosts.

An extra place at dinner, not so difficult. The impromptu demand will be met for your hosts are eager to please you. The dean is particularly eager to please you for you are a famous person who will (very likely) write about them and the college; and it is to their advantage to please you, so far as they can.

Always, people have been eager to please you. Why?

The harder you are to please, the more eager they are to please you. It is something like a law of nature.

And it is a fact, or was—I loved you.

Might have died for you, if you'd explicitly requested it. As it was, your wish was too oblique out on the hiking trail. You'd allowed me to misinterpret. For which I am grateful—*I love you.*

"Remember, Adra—save me a place at dinner!"

You are moving away haltingly, using your cane. I stand here smiling after you, dazed. I pick up my bulky backpack, which I might as well strap to my back. Damned awkward to bicycle so encumbered, especially in the rain.

My pride is such, I will not run after my colleagues to ask which restaurant. They are hoping that I will just vanish, that I will understand that of course I am not invited to this special dinner where I will hope to sit close beside the guest of honor, whispering with her like old, dear friends while others stare in envy at us.

Pride, too, will not allow me to beg a ride with my colleagues. For these are not colleagues but rivals for the fickle admiration of undergraduates. Perhaps not rivals so much as enemies, who would be cheered if I died, or at least was grievously injured, in a bicycle mishap on the highway, in pelting rain on my way to *l'Auberge provençale* at the edge of town—(for I think it must be this restaurant you are going to, I think I'd overheard one of your hosts utter a French-sounding name in a lowered voice, hoping that I couldn't hear); of course, in the rain, as I pedal along College Avenue shakily I am cursing myself for having come to school today without a raincoat crumpled and shoved into my backpack with other essential supplies.

Headlights in my eyes, near-blinding. Like the flash bulbs heralding a new life, that make me smile, and my breath catch in my throat.

Let's try that again, please. Both of you—eyes open and SMILE.

It will be a dazzling sight, to see photographs of the celebrated E__ K__ and myself in the local newspaper, smiling into the flash bulb. My students will be impressed. My colleagues will be impressed. In anticipation I am feeling hopeful, uplifted. My senses are on high alert. I am grateful to be wearing the baseball cap, which prevents my hair from blowing wetly into my face.

Yes, I have aged, since we were girls together. But *you* also have aged, which makes us more like each other.

And so I am hoping that it's the French restaurant at which the dinner will be held, and not the other—Carnival, it's called—on the farther side of town. If I arrive at the wrong restaurant in chagrin I will have to bicycle miles to the other, in the damned rain, and even then, I can't be absolutely certain that the dinner for you will be at Carnival either, if not at the French restaurant; for there are one or two other possible restaurants to which the lecture committee might take you, one of them a steak house, the other a reputedly upscale Italian restaurant, and each of them far too expensive for me to afford even if I were in the habit of going out to restaurants to eat, God knows which I am not.

And if I dine with you, seated close beside you, if through the meal you reach out to squeeze my hand, to exchange intimate glances with me, if we laugh together recalling old adventures and if at the end of the meal you invite me to accompany you to your hotel room for a nightcap, and if I hesitate but say *Y-yes . . . I think I can, Erica.*

Then, we will see what transpires. What surprises the night will yield.

BONE MARROW DONOR

A hospital vigil is notable for sudden interruptions for (often) you lapse into exhausted sleep at the bedside of the patient without knowing where you are or even *why* you are where you have no clear idea you are, and (often) when you wake there is a pulsing pressure in your ears, inside your head trying to determine: *where, why?*

Not at your husband's bedside on the oncology floor but in another place not known to you though also (evidently) a clinical—chilly!—setting. (Why are hospitals so cold?—it's to discourage the [inevitable] growth of bacteria. Colder the temperature, less bacteria fecundity though never [of course] no bacteria fecundity so long as there is the warm pulsebeat of life.)

Roaring in your ears through which you are having difficulty hearing a doctor's jovial voice.

Good news, Mrs. __ !—there has been a new development in the patient's prognosis.

Good news, Mrs. __ !—bone marrow transplant has been approved provided you are still willing to donate bone marrow for your husband.

Good news, Mrs. __ !—there is a strong possibility that you can save your husband's life.

You are very excited to hear this. Yet, you are terrified.

You are in a conference room in the hospital. Several staff physicians are in attendance whose names are told to you, which you immediately forget. Oncologist Dr. N___ is explaining the marrow extraction procedure which involves a minimum of two hours of surgery under a partial anesthetic, performed by a bone marrow specialist. There is some risk (of course). There will be some pain (of course).

An eighteen-inch needle will be sunk into your hip bone and a minute quantity of marrow extracted.

In fact, as Dr. N___ points out, the "gravest risk" to the donor isn't the bone marrow extraction itself but the anesthesia.

Dr. N___ makes this pronouncement in a voice of such flatness, you understand that it is a witticism of some sort. Or perhaps it is an affectionate reproach. One of the physicians lifts a rueful hand to self-identity—Dr. T___ , anesthesiologist.

Another physician is the bone marrow surgeon Dr. R___ who waves at you boyishly.

Weeks before you'd told Dr. N___ that you would like to donate bone marrow if it would help your husband. At the time Dr. N___ had shrugged off your request as if its naivete had offended him.

Overhearing, your husband had protested—*Don't be ridiculous! I wouldn't allow you to take such a risk and anyway, it isn't going to be necessary.*

You will note afterward how the prospect of weakening, failing, dying is viewed as "ridiculous" by many of the afflicted daring you to contradict them and so indeed you rarely contradict them.

Now, confronted with the prospect of the eighteen-inch needle sunk into your hip bone you are growing faint. You can feel blood draining from your head. In a voice of the most subtle reproach (for he can decipher your panicked thoughts) Dr. N___ says that the bone marrow transplant procedure is far more dangerous for the recipient than the extraction is for the donor: the mortality rate for the recipient is ___ (you do not hear this mumbled statistic) while the mortality rate for the donor is less than 3 percent.

Meaning, 97 percent chance of (donor) survival.

Such excellent odds of survival, you would be shamed into saying anything less than *Yes.*

Though you are shivering. Though you have begun to perspire. You feel a need to grasp at the edge of the conference table, to steady yourself.

Dr. N___ cups his hand to his ear. *What is your response, Mrs. ___?*

I said—yes. I will.

You will—?

—donate bone marrow for my husband.

There! The words are uttered.

Around the table the physicians stare at you, gravely nodding. In their eyes you believe you see respect, admiration. The (brave, good) wife will donate bone marrow for the husband!

Y-Yes.

A legal document is presented to you by a (female) notary public. It is oversized, with numerous pages and addenda. With difficulty you read the small print which even as your eyes move across lines of type fades rapidly, you cannot glance back to reread. And by the end of the (thirty-page) document you have forgotten what you've read.

Sign here, Mrs. __ . The notary public is witness to your signature.

Though your hand is badly shaking you manage to sign your name with a pen provided for you.

Such hoarse breathing! You hope it isn't your own.

Your skin is burning, the fever has made you delirious. Slick clammy sweat on your forehead, in your armpits.

Mrs. __ ?—this way.

———

You are greatly relieved, a (female) nurse's aide will be bathing you. Washing away the sticky sweat, the embarrassing smell of your (female, frightened) body.

Dry yourself in an enormous scratchy white towel, cover your nakedness in a short paper gown that ties at the back. If you sit on the edge of an operating table, the paper gown crinkles and rides up your thighs white as lard.

Absurdly modest for a woman of your age, a woman no longer young but with pretensions of appearing young.

The last of all pretensions is that of being sexually attractive. At least, to someone.

My husband thinks that I am beautiful. In all the world he is the only person who thinks so.

In all the world my husband is the only person who loves me.

You are urged to lie down on the gurney. You will be transported to Surgery for the procedure. Overhead a perforated ceiling passes in a blur. Your hair falls in tangles over the edge of the gurney. You are helpless on your back as a turtle on its back. You see that you have lost weight since the start of the hospital vigil, you fold your arms across your small flaccid breasts as if to make yourself smaller.

You will be partially sedated, it is (again) explained. You will be partially conscious through the procedure but unable to move. You will not remember most of the experience afterward.

Yes, there will be pain. But if you do not remember pain afterward is it *pain*?

Yes, there will be grief. But if you do not remember grief afterward is it *grief*?

Skilled gloved fingers tap for a vein in the crook of your right arm. Your veins are dehydrated, many (painful) attempts to start a line are made, and fail, before a needle is inserted successfully—*One-two-three! This will pinch!*

A cry escapes your lips. But soon then you begin to float. Though your eyes are not open you see clearly the part-masked faces surrounding you in a ring above you, eyes brightly avid with curiosity.

An eighteen-inch needle is held aloft in gloved fingers, shining. Fascinated you observe it descend. A cold sensation on your left pelvic hip bone, then a piercing pain, and a yet more piercing pain as the needle is inserted deeper, into the bone, into the very marrow of the bone. So extreme is this pain you have no breath to scream. You have no strength to move—you are paralyzed, as it has been promised.

Oh! Oh God help me. . . . But your quaint cries are muted, no one hears.

Perhaps there is a surgical error, your brain seizes, your heart fails, you sink into oblivion: die.

Or, fail to die but wake in confusion in Recovery hours later.

Eyes open, Mrs. __! Eyes open!

Your spine, your neck, and the back of your head ache with pain but your lower body has disappeared in a haze of numbness.

Where is your husband? Vaguely you expect your husband to have been brought to you, to grip your hand and to commend you for being very, very brave.

A sound of crinkling paper, the silly gown you are wearing that is badly smeared with blood has ridden up your thighs.

A sound of muffled coughing. Muffled laughter?

Solemnly you are informed by an embarrassed voice—*Not such good news, Mrs. __! It appears you were not a viable candidate to donate bone marrow after all. It appears that you are paralyzed from your pelvic hipbone down.*

Stunned silence. You open your mouth to protest but no words issue forth.

More sounds of muffled coughing, laughter. You manage to push yourself up on your elbows, with much effort.

Silly woman! Did. You. Really. Think. That. Through. Any. Pathetic. Action. Of. Your. Own. You. Could. Save. Your. Husband's. Life.

You are informed: your husband has died, he has been dead for forty-eight hours. The precious bone marrow extracted from your hip bone is in the process even now of being "donated" to another, wealthier, and more important patient.

You are informed: your husband has been awaiting you in the hospital morgue on Level C. You will be taken to Level C now.

HAPPY CHRISTMAS

She flew home at Christmas, her mother and her mother's new husband met her at the airport dazzling-bright with Christmas neon in the long mall of shops and restaurants. Her mother hugged her hard and told her she looked pretty, her skin had cleared up hadn't it?—and her mother's new husband shook hands with her and looked her eye-to-eye like no bullshit between them telling her Jesus yes, she sure did look pretty, prettier than her pictures where she never seemed to be smiling but frowning and welcome home. He was younger than the girl's mother by maybe six, seven years. His sideburns grew razor-sharp into his cheeks and were jet-black, not a graying hair visible, not the sideburns and not the thick-tufted hair springing back from his forehead as if shellacked. His cologne or aftershave or hair gel cloying-sweet made her nostrils pinch. On his right hand he wore an onyx signet ring. In his lapel, a sprig of mistletoe. In his handshake her hand felt small and moist, the bones close to cracking. Her mother hugged her

147

again, half sobbing God, I'm so happy to see you, almost thought I'd lost you. Blue veins in the backs of her hands startling, the skin looking thin, papery, but her mother was happy, that was a relief. You could feel that all about her like a thrumming of the soul. The pancake makeup on her mother's face was a fragrant peach shade that had been blended skillfully into her raddled throat. On her left hand she wore her new rings: a small glittering diamond set high in spiky white-gold prongs, a white-gold wedding band. The girl tried and failed to recall the old rings like you might try and fail to remember a dream that must not have been important since it faded so quickly upon waking.

The girl was surprised, they stopped so soon for a drink at Easy Sal's at a Marriott off the Turnpike, she'd gathered that her mother and the new husband had had a drink or two at the airport. In Easy Sal's there were more dazzling-neon Christmas lights, a ten-foot silver-tinsel tree with glittering ornaments in the shapes of bottles: whiskey, wine. The girl ordered just Perrier with a twist of lime (*That's* fancy, her mother said with a kissy purse of her lips), her mother and her mother's new husband had martinis on the rocks, which were their "celebration" drinks.

For a while amid the festive buzz of the cocktail lounge they talked about what the girl was studying and what her plans were for the summer though the mother and the mother's new husband didn't appear to be listening to what the girl said and the girl had the impression that they were clasping hands beneath the wobbly chrome table or possibly the mother's new husband was clasping the mother's chubby knee exposed below her tight-fitting gold-lamé skirt, and when that subject trailed off they talked about their own plans, putting the house on the market, that was the first of the chores after the massive cleanup *top to bottom* as the cleaning service boasted which wasn't cheap, not an ideal time to sell a luxury property (as it was called) but now that the grand jury was behind them, that was the next step. A year and a half of fucking hell but no indictments which was what their lawyers assured them of course, not a shred of evidence that could constitute *beyond a reasonable doubt* if there was a trial and why'd there be a trial?—no crime had been committed, that was the bottom line. The insurance company had finally paid, *that* was the bottom line. There's a fantastic new condominium village on the river, the girl's mother said, we'll show you when we drive past, there'll be a room for you whenever you want it, reserved for *you*. Radiant happiness in the mother's face, the girl could not help but see. The mother smiling so hard you'd think her lower face would crack. Giggling, shivery. It's like I died and was reborn. Just makes me so happy, the two people I love most in the world right here with me. Right here right now. So if I died, you would both hold me tight. Wouldn't you? Wouldn't you both hold me tight if I died right now? The mother's new husband laughed, startled, and kissed her saying, Hell nobody's going to die tonight or any other night. That's a promise. A waitress in a tight-fitting satin Santa costume with a Santa hat tilted on her head brought two more martinis and a Perrier though the girl hadn't finished her first Perrier. And a tiny glass bowl of beer nuts. Thanks, sweetheart! her mother's new husband said happily squinting up at the waitress the tip of a pert pink tongue between his lips.

—

The girl had spoken with her mother no more than three times since her father's funeral in December of the previous year, they'd tried Skype but something went wrong or (maybe) the girl had sabotaged the call, she'd been high, but a bad kind of high, a toxic high, started laughing and then crying and had to shut down the computer and her roommate had to clasp her hands tight to keep them from fluttering like crazed birds saying in a calm voice *You're okay. You're going to be okay. We've decided, you are going to be okay. You're beautiful, you don't need them, maybe they are not murderers you can transcend them. You have got to rise above them, you will destroy yourself if you keep on like this* and eventually it was okay really, actually she'd been able to speak with her mother in a normal voice a few days later about her mother's plans to be remarried. Not that this was a surprise, it was not. Not asking is this the one from online. From, what's it for older people, *match.com*. Not asking how can you. Just, how can you. Her mother was maybe a little drunk. Or high too. A different kind of high. Saying, trying not to sound accusing, Oh I understand it's sudden in your eyes but you know, your father is not going to come back, we have to accept that. He is gone, we loved him so much and our hearts are broken but he *is gone*, it was a totally random tragedy, it always seems soon to the children, you are not a *child* any longer you know. You have to understand, Jay was there for me during all that ugliness. He was there for me, he was the *only one*. You were not, I am not blaming you but the fact is, you were not. And all your father's family—monsters . . . But that is water under the bridge, that is over with now, we are here now. All the back tuition has been paid, that's all cleared up now. Your degree—that's the bottom line. Jay said, we aren't going to turn our backs on that little girl, she needs us. This is a time of need. Mutual need. But it's over now, except for selling the house. We love you. Wait and see. *Both of us*—we are here for you. The girl had fallen silent feeling something nudge her knee, possibly it was the knee of the mother's new husband beneath the wobbly chrome table. As if unconsciously the girl moved her leg away causing the chrome table to tilt, fortunately they were clutching their drinks which did not topple over. The girl laughed nervously saying Yes, or maybe she was saying No. Or I guess. Her mother said in a husky voice, He makes me feel like living again, I feel, you know, like a woman again, after twenty-three years, and the girl felt her throat shut up tight too stricken to reply. As long as you're happy, her mouth tried to say.

Now it was 8:30 P.M. and had been pitch-black outside for a long time. The girl was lightheaded with hunger, she'd had just Diet Cokes and pretzels on the plane but her mother and her mother's new husband were on their third round of drinks. Easy Sal's had entertainment, first a piano player with a sad gargoyle face and a red Santa hat drunk-tilted on his head playing background music, old-timey pop songs the girl did not recognize, then a singer, female, ebony-black, V-necked red spangled dress, Santa cap drunk-tilted on her head, then a stand-up, anorexic-looking, of no sex or gender or ethnic identity you could determine, small bony angular face like a wizened monkey face glittering with piercings, no makeup, punk hairdo, waxed-looking purple-pink, black faux-leather jump-suit, pelvis thrust forward in mock-*Vogue*-model stance, delivery fast brash deadpan like rap lyrics: great thing about havin' your abortion early in the day is uh like y'know the rest of the day's uh gonna be fuckin' uphill, right? There's these half-dozen people in a uh Jacuzzi, hot new game called musical holes, uh maybe it just ain't caught on yet in New Jersey's why nobody's laughin', huh? words too machine-gun quick for the girl to catch but her mother and her mother's new husband seemed to hear, and were laughing though afterward her mother's new husband confided in disgust he did not approve of dirty language issuing from women's lips, whether they were dykes or not.

They stopped for dinner off the Turnpike at a brightly lit Polynesian restaurant surrounded by faux palm trees adorned with winking Christmas lights, on the faux-thatched roof a neon-red Santa with sleigh and reindeers at an alarming tilt. The girl's mother was explaining that there wasn't anything to eat at home, also it was getting late, tomorrow she'd be preparing a terrific dinner from Whole Foods, was that okay? She'd wanted to have a welcome-home dinner but ran out of time, then the plane was delayed anyhow, so was it okay? The mother's new husband interrupted sharply to say it's okay, no need to repeat yourself like a parrot, then made a joke of it winking at the girl like they were in it together whatever it was.

In Mauri's Polynesian Paradise they perused menus so large, the girl could barely see her mother and her mother's husband over her menu, the two seemed to be quarreling or maybe not, maybe it was a kind of foreplay, or afterplay, sipping drinks from halved coconuts, laughing together. In high spirits, this was still their honeymoon as the mother's husband said. Holding hands between courses, sipping from each other's tropical-hued drink. When the girl's mother excused herself to use the restroom moving unsteadily on her feet in high-heeled sandals the new husband leaned close to the girl to confide, Jesus I'm crazy about that woman. Your mother is a high-class lady. She was very hurt, he said, very devastated by things said about her. Erroneous charges. Outright lies. Slander. You know, we never met until—until after. It was all news to me. Shifting his cane chair closer, leaned moist and warm, meaty, against her, an arm across her shoulders too heavy for the girl to shake off.

Saying in a lowered confidential voice, there's nobody in the world precious to me as that lady, I want you to know that. I cannot and will not allow slander to be uttered about that woman, d'you understand? No matter who it is and I think you know who it is—was. But never again, okay? Is that an understanding? You and me, an understanding? The girl who had been sleepy-eyed was wide awake now and tasting cold and very frightened hearing herself say stammering Yes, yes I know it, and her mother's new husband said in a fierce voice close in her ear, gripping her shoulders with his arm heavy as a hose, Damn right, sweetheart: you better know it.

THE NICE GIRL

She was not bitter. Not ever bitter.

She was a Nice Girl. One of the Nice Girls.

See how we smile?—Nice Smiles.

You can't fake a smile like a Nice Smile.

———

Her name was Lila Dey. Even the sound—*Li-la Dey*—is a nice sound, the kind to provoke a smile.

"Lila Dey!"

Always she would remember. *Lila! Bring your things, meet your father and mother in front of the school. Hurry!*

In the black nylon graduation robe that fell to her ankles like a slovenly nightgown, in the laughter-filled disrobing room backstage that smelled, not unpleasantly, of excited adolescent bodies. In the heady afterglow of the commencement ceremony in which Lila

Dey had participated as one of several honors students delivering three-minute valedictory speeches, there came a senior teacher to pluck at her sleeve with the urgent command.

Right now, Lila. Your father says it's an emergency. Hurry!

She was stunned. She had not even time to feel the dismay of being cheated.

Only a few minutes before she'd been aware of her parents in a front row of the auditorium amid rows of other proud smiling parents of graduating seniors. Mothers with highlighted beauty-salon hair of the tawny hue of lionesses, fathers with striped neckties. These were parents who'd come to applaud their children and in the course of applauding their children, they would applaud the children of others as well. They were generous, even profligate in their applause.

As the recipient of several awards Lila Dey was feeling thrilled, slightly off-balance as if the tiny maze of bone (what was it called?) in her inner ear were askew. Then amid a buzzing of hornets she'd made her way to the podium, as in a dream she'd stared at the carefully prepared speech in her hand, precisely timed to three minutes zero seconds. During this speech Lila had glanced up several times—(this too she'd practiced, so that it would seem "spontaneous")—not daring to seek out her parents' attentive faces but affixing her gaze to the farthest row of seats where faces were indistinct and expressions indecipherable.

Smiling faces, she'd wanted to think. We all want to think.

Waves of applause followed her speech. As she stumbled from the podium to return to her seat on stage, just slightly panicked that she might trip in the black robe, for she was wearing unaccustomedly high heels, Lila felt blood rush into her face. She had done it!—given her speech. *Do they like me, after all? Have they believed in me—all along?*

From kindergarten onward she'd fretted that, if others knew what she was really like, what mean petty ignorant things streamed through her Nice Girl mind, they would shrink from her. In the yearbook beside *Lila Dey* were the astonishing words *most admired* but if people knew, they wouldn't admire her at all.

Other seniors were *most beautiful, most popular, most brainy, most promising. Funniest, best athlete, math whiz.* But Lila Dey was *most admired.*

(Am I proud? Am I ashamed?)

(If they only knew what a Nice Girl is really like!)

Following the graduation ceremony was an Honors Society luncheon for the most select seniors. Lila Dey had helped decorate the faculty dining room with the flowers of early summer—gorgeous peonies, roses. As an officer of the Society she'd been involved in planning the menu, sending out invitations. Literary awards were to be given out at the luncheon and Lila Dey was the recipient of one of these, for poetry. Mr. Carlson (who taught advanced placement English, was faculty advisor for the Honors Society, and with whom Lila Dey was desperately in love) would announce these awards at the luncheon, and in uttering the name *Lila Dey* he would smile at her, and she would rise from her seat and approach the front of the room where Mr. Carlson would hand her an envelope, and shake her hand . . . *Lila, congratulations!*

Now, that had been sabotaged. That would not occur.

Her parents were taking her away. Not for the first time, with such urgency.

Breathless and sick with dread Lila made her way through the festive crowded corridors. She did not want to see anyone she knew well—none of her Nice Girl friends! It was a cruel joke—she was headed in a direction contrary to the one she should be headed in. She would not be at the luncheon, she would not hear her name called by Mr. Carlson. This was her punishment for being happy, on this special day. And Lila Dey was not deserving of happiness. *If good things happen to you, you will pay all the more later.*

On the front steps of the school jubilant graduates still in their black robes were having their pictures taken. A short distance away her father was leaning out the opened window of his car calling to her—"Lila! Hurry."

Her parents were not vexed with *her*, she wanted to think. But both her mother and father were looking anxious, and harried. Before they could tell her what had gone wrong, why the day's plans had to be changed, she'd seemed to know.

"Is it Sabine? What's happened?"

"Just get in. Fasten your seatbelt. We're driving to Buffalo."

Buffalo? That had to be Sabine.

Her parents knew very little about Sabine's condition. They'd been told very little.

Lila learned that when her father checked his cell phone after the graduation ceremony he'd discovered a message from the Metro Medical Clinic in Buffalo in which his older daughter Sabine was enrolled in an outpatient program for severely depressed/suicidal persons. *Your daughter has failed to attend her morning therapy session. She does not answer our repeated calls. She gave us this number to call in case of emergency and it is our policy to regard such absences as occasions of possible emergency.*

But was this an emergency? What was it?

Lila was too surprised and too agitated to be angry. Too distracted to think, bitterly—*She has done this on purpose. She knows today is graduation for me.*

Calls to Sabine's cell phone went unanswered. Of course, this was not unusual: calls to Sabine were rarely answered, and messages left for her might be randomly answered, but never promptly.

The Deys had no one else to call except old friends of Sabine's who might well be former friends of Sabine's who in any case did not live in Buffalo where Sabine had moved after dropping out of Juilliard two years before.

It was shortly after she'd quit Juilliard that Sabine had shut and locked the door to her bedroom (in a flat she shared on West End Avenue, New York City, with two other Juilliard students), taken as many as thirty sleeping pills, burrowed into the soiled comforter in her bed with a plan, as she'd vaguely acknowledged afterward, of *going forward or coming back, whichever happened.* Fortunately, one of her apartment-mates had come home unexpectedly and rescued her.

The Deys hadn't been involved until after the fact, when they learned that Sabine had been taken by ambulance to an ER and was hospitalized with a diagnosis of "severe depression"; Sabine denied that she'd attempted suicide, and was not cooperative with therapists. Of course, the Deys had had to come immediately to New York City, to oversee her care; Lila had stayed behind, having to attend school. She would long recall the upended household of the subsequent months, as if the very earth had shifted beneath her feet. She, the younger sister, became invisible to her parents; she cast no shadow in their frantic household, and took a kind of meager pride in this fact. The Deys convinced Sabine to return home to Strykersville at least temporarily and during this time, approximately eighteen months, the life of the household, its busy, ever-urgent core, centered upon Sabine who was *in recovery, convalescing.* She'd been indifferent to Lila, when she wasn't frankly contemptuous, for reasons that weren't clear to Lila except (Lila had to think) Sabine saw through the Nice Girl pose.

Sabine had never pretended to be "nice"—yet she'd been much admired for her vivacity, her unusual good looks, and her talent for music; she had, or had had, a strong contralto voice, and had been admitted to Juilliard to study voice with a famous instructor . . . Back home in upstate New York, Sabine seemed to have lost interest in any sort of musical career; she threw out her music books, her favorite CDs; she saw a therapist, but not regularly; out of boredom she took courses at the local community college, received high grades and the praise of her teachers through the semester, then drifted away without explanation, and ended with final grades of F.

It had seemed to give Sabine a prickly sort of pleasure—(so Lila thought, appalled and fascinated)—to receive a failing grade when she knew, others in the class knew, and the instructor knew, that she was the smartest person in the class.

The smugness of self-loathing. The curious *triumph.*

Lila had not said aloud what she'd thought, meanly, and probably accurately, to herself—*She has discovered that her talent isn't enough. So she will give up trying anything, out of spite.*

Back home in Strykersville Sabine had few high school friends—most had "moved on." And so she acquired a shifting circle of (dubious) friends of whom none were known to the Deys. She acquired "work"—part-time low-paying jobs from which she could walk away without a backward glance, or even a courtesy call to an employer. Frequently she stayed away overnight, several times she simply vanished without explanation and without answering calls to her cell phone. The Deys were the ones to make frantic calls to Sabine's therapist and her friends, to local hospitals, to the local Suicide Hotline.

Hello. We want to report—.

We are frightened that our daughter will try to harm herself. That she has already harmed herself.

No. We don't know where she is.

I said no! If we knew, we'd go there to find her ourselves.

This time, they knew where to go to rescue her. They thought they knew where to go.

Just inside the Buffalo city limits, near the intersection with Delaware Avenue, Mr. Dey pulled up to the curb at 1129 Erie Street.

"Is this where Sabine *lives?*"—Lila's voice quavered.

Lila had imagined that Sabine would be living in a more attractive place, in a more attractive neighborhood. For no matter that Sabine claimed to have no money, and had to be, more or less, subsidized by Mr. Dey, she seemed always to look and to dress with striking effect.

Father, mother, younger sister sat in the car staring out at the two-story duplex of aged and weathered brick in a block of near-identical shabby houses built nearly to the sidewalk. The air held an odor of damp rot. Erie Street was badly potholed and sidewalks were puddled. In the next block were small derelict-looking businesses—*Diamond Nail Salon, Ernie's Shoe Bazaar, Delaware Bar & Grill.*

Black children played in the street, loudly. Next door to Sabine's duplex an obese woman with skin so white it resembled laundry detergent was sitting on a small stump of a porch, fanning herself.

Lila steeled herself waiting for her mother to exclaim—*Oh it's a "mixed" neighborhood!*—but Mrs. Dey seemed incapable of speaking just yet.

On the Thruway the elder Deys had spoken of nothing else except Sabine. Particularly, they'd obsessed over whether Sabine's car would, or would not, be parked at the house when they arrived.

If the car were at the house, that would mean that Sabine was inside.

If the car were not at the house, that would mean (probably) that Sabine was not inside.

Hope shifted with the miles, on the part of the elder Deys, like something loose in the trunk of their car. If the Toyota compact which Mr. Dey had purchased for Sabine were parked outside the house, that would (probably) mean that Sabine was home and if Sabine were home, and had not gone to her therapy session, and was not answering her phone, it might mean that she'd taken an overdose of barbiturates, again; or it might simply mean that she'd decided not to go to the Clinic that morning, and wasn't answering her phone for the simple reason that she didn't want to answer her phone.

If the car were not there, it would (probably) mean that Sabine was "out"—had made no suicide attempt at all.

Lila was fascinated by how long, in what varying ways, with what emotion, and contention, this issue was discussed by her parents. In the back seat of the car she might've pinched herself to see if indeed yes, she was *there*; she did exist, to a degree, and was not (totally) invisible.

Neither of the elder Deys asked Lila Dey what she thought. Would the Toyota compact be there, or would it be not-there.

Is my sister alive, or not-alive.

Each time there was a crisis in Sabine's life involving what the parents called a suicide attempt it seemed to Lila that the probability that Sabine would actually *commit suicide* had to be lessened. Unless maybe (perversely) the probability increased.

The Deys, including the younger daughter, had become amateur experts in the phenomenon of *suicide linked to bipolar depression*. So many statistics, so many heartrending case studies and blogs by "survivors"—the more you learned, the less you actually knew.

Sometimes they do. Sometimes they don't.

And sometimes anyway, they do.

It was a game Sabine played with them. A game in which Sabine made all the moves, and knew the ending beforehand.

The Toyota compact would not be parked in front of the house, Lila predicted. Her self-absorbed "sick" sister wouldn't be home but away—(who knew where?). She might have impulsively gone on a trip with a friend—(Sabine never lacked for "friends"). It was hardly the first time that Sabine had failed to call to cancel a medical appointment, nor was it the first time that a medical staff had overreacted as a result.

The Deys had taken some hope in the fact that their daughter had given their telephone number at the Clinic, to call in case of emergency. When she'd been hospitalized in New York City, no one had called them for more than twenty-four hours.

"Oh—is that it? There—Sabine's car . . ."

Mrs. Dey spoke hesitantly. Mr. Dey grunted as if he'd been jabbed in the ribs.

In a flat surprised voice Lila conceded, "It's her car."

Indeed it was the Toyota compact parked not exactly in front of the duplex but close by. Mud-splattered, edged with rust. A neglected car, though still an attractive car, which Mr. Dey had bought secondhand. Lila was the first to hurry to peer into the rear of the Toyota to ascertain yes—this was Sabine's car, no doubt. The rear was cluttered with clothes, shoes, plastic shopping bags. The windshield was dingy with grime and a patina of tree seeds. Naturally, the car was locked.

Lila turned to stare at the duplex, lifting her eyes to the second floor. She tasted something hot and acidulous at the back of her mouth thinking—*But is she inside? Is she—alive?*

At the same time thinking—*Probably just sleeping. Or she has taken some drug. But she is not dead.*

The Deys stumbled to the mud-splattered little Toyota, peered into the windows, near wringing their hands.

"So—she is home."

"Well, that's good—isn't it . . ."

The Deys seemed to know that Sabine was "involved" with—someone. Judging from her parents' worried exchanges on the drive to Buffalo, to which she'd listened with self-punishing attentiveness, it seemed that there was X in Sabine's life, but there was also Y; or there *had been* X, as well as Y, and maybe Z . . .

They did know that Sabine was an outpatient in a group therapy program at the Buffalo Metro Medical Clinic where, last time she'd spoken to them, weeks before, she was reportedly *making progress.*

The house on Erie Street had numerous occupants of whom just one was Sabine Dey. This, the parents seemed to know. But it wasn't clear if Sabine rented just a single room in the house, or an apartment; or whether she rented at all, or was (possibly) staying with one of the occupants. They did seem to know that she lived on the second floor.

Apart from group therapy exactly what did Sabine do in Buffalo, one hundred thirty miles from Strykersville? When relatives inquired—(with an innocent sort of cruelty)—the Deys were evasive. She "took courses" at SUNY Buffalo—maybe. She "worked"—maybe.

Lila had picked up the idea that Sabine "performed"—(sang? danced? in a nightclub? a "gentlemen's club"?)—at least from time to time.

When she'd been living on West End Avenue in New York, it had seemed clear that, at some point, that Sabine had become involved with drugs. Exactly which drugs, and how heavily she'd been involved, Lila had never known. She had not dared to ask her parents who would have turned to her in astonishment as if to say—*But who are you? This is none of your concern.*

Between the older sister and the younger there was an abyss. Lila had long adored her older sister, but her older sister had been impatient and bored with *her.* Once telling her how disappointed she'd been when Lila was born, four years after Sabine. *Then you came along. Bawling, shitting, and puking.* Lila had been stunned by the hostility in her sister's voice, though Sabine had meant to be funny.

At graduation, when Lila had given her three-minute speech, she'd had a fantastical feeling that somehow, without anyone knowing, Sabine had come to Strykersville in secret, to attend Lila's graduation; she'd known that Lila would be giving one of the valedictory speeches and would be the recipient of awards. Sabine would be in the audience, at the rear, observing with her ironic smile. *Yeah, sure—I'm proud of my sister.*

The Strykersville High auditorium was the very auditorium in which Sabine had first performed for admiring audiences, contralto solos at Christmas and Easter. The female lead in the musical adaptation of *Our Town* that had drawn rapturous reviews in local media and confirmed hopes for a professional career for Sabine Dey.

Lila had tried to email Sabine, to give her the date and time of graduation, but her email had been returned as undeliverable.

She had not called for she knew that Sabine wouldn't answer her phone and if she left a message, she would then have to surmise that her sister had heard the message and deleted it; it was preferable to think that Sabine knew nothing about graduation.

It was possible, but not very probable, that their parents had told Sabine about Lila's graduation. If they had, they hadn't informed Lila in any case.

Now that they'd ascertained that yes, Sabine's car was unmistakably parked on the street, they stood on the sidewalk in front of the house staring at the second-floor windows where blinds were drawn. Mr. Dey tugged at his necktie as if he were very warm. Mrs. Dey shaded her eyes, to squint harder.

They were frightened of what they might discover inside, Lila thought.

She was not frightened. *She* was prepared.

Slow-moving as if dazed the father and the mother climbed the front steps of the house where the father rang the doorbell once, twice, a third time. Was there the sound of a doorbell inside? Or was the sound they heard, or seemed to hear, a faint grinding wail like a siren in the distance?

No answer. No one home.

Mr. Dey knocked at the door, vigorously. Mrs. Dey shaded her eyes to peer into a first-floor window, where a broken venetian blind was partially drawn.

"Sabine? *Sabine?*"—Mrs. Dey cupped her hands to her mouth, and called.

"Sabine! Hel-lo!"—Mr. Dey called, hesitantly.

There was no sound from inside the house. Lila had followed her dazed parents up onto the little porch. She swallowed hard as she'd swallowed approaching the podium that morning. Her knees had actually trembled and were trembling now, just perceptibly.

"If Sabine is home she'd be upstairs—we can assume that. She might be asleep."

"At this time of day? That wouldn't be—natural . . ."

"If she's been up late. If she's been insomniac. She might reasonably want to sleep, in privacy."

The Deys spoke randomly, distractedly.

Might be asleep. Might be in a coma.

How many barbiturates? Might be dead.

The Nice Girl stood a little apart from the parents on the rotted stump of a porch. The Nice Girl was smiling—not quite aware that she was smiling. The Nice Girl was hearing that buzzing of hornets again in her head—had to be blood beating in her ears.

And the poetry prize is to—Lila Dey.

Lila?—not here?

Strange! Lila was here just a few minutes ago, we all heard her give that terrific little speech.

She loved him so much!—Laurence Carlson. She would never see him again.

Mr. Dey cupped his hands to his mouth, to call pleadingly: "Sabine? *Sabine?* It's—Dad . . ."

Mrs. Dey called: "Sabine? We're out here, on the front porch. Dad, Lila, me—Mom . . . Can you hear us?"

In the distance, a clattering noise like a freight train. On Erie Street an odor of something dank and rotted like backed-up sewage.

The freight train made Lila think of books she'd read in middle school, a movie she'd recently seen, Jewish teenagers caught in the horror of the Holocaust. She and her sister Sabine herded onto one of the transport trains and at Auschwitz forced to walk the ramp where Sabine (fair-haired, fair-skinned, could pass for Aryan) was selected to live while Lila (dark-haired, olive-skinned, small-boned, could pass for Jewish) was selected for the gas chamber.

Please don't take my sister. Please—let my sister come with me.

So Sabine pleaded. Pale-blue-eyed, with a beautiful soft mouth, pleading for her spindly sister's life.

The Nazi guards had been persuaded by Sabine for Sabine was so beautiful and so fair-haired. In Sabine's arms the younger sister had shivered and wept.

Shhh! We'll be all right, Lila. We're all we have left now.

This was not a new fantasy. This was a ridiculous old fantasy long past its expiration date, forgotten since ninth grade.

There was no reply to further doorbell ringing, or knocking. The elder Deys' voices lifted weakly and faded and there came no sign from within.

"If she's asleep, she might not hear us . . ."

"If she's taken sleeping pills, she couldn't hear us . . ."

"I worry about violating her privacy. You know how sensitive Sabine is, how easily she's hurt . . ."

". . . if she thinks we don't trust her . . ."

". . . if she thinks we're 'spying' on her . . ."

They tried the doorbell again. They tried knocking again. They tried shouting again. Then, they decided to go to the rear of the house. Very likely there was a rear door, or a side door, and this was the door occupants of the house might commonly use.

They walked in that slow dazed way, Lila was made to think of cattle that have been stunned as they emerge from a chute. The cattle would take a step or two, before they fell.

Lila thought—*I am not really here, am I. This is something of Sabine's she is doing to us, as a joke.*

Older siblings cultivate cruel jokes. Lila knew this from Nice Girl classmates with older siblings.

Once, when Sabine had been a junior in high school, sixteen years old, she'd cut herself with a razor not seriously, not deeply, but feathery-light multiple cuts on her left leg and arm. Lila had happened to overhear her mother's stunned voice, in Sabine's room.

"Sabine. My God what have you *done*."

Soon then there were uplifted voices. The alarming sound of her mother weeping. And Sabine's voice raised in childish anger.

Lila had hoped to see what had happened to Sabine but her mother shut the door against her—"No. Go away, please. This isn't for you."

In the corridor outside her sister's room Lila shivered with fear. And the bafflement of fear.

Go away. Go away. This isn't for you.

It would turn out that Sabine had been "involved" with one of her teachers at the high school, a married math teacher in his thirties who also coached boys' basketball and track. He'd subsequently denied any involvement with his student and had claimed that Sabine had virtually stalked *him*.

The teacher, the married math teacher, had left the Strykersville school district at the end of the semester, whether voluntarily or because he'd been asked to leave Lila never knew. She'd been in eighth grade at the time, in awe of her beautiful willful sister who wielded such power over adults, and who'd wantonly disfigured her own flawless skin with a razor.

Lila had never dared ask anyone what had really happened.

Had that been a *suicide attempt*? Sabine had refused to meet with a therapist at that time insisting that she was the "sanest" person she knew.

How many *suicide attempts* had there been. Lila tried to count but her thoughts were rebuffed as in a gusty wind.

Another time, shortly after graduation from high school, when Sabine should have been looking forward to attending Juilliard, she'd disappeared from her room for no apparent reason; no one knew where she was for a day and a night and part of another day until a neighbor discovered the girl "looking like she was asleep" wrapped in a dirty tarpaulin lying behind the neighbor's garage in a tangle of rancid and ill-smelling cut grass. In the morning sunshine flies, butterflies, mosquitoes had buzzed about her sleeping face. It would turn out that Sabine had self-medicated with a powerful dosage of antidepressants.

Definitely this had been considered a *suicide attempt.*

Lila had been aghast at Sabine's boastful remark afterward—*My advantage is, I play for high stakes. I don't play for low stakes like the rest of you.*

The driveway beside the weathered-brick duplex was badly cracked. Strewn alongside it was litter that looked as if it had been there for a long time.

It did not seem real to Lila, that her sister was living in such a place. Now she wondered if the apartment on West End Avenue had been shabby as well while in her naivete she'd supposed it had to be in some way glamorous, as Manhattan is glamorous to upstate New York.

Nor did it seem real to Lila, that something terrible might have happened to her sister. That in some way it might be Lila's fault that this terrible thing had happened.

At the rear of the shabby brick house the parents were calling, pleading: "Sabine? *Sabine!* Are you there?"

How abject the parents were, devastated by love. It was appropriate, the older sister felt contempt for them, as she did for the younger sister.

The rear stoop was cluttered with debris. Trash cans, rotted cardboard boxes, tin cans. In the weedy grass was a part-collapsed storage shed. Windows to the basement of the house were broken and crudely repaired with plywood. The thought came to Lila—*I could crawl inside one of those windows. I could go upstairs and find her.*

She would not do this! The very thought made her sick with revulsion.

If her parents asked, she would refuse.

Seeing the broken and haphazardly repaired cellar windows Lila began to recall—something . . . Memory rushed upon her rife and powerful as nausea.

The old, sick fantasy of confinement—being held captive—her (faceless, anonymous) tormentors shoving her into a dark cellar, a kind of dungeon, binding her ankles and wrists, tying up her jaws so that she couldn't scream, but leaving her otherwise fully conscious, in terror. Her punishment was to be captive in a hollowed-out space in the very earth beneath her house while her parents and sister lived obliviously above her, in daylight.

How many years, that horror-fantasy, that had begun when Lila had been young—as young as eight or nine. She wondered if Sabine had encouraged it. Had suggested it . . .

But pointless to blame her older sister. By the age of eighteen, she should have outgrown the nightmare.

On the Thruway a bright sharp sun had exposed all things visible but now the sky was becoming overcast and heavy. Gigantic clouds like shaggy bison shambled east from Lake Erie turning the sky inky blue. In puddles on the ground were razor-sharp reflections and in patches of wet on the shingled roofs of houses were duller reflections, that yet caught the eye. In the misery of anxiety the father was saying, "Should I break in—here? The door—here?" Tugging at the doorknob but the door gave not a tenth of an inch. With the toe of his shiny leather dress shoe he kicked at the door (which surely caused him pain) but still the door gave not a tenth of an inch.

The mother was pleading with him, "No—please don't. There could be someone inside with a gun. You don't—we don't—have any idea who lives in this house."

"But our daughter is inside. We have to help her."

"You could be arrested, breaking in. You could be shot by someone inside who has no idea who you are. This isn't Sabine's house."

"But they would know, we're looking for Sabine. It's an emergency. Sabine is *in this house.*"

Desperately the mother cupped her hands to her mouth another time: "Sabine! *Sabine!*"

And the father called "*Sabine!*"

As their cries came to seem ever more futile, so their cries were growing louder, shriller.

Lila was deeply embarrassed, mortified. Lila was trying not to be murderously bitter.

Only one window on the second floor, visible from the rear stoop. The glass of this window looked opaque, grimy—you could see nothing within.

Lila was thinking—*It's all right to be invisible. I don't mind.*

Lila was thinking—*Sabine please! We love you.*

Things had come too easily to Sabine. Like an upright flame drawing all eyes. She'd won every game in childhood. Infatuated with the beautiful girl in the mirror, she'd scarcely noticed anyone else.

Sabine's disappointment was with others who'd let her down, expected too much of her, failed to love her enough.

Yet they'd all loved her. They loved her now.

Even Sabine's absence was a powerful presence, more than the younger sister's actual presence could ever be.

How quickly the applause had faded, after the Nice Girl's speech. No one had listened to a word.

"But if she has hurt herself . . . If she has taken drugs she might be dying. And we are standing here . . ."

"We can call 911. Give me the cell phone."

"I can break down the door . . ." With dogged persistence the father spoke as if it had not already been demonstrated that he *could not break down the door*. The father's forehead was damp with perspiration and an artery throbbed visibly at his right temple.

"Should I—should we—call 911? Is that what we should do?"

"We don't have any choice, I think. If you don't want me to break down the door."

"But if we make the call . . ."

"I just have to break the window, and I can reach around and open the door—maybe . . ."

"Try calling her again. Maybe she'll pick up."

"Possibly her phone battery has run down. Possibly it isn't her fault, she's just sleeping . . ."

"But if she has taken pills, if she has lost consciousness . . . she would be 'sleeping' . . ."

"We'd better do something . . . We can't just stand here and let her die."

It was a terrible admission for the mother to make. As soon as the words were uttered, the mother burst into tears.

Lila heard herself say what she'd foresworn saying: "Maybe I could crawl through this basement window? Here? Then I could come up the stairs and let you in . . ."

The parents looked at her as if they'd forgotten she was there. It did not seem that they heard what she'd said.

How like Sabine it was, to have reduced them all to idiots! To have brought them here on this day in early summer, to a place unknown to them, that smelled of rot, incapacitating them for coherent thought and speech.

It had to be out of spite, Lila thought. One of her sister's games! Sabine could not bear the thought of another's happiness: Lila's graduation day, Lila's graduation prizes.

Nice girl, boring girl. Loser-girl. *You.*

They stood, staring at the house. The implacability of the house, its (seeming) obduracy and emptiness, was the riddle.

How to enter?

How to enter without breakage, damage? For if Sabine were not in need of their help, what they did would be mere trespassing . . .

Lila noticed that one of the second-floor windows overlooking the driveway was opened several inches, and fitted with a screen.

This was not a good sign: the window open. For if Sabine were inside, she should have heard her family calling to her by now.

If she'd been sleeping a normal sleep, she would have been wakened by now.

And again it was astonishing to Lila, it filled her with a strange calm chill, the likelihood that her sister was indeed *inside this house.*

They could not see her, they had no idea exactly where she was. Yet Sabine had to be *inside this house.* As in the famous paradox of Schrödinger's cat, the sister had to be *alive* or *not-alive.* But this could not be known until they discovered her.

She was lying down, probably. In her bed. In a bed.

She was lying down, and she was breathing. Or she was not breathing.

How remarkable this was! The younger sister could not have said exactly why, like one who has stumbled upon a principle of logic without any clue what "logic" is.

In the game of zero-sum there is but one winner: but there can be many losers.

As if they hadn't heard Lila's (impulsive, generous) offer to climb inside the house and end the mystery, the parents returned to the front of the house to call to Sabine again. In the street children continued to play, careening on child-sized bicycles. Who cared about the Deys' mounting desperation? Next door the obese, white-skinned woman reclining in her chair regarded them with mild bovine interest.

"You lookin for somebody?"—the woman called out.

Lila's parents tried to explain: their daughter Sabine rented a room in this house, she wasn't answering her phone, they were worried that something had happened to her, that was her car at the curb . . .

"Who? What's the name—'Sable'—"

"'Sabine.'"

"*Who?*"—the woman cupped a hand to her ear, grimacing.

A lank young man had joined the obese woman, in jeans, grease-stained T-shirt. His thinning dark hair was tied back in an abbreviated rat-tail.

The father was knocking at the front door again. "*Sabine!*"

No answer. No face at a window above.

Lila's heartbeat was unpleasantly accelerated. In her mouth, a taste of something sour. Even now, her classmates were at the school, beneath the big striped tent, being congratulated, signing yearbooks, posing for photographs, laughing, hugging, and kissing and being hugged and kissed as Lila, marooned with these people, the very picture of pathos, failure, grief, *was not.*

The situation was very like a game: Sabine's game.

If Sabine's life were at risk, they must break into the house to save her; but if Sabine's life were not at risk, and they were overreacting (as usual), they did not want to offend their (easily offended) daughter.

And what was at risk, essentially? That she would refuse to love them as they wished to be loved. As loving, protective, responsible parents wish to be loved. Indeed, they feared that Sabine would lash out at them to punish them. *You have no faith in me. You don't trust me. You treat me like a child. I hate you, you are always spying on me.*

For as long as Lila could remember, the parents had quarreled about one thing only: the older sister.

If one thought the other was overly harsh, the other thought that one was far too lenient. One accused the other of "enabling" Sabine to behave as she did, and that one accused the other of "irresponsibility."

It was "enabling" to continue to support the older sister, and to fly to her rescue whenever she *attempted suicide*; but it would be "irresponsibility" to pretend that nothing was wrong with Sabine, and that she could live a normal life without her parents' support.

The thought came to Lila, swift as an arrow—*If she kills herself, it will at least come to an end.*

This was a shocking thought. For Lila understood that her parents and she would not ever survive Sabine's death.

Yet, Lila had long felt a precocious sort of despair at the realization that nothing she did, her academic achievements, her prizes, her scholarship to Cornell, her (uncomplaining) behavior as the secondary, invisible daughter, her very Niceness—nothing mattered set beside the drama of the older sister.

My advantage is, I play for high stakes. I don't play it safe.

Boastfully Sabine spoke. Lila wanted to press her hands against her ears.

All this while, still the parents had not decided: should they call 911.

They were very reluctant to involve "public" assistance. You heard so much about people who'd made terrible errors, calling 911 and bringing police officers to a scene who might be armed, hyper-prepared for a violent confrontation.

Domestic calls, the most dangerous.

They were standing awkwardly in the driveway, that was made of badly cracked asphalt. The father squatted in front of the broken window, trying to peer inside. He began to pull at the plywood strips.

The mother stood close behind him. Lila saw the mother's face wet with tears and yet her eyes shining with a sudden hope.

"Maybe she could climb inside. She's small."

"Maybe."

Lila stood very still, invisible. Hearing them speak of her—*she's small.*

As in a dream in which words are uttered out of nowhere, yet fluently, as if such words had been prepared a long time ago, one of the parents said, in an even voice, "Lila, dear—maybe you could climb inside here?" and the other said, with a quick smile, "We can help you, Lila!" and the other said again, in a voice of calm resolve, "You're so small . . ."

No. I will not.

You can't make me. Why should I. You love her, not me. No.

Yet Lila was thrilled. She was not invisible now!

Kneeling in the driveway, for she had no choice. In her graduation clothes, so carefully chosen kneeling in the oil-stained asphalt driveway helping her father pull away the flimsy boards covering the basement window.

The stench of the underground was released, chill and earthy. In the window frame were shards of glass like wicked glinting teeth, they tried to break off with the plywood strips.

Her mother was cautioning her to be careful. Not to fall and hurt herself. Her mother, with that look of sick, radiant hope.

Mr. Dey was the practical one. Directing Lila to make her way carefully in the dark to the stairs, which would (probably) lead into the kitchen—"You can open the door for us, then. That's all you need to do."

She wanted to scream at them—*I will not! No.*

Wanted to scream—*I hate you all. I wish she was dead, and you were dead.*

Instead she smiled at the parents, a ghastly Nice Girl smile, to assure them that she was all right, she would be all right, there was no danger.

How important it was to comfort *them*.

"Oh, watch out for the glass! Be careful . . ."

Crawling headfirst through the window would not work so she managed, squatting awkwardly on her haunches, to maneuver her legs inside the window, and to lower herself in, as her parents fussed and chattered; the foul chill air made her nostrils pinch. *Why are you doing this, why for* her. *She would never do this for you.*

Her skin prickled with fear, and the keen attentiveness of fear. The thought came to her that possibly Sabine was close by, in this dank cellar. Sabine had much admired the poet Sylvia Plath who had swallowed dozens of sleeping pills, wrapped herself in a tarpaulin, crawled into the darkness beneath a house porch to die.

"Lila! Careful!"

"Oh—maybe you'd better come back . . .

Damn them! They had coerced her into this folly, she would follow through as they'd bidden. If something happened to her, it would be their fault.

She pushed away her mother's hand. She was easing herself inside the window, lowering her legs, cautiously releasing her grip on the windowsill though she couldn't yet touch the floor—then suddenly she was slipping, falling, in so doing (somehow) she cut her right knee on the window frame where small shards of glass remained. At once cat claws of bright red appeared on her knee. She felt a strange stinging salty pain like jeering.

Behind her, above her, her ineffectual parents were concerned for her—"Lila! *Lila!*"—but Lila paid them no heed.

She fell, hard, against the floor of rough, damp concrete that was farther below than she'd expected. Six feet, eight feet. The breath was knocked out of her, and her ankle twisted beneath her. Her eyes were widened in the dim light of the cellar but she couldn't see clearly, as in her turbulent dreams she could not be sure if she were even alive.

About five feet above her head the window through which she'd lowered herself so clumsily was a square of light. A face occluded with shadow like a death's head was peering anxiously inside—might've been the father.

Whatever they were saying to her, she could not make out. How exasperating they were!—weak, well-intentioned people who had failed at parenting, but could not give up; begging their younger daughter now to come back, to come back outside, they were frightened for her.

But no. She would not.

Stupidly she'd cut her knee. Jagged bits of glass, caught in her skin. She tried to pick the glass shards out but her fingers were slippery with blood.

That seemed to her silly—*slippery silly blood.*

And she'd struck her head in the fall. Banged her head on the concrete. Her eyes filled with childish tears. Only children cried. You did not cry if you were not a child for you understood that tears could not help you, what was the purpose in crying?

A Nice Girl is always *all right.* A Nice Girl is never *not–all right.*

A Nice Girl will cross into that other world with a Nice Girl ghastly smile.

By degrees her eyes were becoming accustomed to the dark. There, shadowy stairs against a wall.

Her foot found a step, a first step, her groping hand found a railing. Cautiously she made her way up the stairs. Her heart pounded in exhilaration and a determination not to fail—she could not live with herself, if she failed.

She was in a narrow hallway. Before her was another flight of stairs, leading to the second floor. The walls here were a dingy stained wallpaper. Behind the stairs was a baby carriage—not new, leathery and old and grimy with dust.

Her voice lifted faintly—"Sabine? Hello? Are you upstairs? Sabine, it's me—Lila . . ."

Gripping the railing to steady herself she climbed the stairs to the second floor. The pain in her knee was in her control: she would triumph over mere pain. It was a trifle, that blood leaked thinly down her leg. For it was tremendously exciting to her, that Sabine had to be upstairs. Her car at the curb, they didn't want to think that possibly Sabine had been taken away, or had gone voluntarily away.

If she found Sabine for them, their parents would love Lila so much more. This was a fact, inescapable.

Hesitantly she pushed open a door: she'd come unerringly to her sister's room. Must've been the smell that drew her, a faint smell of cigarette smoke, vomit. For Sabine had often been sick, in her room in their house in Strykersville. Often, the bathroom smelled of vomit after Sabine had used it though a window would be shoved open and a fan turned on high.

"Sabine . . ."

In a tangle of bedsheets her sister lay partly clothed, unmoving. Unconscious. One slender arm outflung, and her head at an awkward angle for there was no pillow. She was breathing erratically, faintly.

Breathing! Alive.

A trail of vomit on her chin, and on the bedsheets.

"Sabine! Oh God."

You can smother her, now. No one will know.

In the smelly bedsheets Sabine lay sleeping, moaning. Her skin was sallow, blotched. She was not a beautiful girl now, you would pity her, seeing her. The skin around her eyes was puffy and there were bruise-like indentations beneath her eyes. Her mouth was agape and wet with saliva. Her streaked-blond hair was stiff and matted. Her forehead was creased in anguish. Her eyes appeared to be partially open but were unfocused, rolled back into her head like the eyes of a giant doll that has been thrown down and discarded.

Lila gripped her sister's shoulders to shake her, rouse her— "Sabine! Wake up! It's me."

Now. Now is your chance. No one will know.

Smothering the sister who wanted to die. Perhaps not easily but it could be done. Many times such merciful deaths have been executed.

You have only to grip the pillow in the stained pillowcase and lift it and lower it onto the face, the face with the contorted expression, the face that has been beautiful but is beautiful no longer, the pillow would hide the face, you would not have to see the eyes, the eyes would not open to identify and accuse, the eyes would never again *see*. Possibly you'd have to straddle the body, and if the body began to thrash and fight for its life you would have to be resolute, fearless, you would have to grip the body tightly with your knees and you would have to lean onto the struggling body, with all your weight you would have to press down, you could not weaken, you could not turn back until the frenzied struggling ceased and *in this way you save your own life.*

"Sabine! Please . . ."

Shaking her sister, speaking sharply to her. It did no good to plead or to beg, Sabine would not listen. But speaking sharply, shouting into the slack feverish face, shaking the alarmingly bony shoulders seemed to be having some effect.

"It's me, Lila. Open your eyes, please. *Look at me.*"

Lila had pulled Sabine into a sitting position in the rumpled bed. Sabine's head slumped forward as Lila held her. How thin Sabine was! *Eating disorder* was another of the diagnoses that Sabine had laughed at but it seemed clear that she'd lost a good deal of weight. Lila was shocked to feel her sister's ribs close beneath her burning skin, the prominent knobs of her spine.

Lila had never dared touch her older sister so intimately, and so forcefully. She felt how the sister's power was passing over, to her.

(What had Lila forgotten?—she'd forgotten to let her parents into the house.)

(They were calling to her now, at a distance. Weak pleading frightened ineffectual adults for whom she felt pity.)

At last!—Sabine was regaining consciousness. She was breathing, she would not die.

Trying to speak. Trying to explain—something.

Like one who has dived too deeply into dark water, whose breath has been squeezed from her. Like one who has dived so deeply, she can barely prevail against the paralyzing weight of the water.

Near inaudible her words—*I didn't . . . I wasn't . . .*

"Just open your eyes, Sabine. Okay? Keep your eyes open."

At the window she called down to her parents in the driveway below. She'd found her sister! But they had to call 911, Sabine was in need of emergency help.

"Is she alive? Is she alive?"—the parents cried in a single voice and Lila told them, "Yes. She is alive."

In their vehicle the Deys followed the ambulance through the unfamiliar streets of Buffalo. Mr. Dey driving, Mrs. Dey beside him and the younger daughter in the back seat.

She was the Nice Girl! In the back seat.

A Nice Girl is uncomplaining even when in pain. Pressing wads of tissue against her bleeding knee (which she hadn't wanted to show the EMTs and her parents had not noticed of course), all focus on Sabine half-conscious, moaning carried down the stairs on a stretcher, out onto the rotted stump of a porch and to the ambulance in the street with the flung-open rear door.

A shock to the parents to see how thin the once-beautiful daughter had become. Only partially clothed in a soiled pajama top, underpants.

Sick, sallow skin. Filthy matted hair. Rank animal smell.

By this time, the rat-tailed boy next door was recording the scene with his cell phone with unabashed openness. Deafening wail of a siren as the ambulance arrived. A Buffalo police squad car with one senior officer and two young officers. Still seated the obese white-skinned mother stared agape at all this commotion.

The ambulance had arrived just seconds before the police. Three EMTs bounding out of the vehicle and directed to the house, to the upstairs, by the distracted Mr. Dey.

My daughter. We think she has taken an overdose . . .

Is it heroin? D'you know?

N-Not heroin. . . . No, I don't know.

The Nice Girl had tried graciously not to note, and not to feel bitterly about not-noting, that the excited father had referred to *my daughter* as if he had not two but a single daughter.

Young Caucasian woman, early twenties, suspected drug overdose, suspected suicide attempt. Psychiatric history.

The Nice Girl was still in a state of excitement, exhilaration. Her heart was still pounding rapidly. Her fingers tingled, with the memory of having taken hold of a pillow, a badly stained pillow, to lift, and lower. . . . But no, that had not happened, had it.

The Nice Girl foresaw: a lifetime of the Older Sister.

Sick, suicidal, bipolar older sister. A lifetime.

For the Nice Girl there was no (reasonable) way out. As for the parents there was no (reasonable) way out.

She was not angry. She was not even resigned.

It would be *what it was*. For she was the Nice Girl, and that was a lifetime.

Her eyelids shut, it was another time. It was a future time, or maybe it was a past time. They were in a shadowy place. Possibly Sabine's girlhood room, all but a single lamp extinguished. A cigarette hung loose between Sabine's fingers. Sabine had polished her fingernails, Lila was in awe of the sparkly polish, the beautifully shaped nails. Lila was just a little girl and easily awed. Sabine picked a speck of tobacco off her tongue, bemused.

There's just not room for two of us, y'know?

Like, before we were born. It's too tight, there's not enough oxygen.

MICK & MINN

In the beginning there was Mick! There was Minn!

In the beginning was Mick!—was Minn! Nothing and nobody that was not Mick! not Minn! for how could there be anything not Mick! not Minn! for there was nothing before the beginning before his pus-stuck-together eyes were gently opened/washed with a damp cloth as there could be nothing beyond the blunt end of never seeing Mick, Minn again.

There was not God. He had not seen God's face. He would not see God's face. He saw Mick's face. He saw Minn's face. Before he knew *Mick, face* he knew Mick's face. Before he knew *Minn, face* he knew Minn's face. He knew Mick's voice. He knew Minn's voice.

Where's your Momma? Who's your Momma? Fuckin Momma, who's your Mommy crazy for Baby? Who loves you most? Who loves you best? Who's gonna gobble-gobble Baby, lookit Baby's little toes, Baby's sweet little hinder, who's gonna gobble-gobble Baby's sweet little weewee?

Who's your Dadda? Baby got a Dadda, Baby got a weewee like Dadda, where's Baby's Dadda, right here's Baby's fuckin Dadda.

He's seein us. Lookin right at us. Shit, he can see. Sees us.

Minn-Momma loves Baby to *pieces.*

Mick-Dadda loves Baby *like to fuckin death.*

Soaked into memory. Like babyshit and babypiss soaking his diaper. Bedding of his crib, whatever it is, a broken crib, or cradle, wadded towels, blanket stiff with filth on the drafty linoleum floor.

Whatever *is*, prepare for it to change. Quick.

Those long hours, might've been entire days/nights lying in babyshit and babypiss until the initial heat of it was lost and the soft skin at his thighs, tender cheeks of his baby ass chafed and throbbed with pain of open sores, sores that became infected, but even so, he knew not to cry.

There were those others like himself (he guessed: how'd he know if any were like him*self* when he had no more idea of him*self* than of the vast desolate city sprawling out beyond the walls of the frantic household of Mick and Minn) who wailed too loud, stank too much, flailed stunted little arms and legs and dared kick when Mick came near, this was a mistake. For Minn might cuddle and coo *Who's your Momma? Who's your Momma?*—Minn was soft for babies. But Mick had a temper quick to flare up as a struck match, can't blame Mick on his feet eight hours of the goddamned day, if overtime as many as ten, twelve fuckin hours at a shit job he hated where he had to wear a fuckin olive-gray uniform like a fuckin janitor. When Mick came home for Christ-sake he wanted some peace-and-quiet and a can of Molson's not fuckin babies screaming and so would shout into a baby's contorted face *Shut the fuck up!* Or to Minn in a fury *Shut his fuckin cryin, I'll break both of ya faces.* Precarious as lifting a long-handled axe and balancing it in the palm of your hand it was (Minn thought) whether her husband (the only man she'd ever loved in her life or would ever love) would get so furious he would call her the nastiest name any husband could call his wife, the *c-word*, preceded by *stupid* and so if Mick did not devastate Minn with *you stupid cunt*, Minn backed away apologizing, grateful. Smiling foolishly for the man for all his flaws and foibles *was* the "love of her life."

It was his Irish temper Mick said, not good to provoke. For Mick was known to lose patience altogether, the patience of Job he'd have had to be born with, to seize a wailing baby in big-Mick hands and lift it and in a fury shake-shake-shake until midwail the baby went abruptly silent with spittle-wet muted mouth like a fish's and eyes rolled back in its head that would never roll back in quite the right way.

Too fuckin bad but these were *brain-damage kids*, everybody knew.

These were *crack babies, FAS (fetal alcohol syndrome) babies*. Everybody knew.

Trash babies. Thrown-away babies. Babies nobody wanted, for sure not their slut mothers.

Caught their heads somehow in the damnedest places like the rungs of a staircase or the mouth of a bleach bottle. Climbed up on a chair or a table or a kitchen counter or the fuckin stove and fell on their heads, cracking their damn skulls. Knocked out their front teeth. On the (gas) stove with burners lit, catching their hair on fire, burning their fingers, screeching like a stuck pig. Some of them born without their brains entirely *inside* the skull, or their heart or lungs wrong-sized so they'd be wheezing and blue in the face, fuckin shame. Or swallowed Lysol, or thumbtacks. Or stuck their mouths tight-shut with Elmer's glue, having found the tube in some drawer they weren't supposed to open. Foster kids! But none of it Mick's fault or Minn's fault, as everybody knew.

Of course not *him*. *He* was special.

Beside the crib Mick squatted. Right away he'd been brought to the house on Wyandotte to be left with Mick and Minn, Mick had an eye for him. Broken-tooth grin, glisten in the man's eye like varnish on a hard surface. Breath fierce with gassy beer like a special gift from Dadda. *This little fucker's taken after me. See?*

Who's your Dadda, Ba-by?

It was so. *He* had Mick's eyes—what Minn called *robin's-egg blue*. Of all the kids, *he* was the one. "Little Mick."

Could be, Mick and Minn had hoped for their own Little Mick. Could be, Mick and Minn had hoped for their own Little Minn.

Hadn't happened, not yet. Nooo. Fuck it, for the best, maybe (as Minn said wistfully), the doctor said of her she's *prediabetic*.

Also, *obese*. And also, *high blood pressure*.

On the sensitive subject of fertility Mick was quiet. Not wanting to think possibly it was *him*, something wrong with *him*, what spurted out of his veiny engorged cock was watery not thick like you'd expect seeing Mick, the size and heft of Mick, he guessed it wasn't 100 percent what it was supposed to be (he'd seen his brothers' and cousins' cum when they'd been kids, plenty of times), winced at the clinical term *sperm count* but sweet dumb-cluck Minn hadn't a clue, wouldn't occur to Minn, whose skim-milk girl face mottled with embarrassment at such words as *ovulate, menstrual period, fertilize, fetus*.

Minn was Catholic, and Mick was Catholic. Not what you'd call "practicing"—but yes, Catholic.

Hell, Mick hadn't *stepped foot inside* a church in twenty fuckin years. Hadn't *taken communion, gone to confession* for longer than that. Bullshit, it was. Sight of a priest made him want to spit. But still, Mick was Catholic, sulky set of the mouth, jerky nod of the head, begrudging, reluctant, yah sure. Sure.

He wasn't anything. Goddamned lucky to be alive. Less than a day old (it was said) when he'd been discovered barely breathing wrapped in bloody towels left like trash in a stall in the women's restroom at the Decatur Street Greyhound station.

Given over to Minn. Newest arrival at Mick-and-Minn's. *Ohhh lookit this! Somethin happen to his head it looks, like, pushed in . . .*

Lifted in Minn's arms. Fat-muscled arms of Minn. Flabby upper arms of Minn swinging loose like a bat's wings if a bat's wings could be white.

Minn with folds of chin. Minn with shining honey-brown eyes. Minn with shining eyes lost in fat folds in Minn's face. Minn with a flushed pretty-fat-girl face. Minn with frizz-hair dyed bright carrot-orange. Minn open-mouth breathing and giving off heat like a steam radiator. Minn with lollipop-crimson lipstick eaten off through the day, she'd have to replenish it every few hours frowning at herself in her upstairs "vanity" mirror. Minn with pucker-kiss lips. Minn in a pout. Minn in a giddy mood. Minn "stuffed"— "couldn't eat another thing." Minn wearing a Sacred Heart of Jesus medal on a short chain around her neck. Minn with small fleshy hands dimpled on their backs, palms chapped and calloused and fingernails painted fire-engine red beginning to chip. Minn with breasts big as pillows sloping to her waist. Minn with hips in layers like pancakes stacked asymmetrically. Minn walking with surprising swiftness on the heels of her corduroy bedroom slippers, causing the floor to quake when there was urgent reason for Minn to walk swiftly, like a small landslide. Minn lifting Little Mick in midwail. Minn lifting Little Mick with a grunt. Minn *shhhing* Little Mick so (Big) Mick wouldn't hear. Minn belching beer. Minn giggling like a girl. Minn kissing Little Mick's (fevered) forehead. Minn near to dropping Little Mick. Heat of something solid-liquidy in Little Mick's diaper. Dripping down his thighs.

Minn biting her lower lip, dropping Little Mick back in his crib. *Oh shit. Not again. What's it—didn't I just . . .*

In the kitchen scolding herself at the (opened) refrigerator. Terrible craving, her gut is the Grand Canyon, nothing can fill it.

Lie in the crib in babyshit and babypiss until it goes cold and you sleep anyway because you always do.

Mick and Minn!—sweethearts since sixth grade at Saint Ignatius Elementary School, Hamtramck.

Mick and Minn!—Mr. and Mrs. Flynn! Minn was "Minn Flynn," which always got a good-natured laugh.

For most of their married life of twelve years living in a (rented) brick row house on Wyandotte Ave., Detroit. Neighborhood used to be all "white" but now what's called "mixed." Realtors block-busting pushing north through residential Detroit scaring white homeowners into selling because *Negroes are moving in* but Mick-and-Minn refused to panic. *This is where we belong, this is our honeymoon bungalow.* Upstairs were three small bedrooms, plus bathroom, downstairs living room, kitchen, back room, and half bathroom, plus down steep stairs a cellar considered "unfinished" smelling of dank dark wet earth and oozing-damp foundation nonetheless put to good use for purposes of what Mick called *discipline.*

On Wyandotte were small front yards mostly grassless, mud-rutted, or littered with trash but 2284 where the Flynns lived stood out, photographs of the dark-red-brick facade would appear in local media: plastic flowers stuck in the ground, pink flamingo, plaster of paris Virgin Mary in flowing blue robes. On the front door the desiccated remains of a Christmas wreath tied with a drooping red velvet bow.

Minn was crazy-soft for babies, that went without saying. Mick was choosy but you could win Mick's (big) heart if you knew how.

A man needs a son, Mick was heard to declare. Especially if he'd been drinking and was feeling what he called *shithouse*. You want to pass on your fuckin heritage. Your name.

Foster parents usually had their own kids mixed with the "fosters." Mick and Minn, no kids of their own. Maybe adopt one? Maybe *him*.

Problem was, *so many babies*. Each baby blessed by God but God wasn't taking such great care of them, was he?

Such questions Mick pondered. Why it wasn't good to be *stone-cold sober*. Picking at the cracks between his teeth with a blood-tipped toothpick.

Minn never asked such questions. Minn was just a girl at heart. Minn loved dolls and still had every doll she'd ever had as a child, positioned on tables, shelves, windowsills through the house. Minn loved to push you in a stroller. Minn loved to dress you "special." Minn loved to feed you. Minn loved to feed you as Minn loved to feed herself. Snacks were secret, though. For Mick was encouraged to believe that *Minn's on a fuckin diet!* Minn devoured waffles and maple syrup, blueberry pancakes, thick wads of butter. Bacon strips eaten daintily by hand, Wonder Bread toast and jam, jelly. Peanut butter spooned out of the jar, luscious-thick, thick as shit, with a tablespoon just the right size for Minn's hungry *O* of a mouth.

Not everyone was given Minn's special foods. No!

Discipline was necessary, some of the children were *bad*. Mick was the overseer of what he called *corp'ral punishment* while Minn was the overseer of meals.

Special foods were shared with Little Mick and only one or two others who were Minn's favorites. One of them was a little "light-skin" girl named Angel whose beauty was mesmerizing to Minn. Spooning peanut butter from the jar to her mouth Minn would just stare and stare.

Saying tearfully if she had a baby, it wouldn't be *her*. Not Angel.

For Angel wasn't *white*. Exactly what Angel was, who her parents were, her ancestry, no one seemed to know.

Minn felt the same way about Little Mick. *If I could have him, y'know, or her, if they'd be mine, and Mick's—Christ! I would . . .*

Stroking her big booming breasts, the swell of her belly through her clothes. As if inside her were these other babies yearning to be born.

There was Angel who was smoke-color, there was Bitt who was pasty-white, there was Jojo who was cocoa-cream, there was Tommy who was Black, there was Eula who was jaundice-color, there was Elijah who was brick-color, there was Esdra who was dark-smoke-color, there was Marilee who was smudge-white, there was No-Name Baby who was red-puckered, all of them mixed together in memory like switching rapidly through the TV channels until your brain just switched off.

Why was Bitt "upstairs" and Esdra "cellar"—why was Eula one of those whom Minn liked to cuddle but then, later, overnight it seemed Eula was one of those shrieked-at for being bad, relegated to "cellar."

This was a fact: Little Mick was fucking slow to comprehend that Mick and Minn were not Little Mick's parents but something called *foster parents.*

For a long time confused thinking that Little Mick and Angel were "twins"—somehow.

Hearing Minn boast over the phone how *valued* her and Mick were, at Children's Services.

Something called *foster parents*. But not *his parents*.

How many times Minn cuddled Little Mick breathy-singing *Who's your Momma? Who's your Momma?* How many times Mick leaning over him grinning all teeth *Who's your fuckin Dadda, kid?*

One day Little Mick would learn to his astonishment that there had been an individual who was his actual mother. Somewhere there'd been an actual father.

No one knew their names. If they were alive or dead—he would never know.

All he knew for sure: Mick and Minn loved him like crazy. Loved him more than the other kids.

Why?—because you're special.

Got Mick's eyes. And smart like Mick.

Well—probably Minn loved him more than Mick loved him. Minn's love was *steady.*

Nights Mick wasn't home they'd cuddle on the sofa watching TV, eating snacks: potato chips, pretzels. Greasy onion rings Minn loved but Little Mick did not.

Nights Mick was home the TV was turned to Mick's programs: wrestling, baseball, football, mostly.

Only the top teams held interest for Mick. Other players, he called *chumps.* Even with his favorites Mick would click the remote restlessly. One channel following another. Cursing every time an advertisement came on.

Wayne County Children's Services sent checks, paid (some) bills but not enough. Fuckin fact was, the house needed constant maintenance. Rotting front steps, rotting back steps. Leaking roof. Leaking cellar. Furnace needing to be replaced. Shit-refrigerator breaking down. Mick was no goddamned handyman. Mick wasn't going to climb up on the fuckin roof with a hammer, fall off, and break his fuckin neck.

All the work they did for the county, never saying *no* when some special favor was asked of them, yet they were paid below the minimum wage. Needed two paychecks just to keep going, so it was lucky Mick worked at Men's Detention.

Not that they took in foster kids for the money. *No.*

Maybe when they were younger, it was easier. Now Minn got short of breath, having to sit down sudden and hard, the kitchen chair trembling beneath her weight. Minn "saw stars"—fumbled at the medal around her neck—"Jesus, Mary, and Joseph!"

Lit a cigarette, sucking the smoke deep into her lungs. Cracking open a can of Coors. On her feet (she said) twelve hours a day why her feet were so damn swollen. And her ankles swollen worse than her mother's.

Mick whistled through his teeth, seeing how Minn's ankles *were* swollen. What the hell? The left one more swollen than the right, near as big as his own.

Massaging Minn's swollen ankles, in his lap. Fleeting look of something like fear, that something might happen to his wife Minn.

That way Mick looked at Little Mick, sometimes. If Little Mick was coughing, had a fever. Christ-sake, how kids pass sickness among them. There were older kids who went to the public school around the corner, had to go because it was the law, fuckin social workers stuck their noses in Mick-and-Minn's business, fuck they knew about taking care of children. It was at school kids picked up bad habits. It was at school kids picked up head lice. It was at school kids got bullied, beaten.

A dozen times a day Minn would declare she was going to keep Little Mick out of school as long as she could. *Those little shits, they'd be all over you. Beautiful baby-boy like* you.

Some nights after his shift Mick came home late, slamming and cursing through the house. He hadn't come directly home—why Minn was so hurt trying not to cry. Footsteps like trucks rumbling. Floor quivering. Mick liked to squash cockroaches flat with his fist against the kitchen wall or with a booted foot against the linoleum floor. *Goddam filthy motherfuckers.* This was pleasure.

Mick liked to gobble-bite Minn on the neck to make Minn squeal and shimmer, grabbing Minn's pillow-breasts in both big-Mick hands and squeezing, hard.

Oh hey, Mick—that *hurts*.

No it don't. You like it.

I *don't*, it *hurts*.

Fuck that shit, baby, *you like it*.

You are—*not nice!*

Shit I'm not. *You* like it.

I mean it, Mick! That *hurts*.

Since when?—laughing in Minn's face.

Trying then to grab Minn's big fat ass to squeeze even harder.

If Minn play-slapped at Mick he might laugh and play-slap back. Or Mick might not laugh and slap Minn full in the face, spilling shocked tears from her eyes.

Slamming out of the room muttering *Stupid cunt*.

Except if Mick chose to soften the blow not in any lessening of disgust/contempt for Minn but in a sudden release of mercy like rain you'd expect to be cold but was warm he'd say laughing—*Stupid cluck*.

Oh but *why?* Minn staggering to a chair half fainting. Like a wedding cake collapsed on itself.

Little Mick nudged and squirmed at Minn's thick legs. Little Mick needing Momma to hug *him*.

Oh you kids! Jesus.

Better for you, you'd never been born. Me too.

Oh but he loves us. I guess.

If Minn was needing consolation she'd hoist Little Mick onto her lap, swell of belly and pillow-breasts, so warm, yeasty-warm, feed him cold pizza slices for a midnight snack.

Minn laughing to herself, breasts jiggling—Is a *cluck* nicer'n a *cunt?*

Half singing, like it was an ad jingle on TV, or a special lullaby just for Little Mick—*CLUCK'S NICER'N A CUNT!*

Upstairs Mick was "out like a light" on the bed—drunk-snoring, could sleep for twelve hours. In just underwear, wool socks Minn couldn't pry off his size-twelve feet they'd sweated and dried like glue.

Mick was a guard at Wayne County Men's Detention. A prison guard was a "CO"—corrections officer—but nobody called them that. *Guards, screws.* Prison guards were granted no respect like cops with their cop uniforms. Mick hated the olive-gray uniform he had to wear at Men's Detention. Two cousins of his were Detroit PD, he hated their guts and told Minn every chance he could, he was living for the day those assholes got theirs.

As a CO Mick had to keep his hair trimmed like a marine. So short you could see his scalp through hairs like bristles on a brush.

Mick liked to scare Minn saying how, at Men's Detention, it was *kill or be killed.*

You're *white*, the young Black kids would slash your throat any chance they got.

Except white trash up from West Virginia, Tennessee—*they'd* slash your throat any chance they got.

Minn shivered and shuddered. Minn believed any bullshit (Mick's word) anyone told her, including him.

Not too smart. Why he was crazy for Minn, the last thing a man wants is a woman smarter than him.

Why he was crazy for Minn, Minn was the only girl crazy for *him.*

And his cock too, Minn loved. Or anyway said so starting in seventh grade.

Some of this, how shitty Mick's job was at the men's detention, Little Mick came to know long before he had any idea what *men's detention* could mean. Absorbed information like you'd absorb a strong smell on your skin and in your hair, unquestioning.

Minn's cigarette smoke in the tender pink lining of his lungs. Cellar stench, seeping up through the floorboards.

Not at the time, not completely. Years were required. What you knew came at you in pieces from different directions. Never knew what you knew or what you didn't know. What was secret. What was lost. What might return.

It doesn't return. It has never left.

Children's cries, screams: there may be differing intensities, modalities. The cry of vexation, joylessness. The cry of aloneness. Cry of terror, and cry of agony.

You never know when a scream *ends*. When you will never hear it again.

He would be asked. By adults who were strangers to him. By social workers whose faces were known to him. But how could he answer? *When* was impossible to recall.

What Mick claimed: it had been the child's fault, that little what-was-his-name not Elijah, no: Esdra. One of the foster kids the County designated Black. *Scalding himself in the tub.*

Hot-steaming water burst through the pipe in the upstairs bathroom. It was an old pipe, you'd stare at it pulsing and throbbing with a kind of indignation, rage. Rarely did you see such indignation and rage that was not merited. No one's fault, how could it be anyone's fault, the money the county paid them, fuckin joke, *chump change* not enough, not nearly enough, who could afford a fuckin plumber even if you could get them to come, in this neighborhood, if it's a white plumber forget it, he won't show up. No one's fault goddamn Mick would swear except the kid's fault, that touched the pipe.

Must've been, he'd turned on the faucet.

The *hot faucet*. He'd been warned, Esdra. That was his name though Mick rarely called him by any name, or any of them by any names, pissed Mick off the little fuckers *had actual names* you were expected to remember.

Jesus, look: Mick explained they'd all been warned. Three years old that was fucking old enough to know. Old enough to remember. Playing in the tub like they were forbidden, naked in sudsy water and splashing. Certain rules and regulations. Some kids, they disobeyed. Like their brains were wired wrong.

No: not a matter of *skin color*. Mick and Minn Flynn were known to be *color-blind*.

Sure, Mick and Minn were what's called *white*. That kind of *white*, like opening a cellar door and what's down there in the pitch-black looking up at you, that face, that kind of *white-white skin*.

He understood, they weren't seeing skin color. Skin color meant nothing to them. It was something else, indefinable. Kids that, just, Mick would say, *pissed them off*.

Rubbed them the wrong way.

Minn would say, making a face like a fist closing tight—*Had the devil in them*. Maybe half the kids in the Flynn household were "white"—like Little Mick. But it didn't mean they'd stick up for you, the other "white" kids.

Jesus it was a while before Little Mick caught on, he was *white* in the way that Mick and Minn were *white*.

It would be charged against the Flynns that they were *vicious racists*. In the newspapers and on TV much would be charged, vehement and excited and self-righteous indignation claiming *monsters, child-murderers* but nothing more hurtful than *racist*.

Mick claiming aggrieved he didn't fucking *see skin color*. Ask anybody who knew him. Guards at the facility, Christ even some of the inmates they'd swear Mick Flynn didn't give a shit what your *skin color* was.

Saying, laughing that motherfucker Mick Flynn was as hard on white guys as on Black. Sure!

At the trial, sidelined for hours on this issue. *We are not pree-judiced, we are not racists.*

But what was the reason, were there actual reasons, for what you did to the children in your custody?—questions posed as if out of curiosity, as an entomologist might pose a question to a particularly virulent venomous insect if such were possible.

What were the reasons?—lots of reasons.

Yes. Those kids were *bad.* Needing *discipline.*

Or, no: they *hurt themselves.*

Why was anything that was, no idea. Minn had a way of jiggle-giggling so the parts of her big body shimmied like in a dance: Hell, some things just *is.*

From the beginning of Time, you could say. *In the Beginning was the Word, and the Word was with God, and the Word was God.*

No arguing with that, right?

No reason why the child they steamed to death—identified as "Esdra" but no one called Esdra—(not a fast death for Esdra: slow with agony, high-pitched shrieks at the start then gradually weakening, fading)—was the one, and not *him*—the favorite of Mick because why?—robin's-egg blue eyes of Mick mirrored in him, weird to think so but that was probably so.

A man needs a son. That's in the Bible.

Not at first. Little Mick didn't think so. (But how'd he *know?*) But later, maybe gradually. Not sure. Time was more a tangle of knots than anything you could track moving in one direction.

Cellar-kids just seemed to happen. Nobody set out to starve them, only just to "punish" them dragging the sobbing/screaming kid into the cellar, down the wobbly steps into the dark, giving a kick to loose a child's desperate grip on an adult's hand.

Little cocksucker, see how you like it.

How it happened there came to be *cellar-kids* sleeping on pieces of cardboard on the filthy cellar floor, coughing and wheezing, too weak to cry. Ever weaker since they were fed just leftovers, cold pizza slices, scrapings from plates.

The others, kids privileged to live upstairs, Jojo and Tommy, Eula, Bitt, Angel got to sleep in actual beds cuddling with one another beneath shared blankets and pillows and to eat at the kitchen table if there was room, tenderly fed by Minn. Not only allowed to watch TV but invited by Minn to watch with her, Minn's favorite programs, no fun for Minn to watch alone when Mick was on the night shift.

TV snacks, potato chips out of the bag, the ripple kind with salt so visible it was like sand, gritty on your fingers and burning inside your mouth, a powerful thirst only the eight-ounce sugary Pepsi could quench. Cold pizza slices.

Was there a day, an hour, an actual minute when Mick and Minn decided okay, we will starve this one, little pike-face bald baby, bulgy-eye baby, crack baby, or was it gradual like erosion, like sediment, like leakage, like goiters, like ulcers, like bunions, like warts, like mold, like tiny baby mosquitoes hatching in the fetid puddles beneath the eaves, rusted gutters gorged with leaves. Was it just God's will: accident.

Minn was not a monster (it would be argued in court) but a girly-girl growed up too fast. A little flame of a brain trapped inside a big blow-up rubber female jiggling, shimmering, shimmying to loud thrilling Motown music out of the plastic radio. A flame quivering, widening and pulsing and ready to burst, a pent-up flame, blown like bubble gum out of the mouth shaped like an *O*, obscene and beautiful, unspeakable. *You'd have to have been there. Playing Parcheesi with Minn. Watching TV. Butterscotch ripple ice cream. Never so happy in all of our lives to come.*

What Little Mick did was sneaky. Risky. Risking the wrath of Mick, which was a serious wrath to risk but not Minn, Minn would look the other way, humming to herself preoccupied with whatever it was inside Minn's carrot-red head behind the sweet-vague lipstick smile that was Minn's face. Little Mick felt sorry for the *cellar-kids* so he'd sneak food down to them, pizza slices, leftover meatballs, chips and crackers, big boxes of Ritz crackers, the *cellar-kids* devoured like animals, ate off the floor, plastic plates like dogs, paper plates, ravenous so they paid no mind to flies, ants, roaches.

Daring to tell Minn, one of the children was too weak to eat. Couldn't lift his head. Mucus in his eyes, nose. Just lying there with his eyes closed. Minn hummed louder, not seeming to hear.

Later saying to Little Mick in an undertone, *Ever hear of "make your own grave, now you got to lay in it"*—with a level look at Little Mick he'd never forget.

One thing Mick didn't like, any kind of opposition. Interfering. That was a principle of the household. That was the crucial principle of the household.

Keeping on the right side of Mick. Minn knew how. Well, sure!

Advice to Little Mick. *Just—y'know: stay on the right side of Mick. You'll be okay.*

Like knowing to drive on the righthand side of the road. That simple: how you kept from being dragged into the cellar, left to starve.

How you kept from being dragged to the bathtub, scalded to death.

Deep in the gut Mick laughed. Mick was a man who liked to laugh. Laughter to blaze like a chainsaw through the lives of those who survived him no less than those who loved him.

When the blood was up in Mick's face you shrank from those ice-pick eyes. Not robin's-egg blue now, no-color now, pupils the size of caraway seeds. So Little Mick knew to go limp. Raggedy-doll limp. (Minn had girl raggedy dolls perched pert and sassy on a high shelf, big round button eyes and savage-bright clothing, only just feet peeking out from beneath the clothing. No legs.)

Knew not to struggle. That was the worst mistake—struggling. He'd been a witness, he knew. Before he could have understood, he knew.

By instinct knew not to cry, not to whimper, a little low groan, a moan, that was okay. His face in the pillow. Mouth muffled. *O-kay* not too hard, not too fast, then harder, harder still as with rough Mick-hands Mick gripped the cheeks of the tender baby-ass, nudge of Mick's veiny engorged thing between the cheeks, into the tight-panicked anus, astonished flesh cringing, shrinking would only cause more pain, and more annoyance to Mick therefore more pain, this Little Mick understood. The cunning of such instinct for survival could be traced through centuries borne in the chromosomes and genes of the child's ancestors, a wavering but stubborn-steadfast course like a thread of glittering mica in a wall of granite.

It wasn't punishment. He didn't think so. It wasn't punishment for *that*—feeding the doomed children in the cellar. (Of which Mick didn't know, evidently. Meaning that Minn did not tell him.) Might've been punishment for something more obscure, a shifting of Little Mick's gaze from Mick's at the wrong time, stiffening of the child's face, smile belated by just a second, not *Dadda's little boy* just then.

Or maybe not punishment at all. Maybe something else.

He never resisted. Slammed against the mattress and the pillow sopping with saliva and sweat, bedclothes bright with his blood, little fucker see?—get what you deserved.

And it was kind of okay, wasn't it. Hey.

I said—it was okay, yah?

Teach you a lesson. That's the point.

That's the entire point. Discipline.

(Movement of his head, *yes.*)

What'd you say?

(Yah. Yes.)

What'd you say?

(Yes.)

Fuckin little bugger, needing to be disciplined. Right?

Where was Minn at such times, had to be downstairs. You could hear Motown turned up high in the kitchen.

Mick would protest: we love *our kids* all equally. Minn would protest: crazy about *our kids* all equally.

Fierce as a lioness protecting her cubs, Minn fought the officers barging into the house with a search warrant screaming at them get the fuck out of my house, we are licensed by the county, we provide foster care for Children's Welfare, fuckers get the fuck out of here, you are scaring my children, you have no right. This is our home, you have no right. In the scuffle chairs were overturned. The kitchen table on its tubular legs. Dishes soaking in the sink, paper plates encrusted with food on the floor. Plastic radio turned high. Windowpanes rattling. A lone Molson's can rolling across the floor. Children cowering, crying. Babies crying. A rank smell of baby diapers, ammonia, and bleach. Bright-pink sponges, sopping wet, soiled. Fierce and fearless Minn protected her brood. Mad strength, clawing at the intruders, breaking her fingernails, the obese female body aimed as a weapon. Toppling to the floor two of the officers of whom one is a female. Shouting, tangled feet, a third officer crouches over them trying to get a clear aim with his stick, striking furiously, by accident strikes the female officer on the shoulder, rears back and strikes again this time harder, hitting Minn's dyed-carrot head and wounds her, blood gushing from a deep scalp wound, sudden alarm among the officers, for Christ-sake what if she's got AIDS, HIV-positive, one of the officers is trying to restrain her, furious at Minn, two officers are grappling with her twisting her arms behind her body but Minn's wrists are too fat to be cuffed, officer on his back on the floor trying to push himself free of Minn's sprawling bulk, one is twisting her leg, has never seen such an enormous thigh, skin so white-white it's blinding, a tear in Minn's clothing exposes layers of dense-marbled flesh, lard-flesh, a fleeting vision of silky lacy panties cut high at the thigh, voluminous pink-nylon panties, voluminous thighs, Minn is screaming, yelling as if she is being killed and in the doorway Little Mick screams *Don't hurt her! Don't hurt her, she's my Momma!*

Several miles away Mick Flynn has been summoned to the front entrance checkpoint at Men's Detention, arrested, cuffed, led out like a captive animal by Detroit PD officers, struggling and cursing.

It would be remarked how innocent of guilt or even chagrin or shame Mick Flynn was confronted with charges of second-degree homicide, abuse of children, sex abuse, endangerment of children. Defiant and protesting, exasperated having to explain repeatedly how civilians don't know shit about the system and by *civilians* Mick meant anybody not in the employ of Children's Services and this included cops, lawyers, family court judge.

Flush-faced and clearly pissed, indignant having to explain to civilians about the *ground rules* of a foster home, need for *discipline*. That had to be swift, and had to be serious.

About the "scalding" it would be explained. "Malnutrition"—"concussions and broken ribs"—"bruises and burns." If you knew how *brain-damage* kids injured one another and themselves. If you had any idea what it was like trying to keep those little buggers alive.

About the faucet in the upstairs bathroom it had been explained to all the children not to "play" with it. Not to "play" with water. Any kind of water. Not to flush the toilet every time they used it, like if it was just pee—don't flush! To save water, that was the point. Because money doesn't grow on trees. Because money was in short supply. Because Mick had his car loan to repay. Because Minn needed fillings in all her teeth. Because Minn misplaced the oil delivery bill and now they were behind. Because Minn lost a crucial check from welfare and they were slow to reissue a second. Because Minn was too trusting, bringing home food from Kroger's past its expiration date, beginning to rot. Because when Minn prepared hot home-cooked meals not all the children (it was claimed) would eat these meals. Because they'd been warned—finish what was on their plates. Because the "good" children always obeyed, the "bad" children did not.

More and more as time went on, the family divided—*good, bad.*

Not play with the toilet, or the tub, or the faucets, or the stove. Not ever turn on the stove. Gas flames! Blue-gas flames. Play with the fuckin stove, Mick would grab your hand and hold it over the flame, how's that?—Mick liked to say, *Eye for an eye, tooth for a tooth.*

If they'd meant to harm any one of the kids why'd they take them to the ER?—for they took them, or some of them, or two or three of them, eventually.

That was the mistake: caring for the damned brats enough to take them to the ER.

The three-year-old who'd been rushed naked to the ER, straight from the bathtub on the second floor, skin peeling off in flakes and eyes like pitted grapes unseeing rolled back in his head.

Boiled-looking skin reddened like the shell of a lobster, his screaming halted.

Minn's face shiny-wet and her head bowed while Mick's head was held high like a soldier's and his broad back straight. Fuck this hearing, fuck all this, Mick Flynn didn't acknowledge the sovereignty of fucking Wayne County Family Court, fuckers betraying him and Minn after their years of service feeding and wiping the asses of crack-babies, cripple-babies, and trash-babies nobody wanted while pretending they did.

Sad to see Minn's face deflated. Vague, confused, bloodshot-vacant-eyed in a floppy soiled-pink sweater adorned with baby rabbits straining tight against her heavy torso. Minn would plead *not guilty*, tears winking in the fatty folds of her face. Voice so hushed no one could hear, the court-appointed attorney stiffly, reluctantly lowered his ear to her mouth. *Involuntary manslaughter, abuse of a child, endangering the life of a child* but the fact was, none of it was intentional.

None of it had even *happened* in the way it was presented. Stories told in the newspapers and on TV were pure inventions by their enemies and rivals and certain social workers who had it in for them, never gave them a chance.

Anyway, whatever happened took place so gradually over so much time that when you came to the end of it, the ambulance rushing to the hospital, the beginning had been forgotten the way a dream fades rapidly on waking.

We are innocent, we never meant to hurt. We meant to discipline.

Had to discipline! Then the kids started to hurt themselves.

To spite us, hurt themselves in the worst ways like the devil was in them.

Mick persevered defiant, disbelieving. Other foster parents would testify for them, he said.

Look, these were not normal kids. These were *brain-damage* kids. Nothing to do with *race, skin color.*

Marked at birth for trouble. Brain deficit. Eyes not in focus. Crying, puking. Kicking. Wetting the bed. Shitting the bed. Some of them, diarrhea just never stopped seeping into the bedclothes. Who'd want to sleep with *that*? Who'd want *that* upstairs in the kitchen?

The more brain deficit the more the deceit. Already as babies, deceit. Liars. Could not trust. With just milk-baby-teeth those devil-babies could *bite.*

Ate like animals, why their food had to be rationed. Had to be padlocked. They had to be padlocked in the cellar. For their safety. For the safety of the good kids kept upstairs.

A goddamned lie, we are *racists.* Of all charges this was most hurtful to Mick and Minn.

Calculating even at that point how they might salvage their reputation. Which was a goddamned good reputation, acquired over years of conscientious work, loving care of the orphaned.

Nobody else wants these kids, nobody gives a damn if they live or die so now it's on our heads, something happens to them.

They try to kill their own selves, it's on our heads! Bullshit.

Each morning in the fluorescent-lit courtroom Minn's shiny face thick and poreless with makeup gradually melted away. Each morning the wide girl's eyes dimmed. Eyebrows plucked and curved with red-brown pencil in a perpetual look of innocent surprise, bewilderment.

Wise-guy lawyer appointed to represent Minn would claim, for his client, *not guilty by reason of mental defect, coercion. Not guilty by reason of fear of her husband of her life.*

This lawyer!—an expression in his face of such disgust, the slick bastard might've been smelling a bad smell. Aura of Minn's bloated body, heat thrumming outward from Mick's flushed skin. Why's he think he's so superior?—law degree from Wayne State. Why'd he think he was hot shit, wasn't even a Jew-lawyer like the prosecutor, just local Irish like Mick and Minn. Sidebar with Your Honor, Minn's lawyer daring to suggest *alcoholic insult to the brain, feeble-minded*. Mick's lawyer looked on him with outrage, contempt.

Like hell that's going to excuse it. My client is no more guilty than Mrs. Flynn. This is not going to go down, my client isn't taking the blame, don't think it.

The family court judge was a middle-aged Black woman with a deceptively round face, seemingly placid, maternal, malleable; second glance you saw the shrewd eyes, mouth set like stone. Lifting from her head a cloud of the finest gray hair, an Afro to suggest Angela Davis. Regarding both Mick and Minn with barely concealed fury, contempt.

Cutting off the defense lawyers abruptly—*Not in my courtroom. No.*

Few of the Flynns' fosters were capable of testifying. Several had given faltering statements to social workers, psychologists, pathetic recordings played in court. Several, no longer living in the house at Wyandotte, aged-out and living elsewhere in halfway houses, dull-witted, "developmentally challenged," not sure what they remembered but in court fearful of looking in the Flynns' direction.

Fearful of Mick Flynn's flushed face, murderous pale eyes.

"Douglas Resnick"—one of those few enlisted by the defense, to speak on behalf of Mick and Minn.

This was the surprise: Little Mick was "Douglas Resnick." That was his name on a document.

No idea how old he was except there in the courtroom it was said aloud from a document: four years, three months old.

Little Mick's throat shut up tight. Trying to speak but can't. Everybody staring at him. Who's *him*?

Minn's desperate smudged eyes raking his face, Mick glaring at him. All Mick could do to keep from shouting at "Douglas Resnick" in terror of wetting himself.

Take your time, son.

"Douglas"—take your time.

Can you speak up? Just a little louder, "Douglas."

Managing to stammer it wasn't their fault but his voice was too faint to be heard. One of the (female) social workers he almost didn't recognize, her face brightly made up and hair brushed and wavy, gently the woman held his hand to encourage him asking if his foster parents had ever hurt him and he'd said very carefully No, no they had not.

Had they hurt other children?—*No.*

This question Little Mick was asked repeatedly. Shut his eyes and when he opened them no time had passed, the question was being asked again.

Licking his dried and chapped lips saying that Minn had "not ever" hurt him, or anyone. Mick had "maybe" hurt bad children when they were bad.

What did *maybe* mean? Did *maybe* mean *yes*?

Beginning to tremble. Not looking toward Mick, those furious eyes and grimacing mouth.

Not ever look at Mick again. Not—ever.

Just a glance at Minn hiding her face with the dimpled-white hands.

You are certain, "Douglas"? What you are telling us, you are *certain*?

Yes. Yes. Yes. *Yes.*

Because of Little Mick's testimony Minn's sentence was much reduced. Because of Little Mick, Minn was spared the worst.

Guilty of reduced charges—*involuntary manslaughter. Assault (not aggravated), endangerment, abuse of a child younger than twelve.*

Homicide, dropped. *Sexual abuse of a child*, dropped.

Eighteen months in the Detroit Women's House of Correction, two-year probation, mandatory psychiatric therapy. Minn wept, throwing herself on the mercy of the court as her lawyer claimed, almost you could see that yes, Minn was *throwing herself* in this public place shameless and naked beneath her billowing clothes, sobbing and choking, eyes shut and near-hidden in the folds of her face but in the Women's House of Correction she would be many times beaten by sister-inmates, whites as well as Blacks, here was an occasion the races could join forces in an ecstasy of punitive violence as the dyed-carrot hair went gradually gray and then white at the roots where it had not been yanked out from the white scalp. Objects shoved into Minn's vagina, up into her anus, leaving her bleeding with ulcerated guts. Head dunked in filthy toilets, the obese body deflating, skin fitting her like a loose balloon, face no longer a girl's baffled face but the mask-face of a middle-aged woman bruised and repellent as rotted fruit and half her teeth missing from beatings/kickings as (male) guards pointedly looked the other way or on occasion participated in the beatings.

Baby killer. Fuckin bitch cunt white-trash baby killer, think you deserve to live?

None of this Little Mick—from now on (officially) Douglas Resnick—would know until much later. Years later. How Mick Flynn serving two consecutive life sentences at Ypsilanti Maximum Security Correctional for Men would be murdered at last, aged forty-nine. Many times threatened, assaulted. At last shivved in the shower. White-faced big-gut scar-cheeked Mick Flynn fallen heavily, blood spurting from a severed artery in his throat draining away in the slow drain clogged with hair, one of the notorious inmates at Ypsilanti so it was a matter of time, coldhearted *pedophile baby-killer motherfucker* would get what he deserved, the warden had his reasons not to transfer Flynn out of general population.

All this, years later. Telling it now, tonight, his memory is flooded, too much crowding in, not a great idea for him to drink on an empty stomach, in an anxious time in his life, but there you are.

But there *you* are. Listening in astonishment.

He'd never researched the media coverage, Resnick was saying. Not till first-year law. Growing up in Marquette, Michigan, in the northern part of the state adopted by an academic couple at the university there, "stepparents" who knew it was wisest to put the past behind him and beyond him in (literally) the lower part of the state so far away it was like another lifetime entirely.

One of the walking wounded. Hadn't realized at the time. His new parents downplayed anything like that. Cautious, wary. Left-leaning liberals they identified themselves but not naive. Can't blame them, he's grateful for them. Adoption means wanting to start the calendar all over again, at zero.

But okay, he'd survived. One of five, six from his time with the Flynns who'd survived. And he was *loved*, that was what saved him.

Well—he'd been *loved* first by Mick and Minn. They'd been partial to him. Minn had been crazy for him. Mick, if you didn't get on the wrong side of Mick, Mick was okay.

You'd have to have been there to understand. Mick *was* okay, most of the time.

Still, he knows: *why?* That's the question.

Not because he was white. Is white. Some others were white too, *white* didn't save them.

One of those little fish bones stuck in your throat. Can't swallow it, can't spit it up. *For God's sake why. If you could explain.* Why did they feed you and starve the others, why did they bathe you and let lice devour the others? Why did they not scald you as well as scold you? Why were your eardrums not punctured? Why were you not beaten, sodomized? *Were you?*

Abruptly then, such questions ceased. As soon as the hearing ended, such questions ceased forever. With the other survivors removed from the Detroit foster-child program in a purge, defunding, reform, and reorganization of County Children's Services, separately relocated elsewhere, Douglas Resnick to the Upper Peninsula hundreds of miles away from the city of Detroit.

In the Upper Peninsula, vast acres of fir trees. Snowy fields, ice-locked lakes. In winter, twenty below zero. Up here everyone was crazy for *winter sports*. Skiing, ice hockey. Skating. Sledding. *Dress warm! C'mon.*

These old questions, memories of a cramped household in a red-brick row house in Detroit did not follow him. Rancid smells evaporated in bitter cold. Unmistakable stench of decomposing flesh, blown away by the wind.

Still, seeing a Christmas wreath on a door, that could do it. Seeing certain TV faces, potato chips. Pizza.

Panic, vomiting. Heart pounding. Weird nerve in his heart—switching *off*, he'd fall in a faint.

Cheap red Italian wine and he's recalling how the child's skin came off in strips, thin translucent-red peels, how he'd screamed and screamed. Had that been Esdra, or Elijah? Had that been both?

He hadn't been present but he'd seen. How they'd pushed the screaming child down into the sudsy-filthy tub water, his face in the water, head beneath the surface of the water so that the screams halted abruptly. Taking care not to burn their hands by using tools to push the child, deliberately chosen claw hammer, eight-inch wrench, Mick the most vehement but Minn furious and petulant too, how steam arose, the baby-face lifting from the scalding water flushed red with blood to burst as the shrieks mounted higher, higher . . . *Why?*

"I tell myself if I knew why, I would know a crucial secret of the universe. I don't mean anything theological. I mean, I guess— 'rational.' If the universe is material, if it's 'determined' . . ."

I'd become silent. Having been listening to him for however long it had required.

In truth, I was stunned. I was sick at heart. I was, well—*surprised*.

Not what I'd expected returning to his apartment with Doug Resnick, whom I've known for more than two years not well, not intimately, until tonight.

Meeting at the law school fall reception. That is, remeeting. Not that we hadn't been aware of each other with some frisson of interest, from our first-year torts class. But it had never advanced beyond that. Never alone together, before tonight.

In Doug Resnick's bed. For what has seemed like hours.

As hours before, it must have seemed like a possible idea. It must have seemed like a not-risky idea. Because Doug is respected at the law school. Well mannered, not argumentative, watchful, wary, considerate, kind. You'd think.

"You won't love me now, I suppose. If there was any chance of that, it's fucked now. Since I told you. 'Mick and Minn.' But I *wanted* to tell you. Maybe—warn you."

Such silence gripped me, a girl who isn't by nature reticent or even shy. A girl who has imagined herself *one of the guys*, when it suited her.

Confident, or if not confident exactly, wise enough to keep out of risky situations.

Most sex crimes perpetrated by (male) acquaintances on (female) acquaintances begin in "misunderstanding." Almost always— "alcohol." Then—"misunderstanding." Then—"escalate."

This hadn't been forced, this had been consensual. I would have said I'd been in control, dominant. Any hesitation on my part, Doug would have drawn away stiff and rebuffed, maybe hurt, but definitely he'd have drawn away.

Asking me now: "Should I not have? Told you the truth?"

Nowhere to look. So close, acutely self-conscious, it is excruciating to be *looked at* in such close quarters.

Here is what I did: I hid my face against his neck. Warm perspiring neck. Sticky hair. This was not a ploy, a stratagem in such tight spots, new to me. This was a disarming gesture that had not failed to work in the past.

Disarm, neutralize. Not blame. Until it was possible to disengage and flee the bed, the premises, disengage and flee, very careful not to suggest disdain, still less disgust.

Until tonight, yes, I'd thought I might love Doug Resnick.

There are candidates, reasonable candidates among any circle of the unattached. Not-yet-married. Not-yet-involved. Doug Resnick was one of these, one of the more attractive.

Often I'd seen his eyes moving onto me, quizzical. Calculating?

Asking: "What are you thinking, Molly? Why are you so quiet?"

Thinking how to reply. My face still buried in Doug's neck, a bare arm across Doug's warm chest, a naked chest, the shock of first-time nakedness gradually abating, almost casual by this time, more of a companionable posture in a stranger's bed, for the woman the sex part is the means to this, casual, companionable. Wanting to think so.

Except: my thoughts are rushing at me too swift to be comprehended like those miniature faces that rush at us when we are falling asleep when we are exhausted. Except: I can feel the artery beating hard and hot in the man's throat. And a just-perceptible stiffening in all my limbs, I know that Doug can feel.

Saying, after a moment, in a voice suggesting a door opening, opening wider, wider than you'd anticipated, before I could manage to reply:

"Or are you thinking that you're grateful, Molly? You've been forewarned? *Stupid cluck.*"

LATE LOVE

They were newly married, each for the second time after living alone for years like two grazing creatures in separate pastures suddenly finding themselves, who knows why, herded into the same pasture and grazing the same turf.

That they were *not young* while described by observers as *amazingly youthful!* must have been a strong component of their attraction for each other.

K__, a widow, and T__, divorced a decade previously from a woman (now deceased), each lonely amid a busy milieu of friends, colleagues. The widow believed herself more devastated by life than the new husband whose reputation as a prominent historian and something of a public intellectual reinforced the collective impression that here was a man whom life had treated well, and had rewarded in visible ways. Only she, once she was his wife, understood how self-doubting the husband was, how impatient with persons who meant well by agreeing with him, flattering and assuring him—"Excuse me, darling, thank you very much but *don't humor me."*

This remark, uttered to the wife in private, was both playful and a warning.

＊＊＊

Soon after they were married, and living together in the husband's house—(the larger of their two houses, the older and more distinguished, a sprawling five-bedroom dark-shingled American Craftsman with national landmark status on a ridge above the University)—the husband began to wake the wife in the night, talking in his sleep, or rather arguing, pleading, *begging* in his sleep, in the grip of dreams that held him captive, from which the wife had difficulty extricating him.

Each time, the wife was wakened with a jolt. Scarcely knowing where she was and who this agitated person was beside her, his broad sweaty back to her, in what felt like an unfamiliar bed with a hard unyielding mattress and an unfamiliar pillow (goose-feather, not at all soft) and in a room whose dimensions and shadowy contours were alien to her.

Thinking—*I am safe, I am married, but to another husband.*

Gently the wife touched the husband's shoulder. Gently she tried to wake him, not wanting to alarm him—"Darling? You're having a bad dream . . ."

With a shudder that rippled through his body the husband threw off the wife's hand. He did not awaken but seemed to burrow deeper into the dream as if held captive by an (invisible, inaudible) adversary; he did not want to be rescued. The wife was fascinated, if alarmed, that the husband had worked himself up into a fever state—the T-shirt and shorts he wore in lieu of pajamas were soaked through, and his body thrummed with an air of frantic heat like a radiator into which steaming-hot water has rushed unimpeded.

Fascinated, too, that the husband's sleep-muffled words were *almost* intelligible. Like words in a foreign language that so closely resemble English, you are led to think that meaning will emerge at any moment thus you listened enthralled, in utter concentration.

Yet, no meaning emerged. And now, the husband had begun grinding his teeth as well as muttering.

He appeared to be cornered, threatened. A low growl in his throat became a whimper, a plea. His legs twitched with the panicked need to run but could not run as if his ankles were bound. Harshly he breathed, panting like a steer in terror of being bludgeoned over the head.

Still, the wife hesitated. It seemed wrong to forcibly wake a person so deeply asleep and yet equally wrong, or worse, not to wake him out of a nightmare. The wife recalled how when she'd been a girl an older relative was said to have died in his sleep of a massive heart attack, claimed by his wife to have been caused by a nightmare . . . But had the wife waking her husband precipitated the heart attack? Or had the impending heart attack precipitated the nightmare?

Cautiously the wife shook the husband's shoulder hard enough to wake the husband in the midst of a whimper.

Sudden silence in the husband, even his labored breathing ceased as if, in an instant, he'd become fully awake holding himself rigid as in the presence of an enemy.

Without touching him the wife could feel the husband's racing heartbeat. The bed quivered with his terror. The wife thought of animals so paralyzed with terror—rabbits, quail—they froze in the presence of the predator about to tear out their throats with its teeth.

"Darling? Are you all right? It's just . . . It's me."

And: "You were having such a bad dream, you were talking in your sleep . . ."

Still, the husband did not turn to her. In his state of animal vigilance the husband did not want to be touched.

How strange this was! The muttering in sleep, pleading and whimpering, and now this reaction. Totally unlike the husband in his waking life . . .

How unlike, too, the wife's first husband, who in thirty-six years of marriage had never once talked in his sleep, at least not like this. Never moaned and thrashed in a nightmare.

Close beside the husband the wife lay hoping to calm, console, comfort not by speaking further but by the solace of intimacy, as one might placate a frightened child; not slipping an arm around his waist (as she'd have liked to do) but allowing the husband to sense her presence. Allowing him to hear her own, even breathing—*It's just me. Your wife, who loves you.*

Naively the wife supposed that in another moment or two the husband (ordinarily affectionate, sensible, matter-of-fact) might grasp the situation, throw off the nightmare, turn to gather her in his arms, and kiss her. . . .

Except: had the husband possibly forgotten her? That is—*her?*

For theirs was a new marriage, not a year old. A lamb with spindly legs, uncertain on its feet.

Vulnerable to predators.

Each day came a flurry of kisses light and whimsical as butter-flies. Silly jokes passed between them, each was grateful for the other. Especially, the wife was grateful for the husband. But how long could this idyll last?—the wife could only hope to forestall the first serious quarrel.

Tension drained from the husband's body. His shoulders relaxed, he'd begun to breathe more regularly. Lapsing into a normal sleep.

Thank God! Enormous relief the wife felt, that she might at last sleep herself.

Enormous relief, as if she'd narrowly avoided danger.

Positioning herself to face outward, staring at a shadowy wall not altogether familiar to her, the wife willed herself to relax, to fall sleep even as to her dismay she began to hear a near-inaudible *click-clicking* sound behind her.

Alert and alarmed the wife listened: was this sound the husband's *teeth*?

His jaws were trembling convulsively, it seemed. As if he were very cold, shivering with cold. An eerie sound that stirred hairs at the nape of the wife's neck.

Again!—the low fearful aggrieved muttering.

What was the husband saying?—the wife listened, now fully awake.

Now miserably awake. Despairingly awake.

Awake awake awake. Never more sleep.

Trying to decipher the garbled words. Rough syllables of sound. Like grit flying in the air. The wife was fascinated, yet filled with dread. Did the wife really want to know what the husband was saying in his sleep?

Wondering, too, with a kind of detached ironic curiosity, if it was even ethical to eavesdrop like this. On anyone, but especially a husband in such a vulnerable state. As if his soul were naked. No protection, no armor. A man's maleness, his dignity. Where?

In their daylight life, the wife would not have eavesdropped on the husband if she'd overheard him on the phone, for instance. Especially if he were speaking with such fervor.

Any sort of speech not directed consciously to her, the wife would have been hesitant to hear.

It was distressing to her, that the (sleeping) husband bore so little resemblance to the man she knew. The (sleeping) husband sounded like a whining/whimpering child, the man she knew had a deep baritone voice and exuded an air of imperturbable calm.

The man she knew stood well over six feet tall, with broad shoulders, a head of thick coppery-silver hair that flared back from his forehead, eyes crinkled at their corners from smiling hard through his life. Swaths of coarse hair sprouted in his underarms, on his forearms and legs, on his back. The wife had never heard this man plead, or whimper or whine.

The man beside her in the bed seemed both shorter than the man she knew, yet thicker, heavier, with a sweaty back that looked massive; his bulk weighed down his side of the bed. The wife seemed to know, the (sleeping) husband's belly would be slack, sagging with gravity. His genitals would be heavy yet flaccid as skin-sacs of something fleshy, reddened with indignation like the wattles of an aroused turkey.

As the wife listened—(for indeed, the wife had no choice: she was determined not to slip away from the bed and sleep elsewhere in acknowledgment of defeat)—it seemed evident that the (sleeping) husband was engaged in some sort of dispute in which he was, or believed himself to be, the aggrieved party; he was being teased, tormented, tortured. He was being made to *grovel*. Was the husband reliving a dispute with someone at the university, or with a relative or a friend—or an enemy? He'd retired as chair of the history department at the university after twelve years, a remarkably long tenure for a university administrator; he was still active in university and professional affairs and published frequently in his highly specialized field of medical science history.

All this, the wife had learned from others, not so much from the husband himself. For the husband's manly vanity was such, he would never stoop to boasting of his accomplishments, nor would the wife have been comfortable if he had.

Of his previous marriage, the husband rarely spoke. Nor did the husband encourage the wife to speak in any detail of her life before she'd met him.

All that K__ knew of T__ in the university community was that his first wife had passed away a decade before, and that T__ had not remarried. The first/former/deceased wife was a person of whom few spoke though she was the mother of T__'s several adult children now living in distant states.

She, the (new) wife was hesitant to ask the husband personal/private questions. Out of shyness, reticence. Out of fear that the husband would rebuke her, annoyed.

Out of gratitude to the man who'd saved the widow's life as if tossing her a lifeline, a rope she might grasp to pull herself out of the seething muck of utter despair, oblivion.

Many a night after the death of her first husband she'd considered taking her own life. Mesmerized by the grammar—*Taking her own life—but where?*

Taking her life in a sort of suitcase?—in a trash container, to be left at the curb?

It was embarrassing to the wife, to hear the (sleeping) husband whimper and beg. Pleading with the (invisible) adversary—for his life? This was no university discussion. This was an ignoble struggle. The husband's sweaty body exuded a dank feral odor of panic, that caused the wife's nostrils to pinch.

"Darling, please! *Wake up.*"

Harder than she'd intended the wife pushed the palm of her hand against the husband's back.

"What!—what's wrong . . ." The husband woke abruptly, with a start.

Again freezing as a terrified animal might freeze in a simulacrum of death, to thwart a predator.

"Darling, please, it's just me . . . Are you all right?"

The wife could hear the husband breathing. The wife could picture the husband's teeth bared in a glistening grimace, rivulets of oily sweat on his face.

"You've been having terrible dreams . . ."

Groping to switch on the bedside lamp which was a blunder: fiercely the husband scowled over his shoulder at the wife shading his squinting red-lidded eyes against the light as if it were, not a soft-wattage bedroom light, the soft-wattage glow of marital intimacy, but a blinding beacon causing him pain.

"Jesus! It's three A.M., did you have to wake me up?"

"But—you've been having a nightmare . . ."

"*You've* been having a nightmare! Every God-damned time I try to sleep you've been waking me up tonight. Turn off that damned light, I have an early morning tomorrow."

Furious, the husband turned from the wife. It was clear, the husband was disgusted with *her*.

Rebuked, the wife quickly fumbled to turn off the lamp. She was speechless with shock, chagrin. She could not even stammer an apology. Stunned by the husband's face in the lamplight contorted with fury and disgust and a kind of humiliation, that she, the wife, the (new) wife, had seen him so exposed, rendered helpless and craven by a nightmare.

The first time we see the other unclothed: the shock of the physical being, the *bodily self*, for which nothing can prepare us.

I am so, so sorry. Can you forgive me!

The wife had to wonder if the marriage had been a mistake.

A *mis-take*: taking something/someone for what he is not. *Mis*-apprehending.

The man whom the wife knew, or would have claimed to know, never behaved childishly, vindictively, foolishly. He was a handsome man who carried himself with dignity, confidence. He was easygoing, gracious, soft-spoken. He dressed casually but tastefully. He wore wire-rimmed glasses that gave him a youthful scholarly look appropriate to his position in life: university professor, historian. If he felt disapproval he was likely to express his opinion quietly. That man did not *make faces*. He did not betray anger, rage.

The face of the man roused from sleep was rawly aggrieved, accusing. It was not at all a handsome face but coarse, fleshy. The flushed skin of the face was creased with fine wrinkles as in the glaze of pottery and the eyes, lacking the wire-rimmed glasses, were puffy and red-lidded as the eyes of a thwarted furious bull.

In such a panicked beast, there is danger. The wife knew, and shuddered.

All this was ridiculous! Of course.

The sort of thing one thinks at night. Snarled in useless thoughts as in a gigantic cobweb.

The husband slept, the wife lay awake listening to the husband's heavy breathing. Thank God the husband was not dreaming: this seemed to be an ordinary sleep.

Now in this precarious calm the wife began to question what had happened. As a chicken pecks in the dirt seeking nourishment however minuscule and demeaning.

Thinking: the husband might not have seen *her*, exactly. He'd been surprised by being roughly wakened, his brain had not been fully functioning.

This was altogether plausible. This was consoling, though problematic.

If my husband is not seeing me, then—who is he seeing?

By degrees, the wife sank into sleep. A warmly murky penumbra rose to envelope her, like muck stirred in water.

On a beach, in cold brittle sand, trying to walk barefoot without turning an ankle, a frothy surf sweeping over her feet washing unspeakable things onto the sand: transparent wriggling jellyfish, squirming dark-splotched eels, ravaged eyeless fish, skeins of fetid seaweed. And one of these unspeakable things the realization that the husband had (possibly) murdered the last woman who'd slept in this bed in the American Craftsman house on a ridge above the university that had come to be a landmark in the university community, at which the wife had herself stared from time to time in admiration, though not envy, thinking, *But who would want to live in a nightmare house!*

This was the explanation! For, seeing the (new) wife in his bed the husband with rage-engorged eyes had seen this other woman, deceased.

The (former) wife, surely. He'd murdered in his sleep in a rage. Because she'd seen him naked, inside the sweat-soaked T-shirt and shorts. Peered into his craven soul.

No man will forgive a woman. For seeing him broken, begging.

Strangled? The husband did have strong hands.

(For how else could a husband impulsively murder a wife in their bed except by strangling her for waking him out of a deep sleep? He wouldn't be likely to stab or shoot her, that would defile the bedclothes, blood would soak into the mattress and box springs.)

Well—suffocation, also. That was a possibility.

More likely perhaps than strangulation which would require manual strength, stamina, patience. *Up close and personal: strangulation.* Having to look into the (dying) wife's eyes as the eyes cloud over, become unfocused.

Pressing one of these thick goose-feather pillows over the wife's face. Over both nose and mouth. Holding down the frantic thrashing wife, incapable of opening her mouth to scream. No mercy, just stamina.

Driven mad by nightmares. Glaring-eyed, suffused with repugnance.

(But which pillow? Would T__ have actually kept the pillow with which he'd suffocated his [first] wife, or would he have disposed of it?)

(An expensive goose-feather pillow, thick as a man's torso, tightly filling out the percale pillowcase which the wife could barely force over it as she struggled to make up the four-poster bed.)

(This bed, a four-poster with carved mahogany headboard and posts, had to be one hundred years old at least. No doubt, more than one person had died in this bed.)

By lamplight the wife had seen the husband/murderer glaring at her over his shoulder. Reddened mad-bull eyes. He'd have liked to kill her but the pull of sleep was too strong for him to resist, fortunately for the wife.

But no. The thought was preposterous, terrible—the thought of the goose-feather pillow pressed over a face.

Absurd, yet also thrilling.

How can you be so ridiculous, ungrateful? This man saved your life.

This is a man who loves you, whom you love. This man who'd hauled you out of oblivion.

Abruptly: it was morning.

The wife's eyes opened amazed. (What had happened to the night?)

Alone in the four-poster bed. Hearing, from the adjoining bathroom, the thrumming sound of a shower.

Hearing the husband, in the shower, humming to himself. The husband who described himself as a *morning person.*

Like warm gauze sunshine spilled through a window.

For this is the logic of *daylight*: whatever has happened in the night fades like images on a screen when light is restored.

Hurriedly, the wife changed the (rumpled, stale-smelling) bed-clothes. Yanked the top sheet from the bed, yanked the bottom sheet from the bed, struggled to shake the goose-feather pillows out of their soiled cotton cases.

Later, on the back terrace where the husband liked to have breakfast in good weather, the wife brought the *New York Times* to him, as soon as it was delivered; the husband glanced up smiling at her, clearly remembering nothing of the night.

The wife delighted in serving the husband his favorite break-fast that rarely varied: fresh-squeezed orange juice, two perfectly poached eggs on multigrain toast, Arabica dark-roasted coffee, black.

"Thank you, darling!"—playfully seizing the wife's hand, kissing the moist palm.

Darling. The wife knew herself vindicated, beloved.

<hr />

Except: several nights later the wife was again awakened by a low guttural muttering close beside her in the dark. And an eerie *click-clicking!* of shivering teeth like castanets.

Awakened with a jolt in the darkness of an unfamiliar room.

And the too-thick, uncomfortably hard goose-feather pillow beneath the wife's head, that made her neck ache; so much higher a pillow than the smaller, more ordinary pillows of her previous life—this, too, was disorienting.

In the early days of the (new) marriage the wife had substituted a smaller pillow on her side of the bed but the husband noticed at once. As the husband was turning out to be fastidious about the furnishings and maintenance of his architecturally distinctive house so he'd objected in his lightly ironic, elliptical way, noting that the *symmetry* of the bed was ruined by placing a flat pillow beside the goose-feather pillow so that the handwoven afghan comforter that covered the bed looked lumpy, *asymmetrical*—"Like a woman who has had a single mastectomy, the *symmetry* of a beautiful body destroyed."

(Mastectomy!—the wife had laughed, wincing. The analogy was so unexpected. But the husband was smiling, the wife saw. He'd only meant to be witty.)

Twenty past one A.M. They'd been in bed for a little more than one hour. That night they'd gone to dinner at the home of old friends of the husband's who'd known the husband's first wife but were cordial and welcoming to the (new) wife. Their names were Alexandra and Agustin. The evening had been a strain for the (new) wife but the husband had been relaxed in a way the wife hadn't seen him before, praising his hostess's cooking (a spicy paella), drinking more than usual—though not excessively, for the husband did nothing in excess. Only just two or three glasses of an (allegedly) delicious Argentine red wine that the (new) wife had found too tart for her taste. (Not that the wife knew much about wine, whether red or white, Argentine or other.)

The husband had fallen asleep as soon as they'd gone to bed, the wife had lain awake thinking over the evening as one might rerun a video hoping to detect small details that had been overlooked the first time, yet nervous at discovering something unexpected; seeing again the genial hosts exchanging glances when the (new) wife was speaking as if—just possibly—they were comparing the (new) wife to the (former, now deceased) wife whom they'd known

229

for many years . . . But how they felt about the (new) wife, what the meaning of their glances was, the (new) wife had no idea.

Do you think your friends liked me?—the wife had dared to ask in the car as the husband drove them home though knowing that the question would embarrass or annoy the husband who did not like his (new) wife to express neediness, or wistfulness, or disingenuous naivete; and the husband had laughed, not unkindly, curtly saying *Of course! Of course they did.*

But not expanding on the subject. Not encouraging the wife to ask further foolish questions.

Not asking the wife if she'd liked his friends, or enjoyed the evening, or hoped to repeat it again, ever.

Her friends, the wife wasn't eager to introduce to the (new) husband. The friends she'd known during her marriage of thirty-six years who did not seem to her nearly so interesting as the (new) husband's friends; nor did the (new) husband express any eagerness to meet them.

And so the wife lay awake tormenting herself with such thoughts. Like fleas or bedbugs such leaping thoughts both inconsequential and stinging, vexing. Gradually drifting into sleep descending a staircase and stumbling on the final step which somehow she hadn't seen for a buzzing of flies distracted her, loud buzzing horseflies; and suddenly she was jolted awake by a person, a presence, close beside her in the dark, a bulky figure weighing down his half of the bed buzzing and muttering to himself, grinding his teeth like (muted) castanets; moving his legs jerkily as if he were caught in some sort of net, or web, or contrivance; which frightened the wife more than she'd been frightened previously for now (she would have to acknowledge) these "bad dreams" were frequent in the husband's (nocturnal) life, and so in her (nocturnal) life as well.

Dazed thinking—*But who have I married? Is it too late, now?*

In the intervening days since the first night of interrupted sleep there had been no (evident) alteration in the husband, who'd behaved as courteously and affectionately to the wife as before. No memory, no shadow of the unfortunate interlude fell between them. The wife felt a twinge of vertigo, almost of nausea, watching the husband's mouth as he spoke to her in his affable-husband manner, recalling the ferocious scowl of the man exposed by lamplight exuding heat, sweat, smelling of armpits, crotch-hair, fetid feral odors though (in fact) the husband in daylight was fresh-showered, fresh-shaved, his silvery-copper hair abundant except at the very crown of his head, flaring back from his forehead, and his eyes of washed-blue glass utterly frank, guileless. It would have taken an effort of memory to summon back the baffled curious bloodshot eyes glittering with rage at her in the lamplight, to what purpose such effort?

Nor had the wife brought up the subject of the husband's "bad dreams"—of course not.

The wife was not a naive young bride but a middle-aged woman who knew better than to dwell upon distressing subjects especially since she was a (new) wife wanting only to please the (new) husband.

Since her first husband had died, and abandoned her, and left her to ponder *taking her own life*, there was now the (new) husband with whom she'd been given another chance: if she could succeed in making this man happy she would save herself as well as him. So very carefully watching her every word, her every step. Quite a blunder it had been, switching on that lamp at three A.M.!

And so, she hadn't said a word to the husband. In fact, she'd forgotten that nightmare-night—or nearly.

Some vague silly dream of hers involving the goose-feather pillow, how such a hefty pillow might be pressed over a face . . .

Her face?—ridiculous.

She rather resented the goose-feather pillow. It was so thick, so *heavy*. Tight as a sausage in sausage casing, a struggle to fit the cotton pillowcase over it.

(It was true, a cleaning woman came each Friday, to change bedclothes, scour, scrub, mop, sweep, vacuum, splash bleach into the toilets, this was Alvira who'd been cleaning the husband's five-bedroom house for many years; yet still, the wife felt obliged to change the bedclothes more than once a week for bedclothes are easily soiled.)

Nor had the wife made inquiries into the death of the husband's (former) wife. The wife hadn't even attempted an online search for an obituary of the (former) wife. For nothing could be more ludicrous than suspecting the husband of—whatever it was . . .

The husband was whimpering in his sleep as if he knew very well what the wife was suspecting him of. Short piteous cries, rueful, wounded. Shifting his shoulders from side to side as if trying to free himself from some sort of restraint that allowed him only an inch or two of movement: the wife envisioned a nightmare cobweb in which the husband was caught like an insect; the more he writhed, the more entangled he was in the web; and the wife too, lying close beside him in the rumpled bed, in immediate danger as well, of being trapped in the web and devoured by—what?

You know, darling: a new marriage is a new life. Requiring a new calendar.

The wife's heart was beating hard, in anticipation of touching the husband. Waking him and incurring his wrath. For the wife believed that she had no choice: she could see that the husband, in his craven, broken way, was suffering.

As you might pity and fear a stricken animal, in the blindness of pain it might lash out, claw and bite.

Tremulously the wife lifted a hand to touch the husband's shoulder. The husband's back was turned to her, she could only imagine his face, the red-rimmed eyes, the mouth twisted in anguish; she felt an anticipatory excitement, or dread, as if with all the best intentions she were about to blunder over a precipice, into an abyss.

An aphorism of Pascal came to her—*We run carelessly to the precipice, after we have put something down before us to prevent us from seeing it.*

"Darling? Please—*wake up . . .*"

Shaking his shoulder. Once, twice. The husband woke with a grunt, in an instant alert, vigilant. The whimpering ceased, at least.

"Are you all right? You've been having a . . ."

The wife was anxious to sound, not accusing, but comforting, protective.

". . . a bad dream."

But the husband denied it, irritably: "God *damn*. I have not. I haven't been asleep."

The husband did sound fully awake now, and very annoyed. Saying that *she* was the one who'd been having a bad dream, whimpering in her sleep.

Whimpering in her sleep! *Her!*

The wife was determined not to argue. The husband would have his own way as a child might, in circumstances that confused and upset him.

Accusing the wife: "*You* woke me. You've been grinding your teeth. . . ."

"I—I'm sorry . . . I didn't realize."

Grinding her teeth! This was pitiful, indeed.

Rebuked, the wife could only retreat. She was one to shrink from confrontation like a boneless-soft slug quickly retreating into its shell at the least sign of danger.

(For there is always the possibility, if we retreat, if we apologize, if we are convincing in our self-abnegation, that the one who has been angry at us might yet be beguiled into feeling sorry for us.)

He is frightened, he will lash out. Do not accuse him.

Whatever had been tormenting the husband faded quickly when he'd wakened. There was that consolation at least.

For some minutes the wife and the husband lay in silence side by side without touching. The husband quivered with indignation, dislike. Unable to acknowledge that he'd been in the grip of a nightmare though he must have wondered that his T-shirt and shorts were damp with sweat.

The wife wanted the husband to know that she'd been protective of him, and that she loved him; but she could not risk antagonizing the husband further.

Wanting to cry. It was unfair, unjust! The husband's perception of her was mistaken and beyond this, *his wish to misperceive her, misjudge her.*

Daring to ask the husband wistfully, "Where do you go? What happens to you? Please tell me"—but the husband, breathing heavily, like one carrying a weight up an incline, seemed not to hear.

Abruptly then standing up, swinging his legs out of bed, with a grunt heaving himself to his feet. In that instant the husband was crass, clumsy as the wife had never seen him before.

Where usually the husband took care not to disturb the wife if he had to use the bathroom at night now he was rudely oblivious of her presence making his way heavy-footed across the room and not troubling to close the bathroom door; the bathroom fan thrummed loudly, the bathroom light glared, the husband urinated noisily into the toilet bowl for what seemed like a very long time while the wife lay miserably awake and finally pressed the palms of her hands over her ears thinking *He has forgotten me! He has forgotten that he has a (living) wife.*

And when the husband returned he half fell into bed making the springs creak in protest, exactly as if there were no one else beside him in the bed: no wife.

Almost immediately falling asleep, his hoarse breath in long slow strokes like a rower plying clumsy oars.

The wife smarted with hurt as if her cheeks had been slapped. No way not to understand that she'd been rebuked, wounded. Effaced.

Like a fool propelled toward a revelation as toward a lethal precipice she would be unable to see until it was too late.

She had no choice, however, but to leave the bed, turn off the bathroom light (which would switch off the noisy fan). Smarting at the husband's rudeness even as (she tried to tell herself) T__ was clearly not fully awake, it was possible he'd been walking in his sleep and so not to blame for his bad manners.

The fact was: if T__ were fully awake he'd have been stunned and mystified by his own behavior.

In the bathroom the wife closed the door. At least the fan had cleared away some of the stale air of the bedroom, the panic-odor that lifted from the husband's skin.

Steeling herself for what she might see the wife peered at her reflection in the mirror above the sink. There floated the pale strained masklike face of a woman terrified that her husband may no longer love her and of what harm might come to her as a consequence.

Oh but why do you care? You have already died anyway. You must make your way alone.

Cooling her face with cold water cupped in trembling hands. In the mirror, the pupils of the wife's eyes appeared to be unnaturally dilated like the eyes of a wild creature.

The wife opened the medicine cabinet, quietly. On the topmost shelf were containers of old, outdated prescription drugs which the husband had never thrown away—painkillers following dental surgery, barbiturates for sleep. The wife was tempted to take one of the chunky white barbiturates, that would surely still be potent enough to help her sleep . . .

Seeing then, in the sink, a dark smudged ring around the drain, as if something darkly oily had been washed down the drain. There was a faint scummy smell as well, as of a sewer.

Seeing then, on the bathroom floor, in a corner beside the sink, a speckled-black thing like a large slug, about three inches in length, with tiny tawny eyes, that gave her a shock; but as she looked more closely the creature scuttled beneath the sink and disappeared inside the grouting.

Barefoot, the wife leapt back. What was this!—the wife stifled a cry of alarm, revulsion.

Recalling having looked through books in the husband's study, in a bookcase filled with old medical texts and histories of medical science. Books so old, they practically disintegrated in her hands. Histories of early medicine, bloodletting, trepanning, drawings of ghoulish procedures long faded from medical practice. . . .

No idea why she was remembering these old books of the husband's, now. For she was very tired, not thinking clearly.

For it was nearly three A.M. For she *must* sleep!

Closing the medicine cabinet. Not returning to the bed to lie beside the snoring husband but slipping quietly from the room to make her way elsewhere in the house, to a guest room where there was a smaller bed where she might sleep undisturbed; in a room also unfamiliar to her, yet not intimidating or discomforting; a room in which she might be blessedly *alone*.

This room, half the size of the master bedroom, had belonged to the husband's daughter when the daughter had lived at home years before.

Trying to sleep, in patches. Making her way across a dark rushing stream on stepping stones unsteady beneath her feet and in that water, swarms of small dark sluglike creatures waiting for her bare feet to slip . . .

Yet, early in the morning, before dawn, waking in time to quietly return to the husband, to slip into bed beside him as he lay sleeping as if she'd never been absent; feeling immense relief, that she'd returned without the husband realizing she'd been gone.

For the wife knew the husband would be hurt if he'd known how she'd crept away out of fear of him, and revulsion for him. As a man is hurt, rejected by a woman.

Not the man but the man's body. For the man identifies with his body, as a woman does not identify with her body.

But he won't know! He won't remember.

Cunning in stillness the wife snuggled close against the husband's back as a one might huddle against a sheltering wall.

And then, it was morning. Sunlight between the slats of the venetian blind like warm gauze bandages.

It seemed amazing to the wife, she'd fallen asleep in the four-poster bed so easily, beside the husband. She had!

And this, the most restful restorative sleep of her life.

And waking now, so very well-rested, alone in bed hearing the husband humming to himself in the shower; and the sound of the shower not disturbing but soothing. Out of consideration for the wife, the husband had shut the bathroom door securely.

Of course the wife loved this husband. Deeply, unquestioningly.

Basking in the luxury of daylight. For whatever happens in the night fades in daylight like images projected upon a screen when the lights come up.

She would change the bedclothes, open a window and air out the stale-smelling room, the pigsty-bed. But in no hurry. After the husband left for the day.

Later, on the back terrace where the husband liked to have breakfast in good weather, as usual the wife brought the *New York Times* to him, as soon as it was delivered, as well as his favorite breakfast: orange juice, poached eggs on toast, Arabica dark-roasted coffee.

"Thank you, darling!" the husband said, kissing the wife's hand.

As if nothing grotesque had happened in the night, to turn them against each other.

As if the husband had not wanted to murder the wife. And the wife, terrified for her life.

For if the husband could so easily forget, the wife was resolved to forget, also.

Would forget.

Except: that evening at dinner the wife heard herself say to the husband, as if impulsively: "You seem to be having bad dreams lately . . ." Meaning to sound sympathetic, not at all accusatory.

Curtly the husband replied, frowning. "Do I! I don't think so."

"You—don't remember?"

"'Remember'—what?"

"A bad dream you had last night?—a nightmare?"

"'A bad dream'—am I a child, to have 'bad dreams'?"

The husband smiled patiently at the wife as if humoring her.

The wife smiled inanely not knowing how to continue.

Not knowing *why* she'd brought up this subject when (she was sure) she'd been resolved not to.

"I—was wondering if—if something . . ."

The wife's words trailed off weakly. Oh, why had she brought up the subject!

The husband was watching the wife with an ironic smile as a parent might watch a child blundering into something easily avoided if only the child would look where it was going or the parent issue a warning.

"Yes, darling? You were wondering—what?"

"If something was on your mind, if—you might want to talk about it . . ."

"'Talk about it'—with *you*?"

"Why wouldn't you talk about it with me?—I am your wife." The wife was frightened suddenly.

(*Was* she this man's wife? How had that happened?)

Thoughts swarmed in the wife's brain like alarmed beetles. She had wanted only to sympathize with the husband, to allow him to know that, if he was troubled about something, if there were dark thoughts intruding upon his sleep, *she was on his side.*

Trying again, in a soft sympathetic voice that was not at all reproachful, "Lately, you've seemed to be having agitated dreams. You've been wakened by . . ."

"Wakened by *you*, as I recall. Last night."

"You've been having nightmares . . ."

"*You've* been having nightmares. Waking both of us."

The wife fell silent. The wife felt as if she were besieged by large buzzing flies close about her head but it was just the husband speaking patiently as if addressing a particularly slow student:

"Keep in mind, darling: dreams are wisps, vapor. Fleeting. Silly. Aristotle thought that dreams are only just remnants of the day shaken into a new configuration of no great significance. Pascal thought that life itself is 'a dream a little less inconstant.' Freud thought dreams are 'wish fulfillment'—which tells us nothing at all, if you examine the statement. But all agree, dreams are insubstantial, therefore negligible. You make yourself ridiculous trying to decipher them."

The wife wanted to protest, it wasn't her dreams she was speaking of, but *his.*

There is nothing negligible about the nightmares you are enduring.

But the wife understood that the husband was threatened by the subject, and quickly dropped it.

Like an apprentice who learns only in the scrimmage of the playing field, and not by any knowledge acquired beforehand, the wife would learn to decode the husband's most inscrutable moods. The wife would learn to anticipate the husband's *bad dreams* before he succumbed to them. The wife would learn how to protect her own life.

Soon discovering that the (former) wife had no history.

No information online. No obituary. When she typed in the (former) wife's name a blunt message appeared on the computer screen in blue font:

> This site has been discontinued. This is due to a violation
> of the terms of service or program policies. Displaying
> this content to users is prohibited.

The wife wanted to protest, the name she'd typed out was not a *site* but a *human being, a woman!*

Yet, to whom could the wife protest? No matter how many search engines she engaged each time she typed the (former) wife's name the same message came up on the computer screen: *Discontinued.*

———

But how was it possible, the husband's (former) wife had no *history?*

When the (new) wife made inquiries about the (former) wife she was met with blank faces like Kleenex.

Alvira who came each Friday to clean the house as she'd done for the past twenty-five years laughed nervously when K__ asked about the (former) wife ("Did you see her, after the divorce? Do you know what kind of illness she had, that caused her death? How long after the divorce was it, when she died?") backing away dragging the vacuum cleaner—*Lo siento, no entiendo!*

(Which was certainly not true for the wife had overheard Alvira speaking English with the husband and, with her, a kind of half English half Spanish such as a child might speak who did not want to engage in conversation.)

In the grocery store by chance encountering her husband's friend Alexandra who seemed at first friendly enough but soon became stiff-faced and evasive when, in the most elliptical of ways, K__ alluded to T__'s (former) wife—*Sorry, I am in a hurry. Another time, maybe!* Hurriedly pushing away her grocery cart as K__ gazed after her stunned at the woman's rudeness.

Only once had K__ met the husband's adult children who were (technically) K__'s stepchildren: and how disorienting, adult *stepchildren* whom she scarcely knew. Even the husband's forty-year-old daughter with whom the wife felt a tentative rapport, she was hesitant to ask about the (former) wife, who happened to be the daughter's mother, dreading the (step)daughter's startled cold eyes—*Have you no shame? Who are you? Go away, we will never love you.*

The wife could not risk it, speaking with this stepdaughter.

Could not risk the daughter telling the husband, and how annoyed the husband would be, or worse.

Why are you asking my daughter such questions?

Who are you, to ask such questions?

In the early weeks of their relationship T__ had made it clear to K__ that the past, to him, was not a happy place nor was it a "fecund" or "productive" place which was why he'd so thrown himself into his work, and had achieved for himself a "modicum of success"; but this was also why he preferred to live in the present tense.

"Which is why I love you, darling. *You* are the future, to me. A new marriage is a new start requiring a new calendar."

K__ had been deeply moved, deeply grateful. K__ had been faint with love.

Soon learning T__ meant exactly what he said. Though not-young they were young in each other's lives. If the wife looked puzzled, or perturbed, or sad, the husband need only laugh and kiss the wife lightly on the lips.

Soon then, the wife began to forget swaths of her own life: exactly where she and her (first) husband had lived, in a residential neighborhood in the "flatlands" of the university town; how long it had been since her (first) husband had died, and since they'd (first) met; where exactly the furnishings of her former house were, which she'd had to put into storage when she moved into the (new) husband's house. A half-dozen boxes packed with K__'s most cherished books she'd stored in the basement of the (new) husband's house but when she'd looked for them she couldn't find the boxes amid a chaos of duct-taped boxes, discarded furniture and appliances (old TVs, microwaves).

Wandering in the cellar of the unfamiliar house, unable to find the stairway leading up for some frantic minutes during which time the wife began to have difficulty breathing.

A new marriage is a new start. A new calendar.

What *is* it?—a curious tingling sensation on the wife's nose and cheeks, a similar sensation in the soft skin of her armpits, on her breasts, her stomach, the insides of her thighs . . . Itching, stinging, not entirely unpleasurable, she tries weakly to brush away, tries to touch her nose where the tingling sensation is strongest but cannot for her arms are benumbed, paralyzed . . .

Help! Help me!

She is crying, wailing—yet, in silence. Her mouth moves grotesquely, opening wide, a gaping *O*, her jaws are quivering, convulsing. Trying to move her arms, her hands, a terrible numbness like formaldehyde has suffused all her limbs rendering them useless. Yet in desperation managing to turn her head to one side, then to the other—shaking her head—thrashing her head from side to side to dislodge something from her face, her nose that is stinging now, hurting.

Waking suddenly, out of a deep sleep. Her exhausted brain begins to clatter like a runaway machine.

"Help me! Please!"

There *is* something on her nose, and cheeks; nestled tight in her armpits . . .

With all her strength the wife manages to stumble from bed and into the adjoining bathroom, fumbles to switch on a light, sees to her horror in the mirror above the sink something stuck to her nose, slimy-dark, sluglike, fattish, rubbery, alive—is it a *leech*?

A half-dozen leeches on her face, the underside of her jaw, her throat . . .

She screams, tearing at the ugly bloated things. Tears with her nails at the leech affixed to her nose until she rips it away bloated with her blood, the thing falls dazed and squirming to the floor. Her nose is reddened where the leech's tiny teeth had sunk into her skin, her cheeks are dotted with bloody droplets, she is frantic with horror and disbelief clawing at her armpits, at her breasts, more leeches fall to the floor where blood leaks from them, *her blood*.

The wife has never seen a leech. Not a living leech. Only just photographs of leeches. In medical history books, in her husband's library. Yet she recognizes these bloodsucking slugs. She is aghast, her face deathly white. Hyperventilating, can't catch her breath. Not enough oxygen flowing to her brain. In terror of losing consciousness. Bones turned to liquid collapsing to the floor where dozens of leeches writhe waiting to attack her anew. Suck all her blood from her as she cries *Help! Help me oh please help me.*

In that instant the light in the room brightens.

Near-blinding as the husband calls her name. Shakes her shoulders. Speaking urgently to her, *Wake up, darling! Wake up!* And she is free, she is awake. Not in the bathroom but in bed. In the four-poster bed where (evidently) she has been sleeping. Rescued by the husband from a terrible nightmare.

The husband with face creased in concern is asking the wife what has she been dreaming? What has frightened her so?—but the wife is unable to speak, she is still in the grip of the nightmare, her throat has closed tight.

No intention of telling the husband about leeches, no intention of speaking the obscene word aloud—*leech.*

Gradually, in the husband's arms, the exhausted wife falls asleep.

Do not abandon me! I have no one but you.

The (former) wife speaks so faintly, the (new) wife can barely hear.

Alone in the house in the dim-lighted cellar searching for her lost, most-cherished books but also for the (possible) (probable?) place of interment of the (former) wife.

Hours prowling the cellar. While the husband is away.

So many duct-taped boxes! So many locked suitcases, piled in a corner!

The (new) wife has to concede, if the (former) wife's remains are hidden somewhere in this vast underground mausoleum she, the (new) wife, is not likely to ever locate them: the husband has covered his tracks too cleverly.

The husband's *daylight self* is the perfect cover for the husband's *nighttime self.* Who but a wife would guess?

It is the (new) wife's guess, too, that the husband must have drugged the (former) wife so that when he'd pressed the goose-feather pillow over the woman's face she was too taken by surprise, too shocked and too weak to save herself.

Too weak to save herself let alone overpower the (much-stronger) husband.

Do not make my mistake. Do not trust in love.

Go to his medicine cabinet, where there are pills dating back for years—you've seen them. Choose the strongest barbiturates. Grind three or four into a fine white powder.

Stir this fine white powder into his food at dinner. A highly spiced dish is most recommended.

Wait then until he is deeply asleep. Have patience, do not hurry before daring to position the goose-feather pillow over his face and press down hard.

And once you have pressed down hard do not relent. No mercy!—or he will revive, and he will murder you.

Render helpless the enemy for self-defense is the primary law of nature.

———

But the next nights are dreamless nights. So far as the wife can recall.

Sleeping guardedly and this time she sees (clearly, through narrowed eyes) the husband approaching the bed in which she, the wife, is sleeping.

It is late in the night. A moonless night. Yet, in the bedroom the wife can see how the husband approaches her side of the bed in stealth, with patience and cunning; how he smiles down at her, the (drugged) wife; how he smiles in anticipation of what he is going to do to her, a rapacious smile the wife has never seen in the husband, in life; and when the husband determines that the (drugged) wife will not awaken, he takes out of a container the first of the dark slimy-black creatures, a wriggling leech of about three inches in length, and gently places it on the wife's nose.

The wife shudders in her sleep. Tries to shake her head, crinkle her nose to slough off whatever it is that has fastened onto her nose, a wee dark creature with several jaws, one hundred sharp teeth on each jaw, in her benumbed narcotized state the wife cannot defend herself against the husband as he carefully positions leeches in her armpits, between her breasts; on her belly, where her skin shivers with the touch of the leech; and in the wiry hairs at the fork in her legs. A lone leech, the last in the container, the husband places on the inside of the wife's right knee where the flesh is soft and succulent.

A dozen leeches, all roused to appetite. Piercing the wife's skin and injecting an anticoagulant into her blood. Fastening themselves snugly, beginning to suck in a kind of choral unison in the wife's deepest sleep.

In agonized silence the wife cries, *No! Help me! Please help me . . .*

"Darling, wake up! You're having a bad dream."

Fingers grip the wife's shoulders hard, give her a rough shake. Her eyelids flutter open.

In the dark that is not total darkness astonished to see a figure leaning over her, in bed beside her. Telling her as one might tell a frightened child, she has had a bad dream but she is awake now, she is safe.

Where *is* she?—in a bed? But whose?

Naked inside a nightgown. A thin cotton nightgown soaked in perspiration that has hiked up her thighs.

Frantically her hands grope over herself—nose, cheeks, underside of her jaw; breasts, belly . . . Only smooth skin, no leeches.

In this bed in this room she doesn't recognize. Then she recalls, she is married (again).

One of them gropes for the bedside lamp, fumbling to switch on the light. Each seeing the other's face haloed suddenly in the darkness.

THE SIREN: 1999

Shouts, laughter. A crashing sound of trash cans overturned in the street.

Some sort of dispute that spills into the vestibule of the rooming house at 229 East Union Street, Oriskany, New York. In his room on the second floor overlooking the street he is determined to ignore.

Twenty years old, just slightly older than most other first-year students at the State University at Oriskany, New York. He's saving money by living not on-campus (as he would have liked, would so have liked to seem like any other undergraduate with a stable family, any family at all) but at the seedy end of East Union in a neighborhood of old once-dignified single-family brick houses partitioned into rooms for low-income residents most of whom are foreign graduate students.

His mistake is: ignoring the commotion out on the street.

His mistake is: he'd promised himself a hike that afternoon.

In gusty November weather along the trail at Flint Kill Creek to clear his head after a difficult week at the university, so yearning for the outdoors after the enforced interiors of lecture halls, headache-inducing lights of the university library, claustrophobia of his small cramped room, eyes smarting from too much close reading, note-taking, squinting into the screen of his clunky old Dell laptop, he has trained himself to ignore noises out on the street, raised voices, laughter; often, drunken laughter; crashing sounds of trash cans overturned on the sidewalk he has trained himself to ignore, in a trance of concentration reading and annotating textbooks for his courses (prelaw, political philosophy, Thomas Hobbes: determinism); in his room with a single tall narrow window overlooking East Union Street he pushes little wads of Kleenex into his ears to drown out distractions as he'd learned to do as a boy in a noisy and combative household in Sparta, New York. So intent now upon hurrying outdoors, in hiking clothes (worn corduroy trousers, gunmetal-gray hoodie, water-stained Nikes), heart uplifted, the only certain happiness in his life is hiking along the Flint Kill trail, a seven-mile loop on both sides of the fast-running Flint Kill Creek, desperate to get outside, to *breathe*, and so what sheerly bad luck (he will see in retrospect) that he is leaving the building at the very moment a new dispute erupts out on the street, he's been hearing loud voices sporadically for some time and now there are shouts of rage and incredulity, protest, a siren splits the air like a machete, an Oriskany police cruiser pulls up jolting to the curb and someone pushes roughly past him to take refuge in the vestibule panting hotly into his face cursing *Out of my way, asshole!*—one of the contentious street people whose faces have become familiar to him as (probably) his face has become familiar to them though he doesn't know their names, doesn't want to know their names, these are not students like himself enrolled at the university though some may be former students, dropouts, flunk-outs, each semester in Oriskany there are those who falter, stumble, fail, and are left behind to swim or sink amid the flotsam and jetsam of a university town, some of them homeless, some of them forced to sell their blood to the Red Cross clinic at intervals while he is a legitimate university student not a *loser*, not a *dropout*, not *one of the formerly promising* like many who continue to dwell in Oriskany though expelled from the university community for reasons of mental health, finances, the simple implacable heartbreaking injustice of life. And among these are drug users, petty drug dealers, who occasionally OD on drugs dying in the university hospital where if no one claims the body in the morgue after six weeks the body becomes the property of the university medical school where medical students will carve it up in the first steps of their careers *but he is not one of these.*

Trying not to think that by the end of the semester he will owe the university eighteen hundred dollars, plus the student loan, eventually thousands of dollars, he has given up thinking about any of this, it is the interest on the loan that will throttle him, he has given up thinking about that too, how many credits he needs for his BA, how many credits yet to go, his grades have been good, mostly As with a sprinkling of Bs; his professors have encouraged him, like boatsmen at the helms of swift-moving skiffs encouraging swimmers in the treacherous waters that buoy up those skiffs his professors have encouraged him to think that he, too, will succeed, has a good chance to succeed, a good chance not to drown in the treacherous waters but to persevere until he, too, is a helmsman in a swift-moving skiff; and so he prefers to live in the present tense, and in the future, like a swimmer intent upon survival he concentrates upon what is before him, and not the past; except sometimes in weak moments, in the early hours of the morning sleepless in his bed he cannot help but think of the past, for the past pulls at him like an undertow; in moments of loneliness and self-doubt, the (modest) scholarship he has to attend the university, the anxiety of the possibility of losing that scholarship, such thoughts like a noose tightening around his throat for sometimes short on cash he, too, has to sell his blood at the Red Cross clinic. His brain works frantically to calculate how he can make a future for himself, if his grades will be high enough for law school, if there will be a scholarship for law school (he guesses *no*, he will have to take out another loan); estranged from his family in Sparta, financially and emotionally estranged from his family from whom (if they'd even offered, at this point) he wouldn't take a penny. If they had a change of heart. He wouldn't forgive. He wouldn't beg. He wouldn't *give them the satisfaction.* They'd resented his paltry scholarship, they'd have liked to *cash it in.* They were petty, ignorant people. They were not even *petit bourgeoisie* they were *lumpenproletariat* not wanting their children to be better educated than they, instilling in him a distrust of others with such ambitions, a distrust of others generally which may be why he is so often suffused with anxiety, afflicted with dreams of someone crouching over him in the dark, terror of cockroaches, the hairs at the nape of his neck stir when he hears scuttling inside walls in the night, a phobia, too, about dying in his sleep, he jokes nervously of *waking up dead, how'd you know if you were or not?* Poisonous cloud polluting his soul except when he runs on the trail beside Flint Kill Creek (where his lungs expand, he can *breathe*) but he is far from Flint Kill Creek now rudely thrown to the vestibule floor by a uniformed police officer breathing hotly into his face, sticky linoleum floor and in the corner trash bags piled eking foul-smelling juices, beneath the wall of tarnished and battered aluminum mailboxes where on a small white square of paper his name *R. Vandeveer* is hand-printed in black ink he lies stunned and speechless as a booted foot kicks him fiercely in the ribs, on all sides deafening shouts, voices of fury and protest, high raw young-male voices, an Oriskany police officer seizes his arm as if to yank his arm from its socket, another stoops over him panting and cursing shouting into his face, no idea what commands they are shouting at him, why they are so furious with him, he who is innocent and utterly bewildered, unarmed, no drugs in his pockets, not even cigarettes, his jaws are clean-shaven he is not one of the scruffy-bearded street people, he is (clearly) no danger or threat to the police officers, he has just come downstairs from his room on his way to hike at Flint Kill Creek, if only he could explain this to the officers, if only he could explain who he is, who he *is not*, it is true that the hoodie makes him look suspicious, possibly this is true but the glasses they have knocked from his face are rimless round glasses surely suggesting *scholar, serious student*, no threat to armed police officers. If only he could declare to them *prelaw*, in some way not threatening declare himself *on the side of the law: lawyer.* Nonetheless he is being unceremoniously turned onto his stomach, onto his face, arms yanked up behind his back causing him to scream in agony, feels as if both his arms are being wrenched from their sockets, though he lies helpless on his belly still the police officers continue to shout at him, his wrists are cuffed together, handcuffs too tight so that he weeps with pain and with the ignominy of pain, face pressed against the filthy floor, dimly aware of others being beaten, shouted-at, handcuffed and arrested, with the others he is forced onto his feet, stumbling he is dragged outside, thrown down concrete steps to the sidewalk, around him reeling lights of police vehicles, deafening siren as another cruiser pulls up jolting to the curb, more uniformed police officers, blinding lights, shouted commands, trying to protest he is struck a hard blow to the right temple, for an instant unconscious on his feet, weak-kneed, swaying, tasting vomit, trying not to choke on vomit, trying to explain to a rage-engorged face that he lives in this building, he'd just come downstairs to go hiking, they could check his pockets, no drugs, no weapons, he doesn't know any of others, he isn't one of them, he isn't involved with them, they don't live in this building, *he* lives in this building, *he* is a student at the university *not a drug dealer, not a drug user, has not done anything wrong* but bleeding from a head wound stunned and sobbing he is herded with five or six others similarly battered and cuffed into a police van, wrists tight-secured behind his back and ankles tight-shackled, brought to the Herkimer County courthouse where in a haze of pain and incomprehension beneath blinding fluorescent lights he is but dimly aware that he is being booked on charges of *drug possession, drug trafficking, aggravated assault against a police officer, resisting arrest.*

Which charges, with the exception of *resisting arrest*, will be dropped after forty-eight hours spent in the Herkimer County detention facility; for *resisting arrest* he will be sentenced to time served plus six months' probation overseen by the Herkimer County Parole and Probation Division.

With the result that, innocent as he is of any behavior that might be called *illegal*, he has now and will have forever a police record in Oriskany, New York, for *resisting arrest.*

Unfair! Unjust!—he will protest. In vain.

With blurred vision and a headache that will persist for months. Aches in his joints, ribs, neck, spine to persist through years. Fear and loathing for all uniformed police officers, a reflexive fear and loathing for all uniformed individuals to persist through the remainder of his life, his career *in law* terminated at the age of twenty. . . .

—∞—

Hearing the siren, just in time.

Out of nowhere, a police siren, scintillant-flashing as a machete blade, at this seedy end of East Union Street it isn't uncommon that Oriskany police are summoned to quell disturbances, more usually at night and not at this hour of the afternoon. He is just about to go downstairs, just finished tying the laces of his running shoes, pulling his hoodie over his head, on his way to hike along the trail at Flint Kill Creek on the farther side of the sprawling university campus, a break in his routine he has been promising himself but wisely now he holds back, he will wait until the police officers have departed, some ten, fifteen minutes before it is safe for him to leave his second-floor room at 229 East Union Street, Oriskany, New York, on a gusty November afternoon in 1999, eager to be outdoors, deeply breathing the fresh chill air, his brain flooded with plans, with hope, with happiness and all his life before him.

ACKNOWLEDGMENTS

Thanks and much gratitude to the editors of the magazines in which these stories originally appeared, often in slightly different versions.

"Flint Kill Creek" and "Friend of My Heart" appeared in *Conjunctions*.

"The Nice Girl" and "Mick & Minn" originally appeared in *Boulevard* and was reprinted in *Pushcart Prize XLIX: The Best of the Small Presses*.

"The Phlebotomist," "The Siren: 1999," "The Heiress. The Hireling," and "Bone Marrow Donor" appeared in *Ellery Queen*.

"Weekday" appeared in *Salmagundi*.

"***" was first published in a different form as "The Appointment" in *Weird Fiction Review*.

"Happy Christmas" appeared, in a shorter version, in *Vanity Fair*.

"Late Love" appeared in *The New Yorker*.